VERGE
OF
CORRUPTION

P.C. STEVENS

Copyright © 2020 by P.C. Stevens

This book is available in electronic and print form.

ISBN 978-1-7351368-2-0
ISBN 978-1-7351368-1-3 (ebook)

Copy edited by Suzanne Johnson

Cover Design by Melody Simmons

Dedicated to my family

GLOSSARY

- **Pirmas**: ancient supernatural race
- **raptatawks** (sometimes referred to as 'tawks): male-only winged Pirmas species; refer to each other as brothers; all are considered sons of the High Lord; possess telekinetic and telepathic abilities; they're the only Light-blooded breed in existence
- **hyx**: grainy silver scrying metal native to Otherworld; operable only by demons and warlocks. Scryers can view any place they wish in real-time. A drop of an individual's blood on the hyx will yield a view of that person in real-time
- *lokoke*: the power used by warlocks to manipulate emotions
- **warlock**: keepers of the First Tribe; telekinetic, telepathic, mentally, and emotionally manipulative magic-wielders capable of teleportation. There is not much they can't do. The first warlocks were humans snatched from their mortal existences by demons who conducted horrific experiments and "treatments" on them. Warlocks can procreate warlocks. Only Pirmas breed derived from humans. They need to drink demon blood to survive. Their eyes, which can become mirrored, are abnormally pale. When hostile, their appearance turns monstrous

- **fae**: keepers of the Third Tribe; each is affiliated with an element—earth, fire, wind, or water—to expertly wield. Mermaids, selkies, and other water-restricted creatures make up the water fae, while the wind, fire, and earth fae live on land
- **elves**: keepers of the Second Tribe; robust immortals with pointed ears whose strength, speed, agility, and endurance are unmatched. The men lead the tribe and are atrociously misogynistic, keeping their women biddable and confined
- **beasts**: shape-shifting Pirmas and keepers of the Fourth Tribe
- **The Corrupted**: collective and individual term for raptatawks who've pledged their loyalty to Darkness, and subsequently, demons. Upon becoming Dark-blooded, their teeth grow pointy and eyes turn red. They retain the supernatural abilities of their former selves
- **Otherworld**: comprises all realms minus Earth
- **Underworld**: Also known as the Dark Realm or Dark Dimension, it's a place of mayhem, depravity, pleasure (if you're lucky), and misery (if you're unlucky); ruled by demons
- **Chosen**: Earth dwellers and victims of fae changeling encounters. They live as humans on Earth and don't know of their true origins. They must cross into Otherworld in order to change into Pirmas. Queen Dia is the only character thus far who was Chosen
- **demons**: hideous, damned souls confined to the Dark Dimension

- **High Lord**: Supreme Light deity worshiped by some Pirmas. He created raptatawks and they know Him as Father. His name, plus pronouns referring to Him, are always capitalized
- **The Ravager**: demon in charge of the Corrupted
- **First Tribe**: first in Pirmas royal hierarchy belonging presently to warlocks. First Tribal leaders are under constant threat of attack
- **Second Tribe**: second in Pirmas royal hierarchy presently belonging to elves
- **Third Tribe**: third in Pirmas royal hierarchy presently belonging to fae
- **Fourth Tribe**: fourth in Pirmas royal hierarchy presently belonging to beasts
- **Noctis**: Home realm of the First Tribe. The nights last as long as three Earth months and the days last the equivalent of three Earth days
- **Four Cherished**: Pirmas royal ranking system presently consisting of the First Tribe of Warlocks, the Second Tribe of Elves, the Third Tribe of Fae, and the Fourth Tribe of Beasts; First Tribe is unofficial leader of all Pirmas

***Note to readers**: you need only read the brief prologue if you didn't read the first book of the Love's Warrior series, *From Here to Eternity.*

PROLOGUE

Six Earth months have passed since Prince Lachlan slew his father King Soren. Now, King Lachlan and his queen, Dia, the wind-controlling fae who lived a human life for twenty-eight years before Soren abducted her and taught her of her true lineage, rule the First Tribe. They've sent search parties to Earth to find the humans who'd successfully hidden from Soren's apocalyptic forces, but the search is proving widely unsuccessful. Humans are craftier than even Dia anticipated.

Lachlan and Dia's other crucial responsibility is to lead the first line of defense against the Darkness.

Demons are growing stronger. They've found a way to use the High Lord's sons against Him, by Darkening their blood and gaining their servitude. The calm that settled over the Pirmas following King Soren's death is due to shatter right… about…

Now.

CHAPTER 1

Even a fifteen hundred-year-old could make lousy choices. In Zestine's case, living with the consequences of one such lousy choice, although sufficient punishment for making it, was beyond intolerable.

Dusk loomed, the surrounding bluish-gray cliffs having just smothered the sun's comfort and guidance. The chill that followed was a perfect match for Zestine's mood.

"I'm telling you, there are no stinkin' mortals left. We're the subject of a corrupt experiment," said Pyko, the warlock and only male in their group. Raising his pale-blue gaze, in stunning contrast to his dark-brown skin, to the sky, he cupped his hands around his mouth. "Are you having fun watching us?"

Zestine rolled her eyes while the two fae, Kas and Richelle, giggled. She knew Pyko was only half serious, but the more time that passed without success, the more she thought he was onto something.

It had been two months since her impulsive decision to volunteer for human search duty. In that time, she and her teammates had failed to locate a single mortal. Apparently, humans preferred hiding in deserted areas, or places that were deserted back when there was a thriving population. This drove the team deep into the mountains of Northern California.

Tired of walking on two legs, Zestine shifted into a leopard and sprinted ahead of the others. She licked her chops, rotating her ears to listen in every direction.

Beyond the sounds of trickling water, birds, scurrying animals, the wind, and cadence of her team's footsteps, a peculiar noise vibrated her eardrums. A harsh smacking and… voices? She listened for a few more seconds. Not just voices…

Screams.

Humans? Her pulse skyrocketed as adrenaline spiked her blood. Zestine shifted back to a woman, turned toward the group, and held a finger to her lips.

They halted, swiveling their heads around to scan the area with hungry gazes.

She frowned. The piercing exclamations approached *fast*, not emanating from underground or the team's current ground level. In this terrain, no mortal could travel that fast on foot. Her flicker of hope that humans were near snuffed to darkness.

A bellow resounded through the peaks. The team glanced at each other.

"What the fuck was that?" Kas asked, her warm, brown gaze darting to and fro.

"Can't be human," said Pyko.

Whoosh, whoosh, whoosh. Zestine held up her hand. "Wait, it almost sounds like flapping… like wings…"

Whoever approached emitted a rough howl. A thump sounded, followed by another scream.

Whoosh, whoosh, whoosh.

Zestine's hand shot to her mouth when the source of the perilous noises came into view. From behind the nearest peak flew a man with black-and-white wings—a raptatawk. He sped by, vanishing into the peaks as fast as he'd appeared. Seconds later, two more arrived, each carrying two machetes and covered in blood, and streaked after him.

"Why would raptatawks be on Earth?" said Pyko.

"And why are they all bloody?" asked Richelle.

Two more came, one right behind the other, and circled the clearing above Zestine and her teammates. The raptatawk in the lead, with white-tipped, midnight-blue wings, carried nothing on his person and cut abrupt paths in every direction to dodge the other. The 'tawk giving chase, who sported red, yellow, and orange wings, brandished a pair of machetes. Face smeared crimson, the pursuing 'tawk's expression was severely contorted, like he flexed all his facial muscles while trying to expel breath between tightly sealed lips. The two men moved through the air with chilling grace. Their figures, against pink-dusted clouds stretching across a deepening cerulean sky, displayed a sight of hair-raising beauty.

Gut squirming, Zestine turned to her fae comrades. "Can't you guys do something?"

Their gazes broke from the skyward altercation to her. "What do you mean? We're here to find humans, not save raptatawks. I don't want to barge in on their business," said Richelle.

Zestine looked at Kas. "C'mon. Do something!" She gestured to the sky. "This isn't right and you know it." She willed her canines to lengthen and claws to unsheathe, ready to make threats if that's what it took.

5

Kas looked from Zestine to Richelle, who shook her head, then back up at the two raptatawks. The chaser hacked at his prey with both blades, missing by mere inches with every swing.

Zestine grimaced. Raptatawks did *not* kill their own. If she wasn't witnessing that very thing about to take place, she wouldn't believe it.

Can I let him die when there's a way to help him?

Strange warmth uncoiled in her belly as she contemplated. Seemed she was the only one who cared this situation was amiss. But she refused to let her teammates' apathy influence her. If she didn't do something, even if that meant forcing another into action, she'd rue it.

The team's failure at locating humans was disturbing in its similarity to her own life. Was this all she had to look forward to, endlessly roaming the world in search of something just out of reach? If so, Zestine wasn't sure she could bear it. She needed… excitement, passion, purpose. She'd thought she'd find those things on Earth. So far, she'd been wrong.

Until now, perhaps…

Baring her fangs at Kas, Zestine unleashed a low growl. Earth fae were formidable, no doubt about that, but they lacked beastly speed. Zestine could rip Kas's throat open before the fae could even *decide* how to defend herself.

Not that Zestine would actually kill her. She, Kas, and Richelle threatened each other more and more the longer they were Earthbound. It had become somewhat of a game during the tedious days and nights of a pointless search.

Kas rolled her eyes and bared her own shiny white teeth. "Fine. But if this backfires, I'll hunt your feline ass down and kill you myself."

Zestine widened her eyes before looking at the ground to hide a smile she wouldn't have bothered hiding if she wasn't desperate for the fae's help. *You'd try.*

Kas turned in place and studied the surrounding cliffs. After selecting a highland area to manipulate, she raised and positioned her hands just so. Willing her power forth, a duplicate pair of humongous phantom hands worked to fracture part of a cliff. The rock moaned, scrunched, then split with a pop, loosening pebbles that clacked against the slope on their way down. With her hands mirroring the wraithlike ones, Kas slowly pivoted; the boulder moved toward the chase in the sky.

Zestine's heartbeat thundered in her ears as the pursuing raptatawk gained on his brother. This time when he swung the machete, it sunk deep into the back of the other's leg.

A roar echoed off the mountainside at the same time Kas released the massive stone several feet above the fiery-winged 'tawk, who'd been too distracted to see it coming. It slammed into him with a stomach-wrenching smack, just missing his prey, who dove into a forest of evergreens across the clearing from the cliff. The machete-wielding 'tawk's wild shriek cut through the air as the rock propelled him toward Earth at breakneck speed. He landed with a sickening crunch several yards away, the abrupt silence prolonged as the group's shock bled into the moment.

"Shit," Pyko said, making his way over to the crushed male. Kas and Richelle followed.

Zestine searched the sky for the wounded raptatawk, but failed to spot him. *I should find him.* Maybe he knew why his brother had tried to murder him and why two other 'tawks looked like they'd just participated in a massacre. Surely he'd bled from the gash to his leg. She nodded to herself. A blood trail would make him easy to find.

She joined the others standing around the mangled raptatawk. Everything besides his arms, legs, and head had been crushed on impact, including his wings. His limbs were severed and his head barely attached to his neck... or was his neck barely clinging to his shoulders? It was hard to tell, but the damage testified to the deadly capabilities of earth fae.

"Whoa. Check out those eyes," said Pyko.

Kas knitted her brows and crouched for a closer look. "Very odd."

Richelle, as if she couldn't help herself, nudged the body with the toe of her boot. "I thought only baseborn creatures had red eyes."

Zestine shrugged. "Maybe he was born with them."

Richelle laughed. "Baseborn creatures are born with them."

"He's obviously not baseborn," Zestine replied. As sons of the High Lord, raptatawks were, if anything, the opposite of such folk.

"They're fucking creepy," Pyko said through a pinched expression, and Zestine couldn't argue. The 'tawk's irises resembled the bright shade of arterial blood and gave her a twisted sense of things to come. She shook off a shudder and averted her gaze.

Need to find that other raptatawk.

Kas focused her power and mimicked rolling the boulder off the soon-to-be corpse while Pyko retrieved one of the dead 'tawk's machetes. In one swing, the warlock severed the vertebrae and hunks of muscle and tissue securing head to body, ending any chance of survival.

"What a mess." He slid the flat sides of the blade against his pants to clean off the blood.

All eyes settled on Zestine, her comrades' annoyance palpable. She liked them well enough, or maybe *respected* was a better word, but an opportunity had just presented itself and she wouldn't let it pass. She was too damn old. It could be a momentous chance leading to something *more*.

Yeah. Sure it is.

"Stay here," she said. "I'm going to find the other guy."

"What? No!" Richelle complained.

Pyko grunted and tentatively pushed his hand toward her. "Sweetheart, let's talk this over."

With a noncommittal shake of her head, she sighed. "Sorry, but I have to do this." She gestured to their surroundings. "Do you see any humans out here?"

Kas and Richelle spun around and meandered away. Pyko dropped his head.

"I just want to check on him. He might need our help." On a whim, she added, "If I don't return, go on without me. Good luck." Zestine shifted into a black panther and put her nose to the ground.

CHAPTER 2

Tris landed in the middle of an evergreen forest, almost doing a face-plant but catching himself just in time. It was crazy other Pirmas were out here, and even crazier that they'd saved his life. But his troubles weren't over. As he craned his neck to assess the deep laceration to his calf muscle, doubts and worries muddled his exhausted mind.

Men he'd trusted with his life wanted him dead. Everything he thought he knew about the world, gone. What would he do now?

Ripping off both pant legs from the knee down, Tris tore the black linen into strips. He tied three strips over the length of the cut and used three more as a second layer. The wound was healing, but deep enough it'd bleed for a while before correcting itself.

He'd fled before seeing if his pursuer, Melvin, survived his fall. A pang of regret sliced through him at hoping the raptatawk hadn't made it.

What's happening to us?

Only a few months ago he, Melvin, and dozens of their brothers had lived it up in celebration of entering the final phase of raptatawk maturity and at last becoming immortal. Then, out of nowhere, everything had changed. The Darkness had intruded, wholly unwelcome, and wreaked havoc the likes of which Tris and his people had never seen coming.

Shaking away woeful memories, Tris started in the direction he'd flown. After traipsing several yards, the hair on the back of his neck lifted.

Someone watched him.

Slowly, he swept his gaze from right to left, hoping to find a curious raccoon or deer, but saw nothing. He spun in place, then jerked to a standstill at spotting a large black panther approaching.

Tris pulled in a sharp breath. Out of all the animals out there to stumble upon, he got a top predator. Defenseless he was not, but his power of telekinesis only worked on non-living things, and defending himself risked giving away his location to lingering, bloodthirsty 'tawks.

Out swept his wings and he poised for takeoff when, before his widening eyes, the impressive cat morphed into a woman.

Well, never mind. He *was* defenseless.

She was a shapeshifter, a beast from the Fourth Tribe and the first of her kind he'd encountered in the flesh. She could shred him to bits in a trice.

The beast sauntered closer.

He backed up a couple of steps.

She stopped.

"Come no closer." He raised his hand, unsure what to do. Going to sky could be a bigger mistake than staying grounded with a beast.

Her ruby lips parted (in surprise?). "I'm not here to harm you."

"Who are you?"

She beamed. "I'm the girl who just saved your life."

Oh. "Why?"

Her smile vanished, eyes narrowing to slits. "You're welcome."

He pulled his wings in, never taking his eyes from her. "Right. Thank you, but why?"

Her gaze drifted to the trees. "It's kind of odd, don't you think, for *raptatawks* to murder each other?"

Tris huffed. "Tell me about it."

She stepped closer, but this time he stayed put. "Why don't you tell me about it?"

Wait a sec. He narrowed his own eyes. "*You* didn't save me." He'd seen enough of the incident to know she couldn't have been responsible.

"I'm not out here alone, and I don't appreciate the change in subject. I asked you a question."

Mouth falling open, he furrowed his brows and broke eye contact to stare at her feet. "There's not much to tell." This woman didn't need him to acknowledge that some of his brothers had turned into bloodthirsty killers overnight. What business was it of hers?

Though it stung to admit, even to just himself, the female was right. Light-born raptatawks didn't slay one another or anyone, period. Needlessly taking lives wasn't part of their makeup.

"Really?" The woman scoffed. "I find that hard to believe."

"Why do you care?"

She didn't answer, instead taking a moment to run her gaze the length of his body, from his head to his toes. "What's your name?"

"What's yours?"

"I asked first."

He narrowed his eyes. "Tris. Now tell me yours."

"It's nice to meet you, Tris. I'm Zestine."

He sighed and put his hands on his hips. "What do you want from me?"

"I work for the First Tribe. I'm sure they'd be interested in the attempted murder I witnessed. Between *raptatawks.*"

Tris raised his eyebrows. "A Fourth Tribesman working for the First Tribe? You must really think I'm stupid."

She rolled her eyes, her lips curving into a disbelieving smile. "No… but now I think you're stupid enough *not* to believe it. There's a new king in power. He doesn't discriminate like the last one."

The First Tribe couldn't help, not with this problem. Tris shook his head. "I can't."

"You can't, or you won't?"

Biting his bottom lip, he closed his eyes and dropped his head. She was skeptical of him, but she shouldn't be. Sure, he could explain *how* his fellow 'tawks' behavior had changed recently, but as to *why*, he was as perplexed as she was.

Tris's eyes flew open at the sudden rustling evergreens and heavy whooshes of air.

His Dark brethren still hunted him.

Heart hitting his throat, he dove under—or more like *into*—the nearest tree. The branches scraped his skin, causing him to repeatedly wince as he buried himself as close to the trunk as possible, then watched Zestine's fierce black panther stroll around the trees as the raptatawks flew overhead. The flap of their wings upset the evergreens and lifted dirt and needles off the forest floor. By observing the size of the disturbance their presence made on the ground, Tris guessed the party comprised three men.

He couldn't detect their voices through speech or telepathy, the latter of which meant they were definitely of the changed variety. At the same time his brothers' behavior had turned baleful, their ever-present mental connection vanished. Though eerie, it'd proven a welcome development. Tris wasn't sure he could bear witnessing the Darkness seep into their minds and raze their Light.

The 'tawks continued on after a couple of minutes, but Tris stayed put. Uncertainty drove icy hooks into him. Even as his blood buzzed with excess adrenaline, the thought of moving an inch nearly smothered his lungs with foreboding.

The panther morphed within a millisecond into a comely redhead and approached Tris and his hiding spot. Standing with her profile to him, Zestine folded her arms over her chest and kept her gaze averted. The woman exuded confidence that intimidated, unnerved, and intrigued him all at once.

"It'll be dark soon. Planning to stay in there all night?" she asked.

Tris had considered it, but she didn't need to know that. Though uncomfortable, he could manage, given his very life was at stake.

"Hello? Anyone there?" She shifted from foot to foot, turned her face his way and then back without looking at him. She was almost close enough to touch, meaning she knew exactly where he was. So why hadn't she looked at him?

He scowled at himself. Why should he care if she looked at him or not? "Go away. I can take care of myself."

She laughed. "Yeah, I can see that."

In the distance a woman called, "Zestine? Zesty-eene? Where are you?"

"Zestine! Fun time's over. It's almost dark," shouted a male.

Zestine cursed. "Hey, raptatawk." She turned her body and faced him head-on. They locked gazes. "I'm not leaving without you. I have a warlock with me. He can teleport us to the king and queen. You'll be safe there."

Tris rolled his eyes and shook his head. What was with this woman? Why did she care what happened to him? "No."

"Why?"

"I don't trust warlocks." He left out, *or fae, or elves, or beasts.* His trust was severely limited. When trusting his own brothers wasn't an option, it was impossible to trust anyone. Surely she could understand that.

"Fine, we don't have to teleport. How'd you get here? I'm guessing by portal?" At his silence, she gave him the view of her profile again and continued. "We'll go to Noctis via the portal that brought you here, okay?" When seconds ticked by without an answer, she heaved a sigh. "All right, you win. Stay here and rot. If you're too imbecilic to accept help, you don't deserve to survive." She scoffed and shook her head, then pivoted and ambled off.

The farther away she got, the more sweat slicked his palms. This was his solution? To hide within a tree the entire night? Pathetic. Surely he could devise a better plan. But help was better than no help, and Zestine was the only person offering. He closed his eyes, treated his lungs to a cleansing breath. Either he was an imbecile, as she'd suggested, or not. The beast would protect him. She'd saved his life once, so why not again if circumstances called for it?

Tris wiggled himself free of the evergreen, shook the tree needles from his hair and wings, then sprinted after her.

Zestine turned and crossed her arms as he closed in on her. The man and woman still called for her, but based on the volume of their voices, it seemed she'd traveled away from them, which struck Tris as odd but was not his problem.

He stopped, grasped his hips, and gave a reluctant nod. "Okay, you win. I'll go with you to Noctis."

~

Zestine smiled and uncrossed her arms. "Good choice. King Lachlan and Queen Dia will protect you."

At least she thought they would. It'd certainly surprise her if they didn't have a problem with what she'd witnessed.

Tris raised his brows. "If you say so."

"You remember where the portal is?"

"This way." Tris headed in the same direction she'd gone, thankfully adding distance between her and her peeved teammates.

He took the lead, and Zestine stood there for a moment beaming at his back. Something told her it was no accident their lives had intersected and that going to

Noctis with him would prove worthwhile. Of course, meeting a beautiful man nearly always carried a positive vibe. She skipped after him and once by his side, pressed her lips together to lose the smile and tried to curb the bounce in her step.

"How far is it?" she asked. The trees' ghostly shadows danced upon the forest floor, dusk's icy breath having rendered a colder bite to the air since she'd first encountered the 'tawks.

"It's a hike."

She halted. "I'll shift, then."

He stopped, locked gazes with her, and nodded. During the moment of eye contact, Zestine noted the color of his: midnight-blue, the same shade as his wings, with the barest of distinctions between iris and pupil. From there, her gaze slid over his prominent cheekbones, five o'clock shadow, strong jawline, and pouty lips that sprung forth wicked sexy thoughts.

"Back up." Tris unfurled his wings halfway, seeming oblivious to her hungry gaze. "I'll have to fly in certain areas." He broke into a jog and Zestine, after ogling his brawny posterior, shifted into her panther and trotted along behind him.

The terrain was challenging, but in beast form she had no problems and whenever Tris flew, he stayed as near to the ground as possible. His mastery of the air rivaled her prowess of the surface.

Tris's wingspan had to be a magnificent twenty feet, and after a while she noticed the coloring of his wings resembled the ocean meeting a white sandy beach.

What would it be like to go to sky with him? How high would he take her before her hands sweat? Would he thrill her by diving full speed toward earth? Risqué thoughts swarmed her mind too, like how it'd feel to be cocooned within his winged embrace while he thrust deep into her.

Seemed her good service came with an inconvenience: a powerful attraction to the person she wanted to help. Though she'd always appreciated their splendor, she'd never gotten close to a raptatawk.

The glittery black of night dominated the heavens by the time Tris led Zestine into the cave housing the portal.

Portals existed naturally in Otherworld as they once had on Earth, but when the Pirmas and their magic left Earth many centuries ago, the portals vanished with them. When King Lachlan came into power, he and a team of warlocks traveled the planet re-installing portals so human-hunting Pirmas needn't rely on warlocks to cross realms.

Tris and Zestine stopped in front of an access covered in puffy white fog. She shifted to her bipedal form and looked at him. "Ready?"

He made a big show of inhaling deep and letting it out. "I guess so." He gestured to the gateway. "After you."

"Noctis, please," Zestine said before offering him a grin and stepping through.

~

Tris didn't waste a second before bolting. Right away, however, he realized his plan was lacking. He needed to avoid the beast long enough for her to give up and return to wherever she came from. Then he'd have the portal to himself.

He scowled and roughly shook his head. Taking to the air was the easiest way to elude her, but flying risked detection by his corrupted kin.

"Tris," she called.

Before he had a chance to exit the cave, she stopped him in panther form, planting herself in front of him and shifting. "What are you doing?" She put her hands on her hips and tapped her foot against the rocky floor.

He raised his eyebrows, suppressing a guilty grin. "Isn't it obvious?"

Zestine's gaze hit the rocky ceiling as a bitter laugh escaped her lips. Her bluish-purple eyes pinned him to the spot. "Not really. Why lead me here if you had no intention of using the portal? Were you planning on going back into the forest and hiding under a tree for eons or until one of yours comes along and kills you? Does that sound smarter than, oh, I don't know, coming with me and telling someone who can help about your problem?"

One of yours? One of yours? His eyes bugged. "I am *not* one of them, and I don't need the First Tribe's help."

"Yes, you do. You just don't realize it, which, considering what you've been through, seriously boggles my mind."

Time to switch tactics. He angled his palm and splayed his fingers at her. "Look, I'm grateful you saved my life, I really am, but I've no desire to visit the First Tribe." He could only imagine the consequences of doing so... *if* they believed him.

Zestine crossed her arms. "What do you have to lose? Do you want to fix what's happening with your people?"

"Of course!" How could she ask such a thing?

Her brows shot up. "Doesn't seem like it."

"You don't know what you're talking about."

"*That's* where you're wrong." She nodded to the outside world beyond the cave. "Go on. Hide if you must, but I hope you understand more of your brothers will die." Zestine squinted. "Has anyone discovered *how* 'tawks are becoming cutthroats, let alone what to do about it?" When he didn't respond, she continued. "Then what's to foil the metamorphosis?" She angled her index finger at him. "Know this, raptatawk: If you walk away, you must live with the fact someone gave you an opportunity to figure out how to stop it. Your dead brethren's blood *and* their killers' depravity will forever stain you."

Tris looked at the ground, swallowing past the lump in his throat. Her arguments struck his conscience like an omen, a little too sound to shun. This fiery-haired woman with arresting indigo eyes was keen. She knew just how to render him vulnerable yet thirsty to act. Well aware of the brutalities his Dark kin were capable of, could he live with himself knowing he'd rejected this chance?

"Now, if you'll excuse me, I have a team to rejoin." Zestine pivoted, then whirled back around. "Oh, and if we run into any blood-caked, machete-wielding raptatawks asking about a guy with blue and white wings, I'll be sure to cover for you... though I can't say the same for my teammates."

"Wait," he said, voice laced with a growl. *Why me?* Of course he was desperate to figure out how and why his brothers were embracing Darkness. But he didn't want to be the one to do it. He thought about his people and their uncertain future... a future suddenly in his hands. *Why us?* Something within him detonated. Tris turned to the cave wall and launched his fists into it, painting his fury onto the stone with blood-slicked knuckles.

Crimson had begun to stream down the makeshift canvas when a nudge to his hip drew his attention. He looked down, where a jaguar with a head as wide as his hips bared a mouthful of spears at him. He staggered backward.

The cat transformed into Zestine, who folded her arms over her chest. "Unless beating the wall is your idea of foreplay, why am I waiting?"

"What?" Tris widened his eyes and parted his lips before jabbing an accusing finger at her. "Is *that* why you saved me?"

She snickered and tipped her head back. "Please. I would have intervened no matter what."

"Okay, but would you insist on bringing me to royalty?"

Her gaze narrowed. "Yes. Now, why'd you tell me to wait?"

Holding out his crimson-smeared hands palms up, he said, "You win. Let's go."

Zestine smirked and started toward the portal. "May want to lose the 'you win' bullshit. Last time you told me that, you *lied.*"

Sidling up to her, he rubbed the back of his neck, pressing his fingers into the muscles, then tossed his head left to right and rolled his shoulders. Hopefully, he'd get ahold of himself before meeting the king and queen.

In front of the portal, Zestine held out her hand, mimicking his gesture from minutes ago. "After you."

CHAPTER 3

He gave her his best glare before walking into the misty doorway.

"Noctis!" she yelled.

Tris closed his eyes and shook his head at forgetting to state his destination. If not for Zestine, the portal would've randomly dumped him anywhere in Otherworld.

Balmy air greeted him as he stepped onto soft, warm sand. To his right, the ocean strummed its ever-present chord as waves crashed upon a glimmering white shore. Above the water, two pink moons floated amid countless twinkling stars dotting a dark-blue sky. He'd never been to the realm and couldn't help but gape at its sublimity. The soothing ambience brought to mind his homeland of Sohvic... before hellish versions of his brethren had infected it with Darkness. Considering that a warlock ruled Noctis, Tris had expected to arrive in a much more unpleasant place.

Zestine appeared at his side. "This way." She headed away from the water.

With a parting glance toward the sea, he followed at a respectable distance. Mesmerizing scenery filled his gaze, clearing his psyche and easing a crushing sense of despair. The hike wasn't long. Sand gave way to spongy, lime-green grass that tickled Tris's feet as they walked by a small forest of unfamiliar trees. Tall and thin, their branches made a ninety-degree angle toward the sky and flourished with giant oblong leaves of bright orange, ice blue, and sparkly magenta. Tiny, glowing-winged beings zipped about the foliage.

On the other side of the forest stood a small white stucco one-story property without windows. Nearby plants and the glow of the two moons provided the only light. Two armed elves guarded the front entrance.

Tris looked at himself, naked from the waist up with nothing on his feet. At least he wouldn't appear a threat to Pirmas royalty.

"Aw, shit," Zestine said, turning to him.

"What?" They were no more than twenty feet from the property.

"Elves," she whispered.

"Elves?"

"Shh. Keep your voice down." She peeked back at the building. "Those guards are elves."

"Um, okay." He lowered his voice to a whisper. "Why are you telling me this? I can see just fine."

She shook her head. "Are you really this dense, boy? Elves hate women. They have zero respect for us. I can't fucking stand them." Her eyebrows furrowed as she massaged her forehead.

Tris ground his teeth. The beast was bold, calling him *boy*. He pressed his lips together and forced himself to take a deep breath. "Seriously?"

Zestine scrunched up her face. "How do you not know that?" She closed her eyes and pursed her lips. After a moment, she opened them. "I need you to talk to them. Just say we're here to meet with King Lachlan and Queen Dia."

He looked at the elves, then at Zestine. "Why?"

Her eyes grew impossibly wide at the same time her cheeks flushed. "Did you not hear anything I just said?"

His gaze narrowed. "Are you telling me if you approach them and ask to see the king and queen, they'll act like you're not even there?"

More eye-rolling. "I'll tell you this once, raptatawk. I hate elves, you got me? They're filthy rapists who think their dicks are status symbols." Her eyes flashed with the ominous glow of her beast. "Killing them sounds delightful, but if I kill these two, I'd get in a lot of trouble, as would you." She stabbed the knuckle of her index finger into his chest. "Do you get what I'm saying, Tris? I'm trying to help you. The least you can do is help me."

Would she freak out if he told her he'd never asked for her help? "Fine." He palmed her shoulder and guided her to the front of the small building. Lord Father, did this female rile him.

Zestine dodged his touch by ducking beneath his arm and allowing him the lead.

The sentries guarded metal gates wrought into intricate designs. With every step nearer, their color shifted. At times the gates even appeared multi-colored.

Upon reaching the access, Tris cleared his throat and smiled. The elves' gazes zeroed in on him. They even slanted their bodies in his direction as if Zestine was invisible.

"Hi," Tris said, clearing his throat again. "So, we're here to see King… uh…" *Shit. What's his name again?*

A few seconds later, Zestine whispered, "Lachlan."

"Lachlan, right. King Lachlan. And Queen… Dina."

The elves eyed one another without turning their heads.

"*Dee-uh*," she said, tone saturated with irritation.

"Oh, sorry. Queen Dia," he finished, nodding.

The guards still exchanged a look from the corners of their eyes, and for a moment, Tris worried he'd destroyed their chances of seeing the king and queen.

"And who are you two?" the elf directly across from Tris, with styled short brown hair and dark eyes, asked.

Two? Shouldn't they know her? His gaze shot to Zestine, who despite her reluctance to talk to the guards, didn't hesitate to answer.

"I'm Zestine Amolora. I've been on Earth searching for humans under the king and queen's guidance."

Already gotten over her seething hatred, had she?

She gestured to Tris. "This is Tris. Tris…"

"Just Tris." His kind rarely bothered with last names, though sometimes they gave their progeny the female's last name, as all raptatawks were males and their mates gave birth to only raptatawks. His parents had never chosen a surname.

"Have you found any humans?" the elf with long white-blond hair and cerulean eyes asked Tris.

"Well—"

"We're here for a different reason, and I assure you the mister and missus will be grateful we've brought this… issue to their attention," said Zestine.

"Why don't you tell us first and we'll decide if it's worthy of their attention," said the dark-haired elf.

Her narrowed eyes relaxed when she looked at Tris. She flicked her head in the guards' direction and mouthed, "Tell them."

Tris tucked his upper lip and bit his lower one, flashing his teeth. *Lord Father.* These men were strangers, *powerful* strangers who didn't need to hear the truth. So he lied. "My father, the *High Lord*, sent me to deliver an important message to the First Tribe. He instructed me to intercept Zestine specifically, knowing she'd get me here safely."

The guards pondered that information for a few moments, sharing another peculiar look as if they were incapable of turning their heads.

"Where's the rest of your team?" the brunette elf asked Zestine, his tone accusing and eyes venomous as he regarded the beast with cutting disdain.

"Earth."

After side-eyeing each other again, the blonde nodded and his comrade turned and entered his side of the gate. It latched behind him with a clang.

"He will summon them," the remaining elf said.

Tris let out a breath, relieved they hadn't questioned him further.

The three Pirmas stood in awkward silence for several minutes before the elf returned. He opened both sides of the gate and moved out of the way to allow Zestine and Tris entry.

"You may enter," he said, his attention on Tris. "At the end of the hall, take a right. They're waiting for you."

Tris nodded and passed the threshold. A few steps later, Zestine's voice stopped him.

"What are you doing?"

Tris turned around, but the guard blocked her from view.

"My job, hussy," the guard replied, his tone heavy with condescension.

"Tris!"

Thinking fast, he said, "Zestine is to stay with me the entire time. Father was clear about that."

A few seconds ticked by before the elf, taking his time, pivoted and allowed her entry. When she appeared, Tris recoiled despite himself.

The beginnings of a muzzle distorted her face, making it protrude slightly from nose to chin. Eyes ashine with feral luminescence bore into the man who'd disrespected her. Gifted three fangs for every one fang of her Earth-dwelling cousins, she bared all twelve while emitting a savage growl.

Tris looked away and hooked his thumbs in his pockets. He hadn't known a beast posed much of a threat when not fully shifted. If the half-turned state equipped Zestine with her beast's speed, that elf would be in real trouble.

But she'd said killing them was out of the question. Looking at her hands, short spikes protruded from her fingertips: evidence she held back. Those claws were pathetic compared to how long, and thus fearsome, they could become.

Note to self: don't piss off this woman… more than I already have.

27

Zestine walked backward, presumably to stare down the guard, until she reached Tris's side. Turning to the raptatawk, she opened her mouth wide as her canines shrank and her features normalized. With snicks, her claws morphed into nails. Her eyes were the last to change, darkness chasing away their wild radiance until he stared into brilliant rings of indigo.

"Ready?" she asked as if she hadn't just openly thirsted for the blood of a royal guard.

He pushed his lips out and nodded, at a loss for words.

"Let's do this." She started down the hallway. Without sparing a glance at the elves, Tris fell into step behind her.

CHAPTER 4

The corridor seemed neverending, growing darker the farther they walked, but upon reaching the end, the air crackled and light enshrouded them.

"What...?" Discombobulated, Tris spun to look behind him. A black screen filled the hallway from wall to wall and floor to ceiling. He thrust his hand into it. Shadow encased his arm to just below the elbow, where an electric flicker hissed and snapped though he felt no pain.

"It's a ward. If you sought to harm the king and queen, it'd feel like jagged razors going to war inside your body, as you flew backward into the guards' care."

Tris dropped his arm. "Hey, why didn't the guards recognize you? I thought you worked for the First Tribe."

"I volunteered to help them find humans." She shrugged. "Call it what you want. I call it work. And I don't exactly hang out with elves." She looked to her left, where King Lachlan and Queen Dia waited, then back at him. "You won't embarrass me in front of them like you did with the guards, will you?"

Tris snorted. "Embarrass you? I did what you asked."

"What are their names?"

"Whose?"

Smacking herself on the forehead, she answered, "The king and queen!"

"Lachlan and Dia."

"How do you not know their names?"

"You said yourself they're new. I don't pay attention to names. Big deal." Did she think he didn't regret that faux pas?

She flailed her finger at him. "When we get inside, we kneel. Don't interrupt and don't speak unless spoken to."

He rolled his eyes, holding back a laugh at how asinine she assumed he was. "Uh-huh. Got it."

Zestine snatched his wrist and squeezed so hard his bones groaned. He stifled a yelp through a grimace.

"What is wrong with you, boy? Do you need a lesson in civility? They're the unofficial *Pirmas leaders*, you know."

Tris bared his teeth as he shot out his free hand and grabbed her shoulder. She dropped his wrist and backed against the wall, where he pressed his palm next to the curve of her neck. He squeezed her shoulder, not too hard but hard enough. Her pupils morphed into thin vertical ellipses and her gums sprouted those terrific fangs, but the changes stopped there, meaning she was leashing her aggression.

To keep from capturing the king and queen's attention, he spoke in a soft tone. "What's wrong with me? How about what's wrong with *you?* You need to learn a little respect, and I'm not a mere *boy*. You've major audacity talking to people like that." Did she whip that sharp tongue at everyone, or just him?

Cat-eyes drilled fiery pique at him. A faint rumble emanated from her throat. Then… she hit him with a true surprise.

His nostrils flared. Was that… *her sex* he scented?

Immortal senses could reveal hidden truths. Tris had socialized with only a handful of women during his short twenty-seven years—had bedded but a fraction of that handful—but he knew when females were libidinous. Their scent was the best indicator during the times they didn't throw themselves at him. It didn't just come from between their legs, but a chemical change from within that—combined with what *did* originate between their legs—produced a unique aroma that was hard to ignore. Zestine's was like vanilla musk. Going straight for his nostrils, it beckoned him forth.

He released Zestine and backed away, bracing for a counter-attack by balancing on the balls of his feet with his legs spread scissor style and his knees slightly bent.

The she-cat didn't lunge for him, but turned away and rolled her head from shoulder to shoulder.

Not that he'd mention it to save his life, but the smell of her arousal filled the surrounding space.

He studied her. *Does she know I know?* She was many things. Bossy. Infuriating. Spirited. But he'd not peg her an idiot.

Zestine turned to him with an averted gaze and gave a terse nod. "Let's do this." She strode to the end of the hallway and turned right into a short corridor leading to the throne quarters.

Tris followed and upon breaching the room, noticed an energy shift. Unlike the hallway, here the atmosphere was thick with regality and honor.

The king and queen sat beside each other in the middle of a huge plush black horseshoe sofa. In front of them was a rectangular hyx-topped table standing no taller than the couch cushions and spanning the length of the couch's middle section. Ribbons of white, gold, and silver, along with chains of precious gems, hung from the ceiling, swaying and clinking to a breeze seeming to come from nowhere. Not until Tris studied Queen Dia closer did he surmise she was the source. Wind blew around her, causing wisps of her golden-blond hair, which was secured into a ponytail on the top of her head and traveled to her waist, to lift and wave. Her shiny blue blouse also fluttered to her command of her element.

She was a wind fae mated to a warlock. A dirty, demon-blood-drinking warlock.

What. The. Fuck?

Tris and Zestine halted a couple feet from the table. He copied her as she knelt and bowed her head.

"You may rise," said the king.

Tris stood and clasped his hands in front of him.

Lachlan's gaze moved over Tris and Zestine several times before settling on Tris. "Yuny said the High Lord sent you here with a message, is that right?"

Yuny had to be the brunette elf guard. Tris inclined his head. "Yes."

Lachlan nodded. "What's the message?"

"I—" Tris held back his next words with a gulp, suddenly realizing his first statement to the king would involve explaining why he'd *lied* to get permission to speak with him. Uncomfortable heat slithered across his shoulders and twined around his neck. He looked at Zestine, parted his mouth, and momentarily widened his eyes, hoping she intuited his predicament.

She rolled her eyes and looked away, then to Tris's relief, spoke.

"If I may speak first, my king." Lachlan inclined his head. "The High Lord did not send us. Tris wasn't willing to tell your guards the true reason we came, so he made up a convincing story to get past them. I'm sorry we deceived you and Queen Dia."

"I see." Lachlan's gaze, not steeped with hostility but with curiosity, settled on Tris. "What didn't you want to tell my guards?"

Where to begin? The terror of remembering cinched his airway and quickened his heart rate. "Well, I… uh…" a strangled noise leaked from his throat, his cheeks warming as his mind drew a complete blank.

"Why don't you start by telling us how you and Zestine crossed paths?" suggested Queen Dia. She smiled, and Tris nodded before switching his gaze to Zestine, then to Lachlan.

"Okay. So I was, uh… My buddy Melvin was chasing me. He was…"—he took a deep breath—"he wanted to kill me. We crossed into dimension after dimension and eventually got to Earth. That's where I met Zestine. She saved my life."

"How did you do that?" Dia asked Zestine.

"My team and I saw raptatawks carrying machetes and covered in blood. Tris and…"

"Melvin," said Tris.

"Melvin were the only ones who lingered. When I realized Tris's life was in danger I, well, I impelled one of my teammates to intervene." She nodded toward him, making brief eye contact before returning her attention to the king and queen.

That single glance reminded Tris of the musky-sweet scent permeating the hallway minutes ago. *He* had aroused her. What had sparked such a reaction at that specific moment?

"Intervene how?" King Lachlan asked.

"One of the earth fae dropped a giant boulder on him... on Melvin." Again, Zestine peeked at Tris, this time out of the corner of her eye. "He didn't make it."

Tris's heart twinged. Though he'd suspected Melvin had perished, having it confirmed still made him ache from the senseless turn to Darkness that'd led to his death.

"Then what happened?" asked the king.

"I left the group to find Tris and convinced him to come with me to talk with you and Queen Dia." She gave him another fleeting look. "He may act like it's no big deal, but raptatawks going against each other—*killing* their own, well... that's not normal."

Tris scowled. "How is that normal for any species?" He hadn't expected to be picked on.

"Perhaps not *normal*, but not out of the ordinary," said Lachlan. "Other species murder their own fairly often. I'm sure you're aware I killed my father and sister recently?"

"Yes, but for good reasons."

The king inclined his head. "True. And please." He briefly lifted his hand in a calming gesture. "There's no need to get defensive. We're not trying to bully or deceive you. Raptatawks differ from other species in this way."

Tris sniffed and combed his hair back with his fingers before holding his head in his hands. Those hands trembled when a horrifying truth struck him: if Darkness could crush the unshakable solidity of raptatawk brotherly love, his people were doomed.

"Tris." Zestine's gentle whisper penetrated his bleak musings.

Remembering his place, Tris dropped his hands and resumed a courteous demeanor.

The king propped his elbow on a fist and brushed his forefinger back and forth over his bottom lip as his eyes narrowed on Tris. "You're rather young, aren't you?"

Just because he'd asked, Tris wished he could say he wasn't.

"How old are you?" asked Queen Dia.

Tris looked at the floor. Their gazes were heavy against his skin as he admitted, "Twenty-seven."

Dia gasped. "Holy shit. Younger than I?" She giggled, her eyes sparkling with mirth. "I don't feel like such a baby anymore!" She gave Lachlan a huge smile. He smiled back and took her hand, interlacing their fingers. Dazed, Tris's gaze fastened on their joined hands.

"Anyhow," said the king, "it's conceivable for you, as a raptatawk yourself and so young, to be naive of certain things. Sometimes the closer you are to something, the tougher to adequately judge it. Your kind does not war with each other, or at least they didn't. Naturally, this warrants concern." He shifted his gaze to Zestine. "I commend you for bringing this to our attention." To Tris, he said, "Now, what happened before you and Zestine crossed paths?"

He nodded, his shoulders lifting in a sigh as he centered himself. "A group of brothers ambushed four of us. They were… different. Someone, or something, changed them. I can't link to their minds anymore, but I suspect they're able to communicate between themselves telepathically as I am with the unchanged."

"Has anything else about them changed?" asked the queen.

Melvin's eyes and teeth flashed through his mind. He pursed his lips and nodded, eyeing the floor. "Their eyes are red. And their teeth, all their teeth, are sharp. Like little needles."

Thinking about their physical changes evoked his brother Quinn, who'd gone missing months ago and had participated in the ambush. Quinn had plucked another brother, Bailey, from the ground and rammed his teeth into his neck. Then, holding him by the teeth, Quinn grabbed the tops of Bailey's wings and ripped them from his body. Tris still heard Bailey's agonized shrieks as Quinn dropped him from high in the air, and the resounding thump of his body hitting the earth. Still he saw Quinn drenched in scarlet, the whites of his eyes stark against all that blood, as he laughed like a maniac at what he'd done.

"They want us to join them and the second we refuse, they're set to kill us. No second chances," Tris said.

"When did this start?" asked King Lachlan.

"I don't know. A bunch of brothers went missing right after King Soren invaded Earth. Some of them were there, so..." He chuckled bitterly and shook his head. So worried he'd been about those guys when they'd disappeared. "Sickening," he whispered to himself, his vision going out of focus as he fisted his hands.

"Where did the attack happen? Are you the only survivor?" Lachlan inquired.

Tris forced his gaze to meet the king's. "It happened in Sohvic, and I don't know."

"Any species besides raptatawks attacking?"

"Not that I've seen."

Lachlan looked at Dia and nodded. "All right. My queen and I will discuss this further in our private quarters. I want you two to stay here. Please make yourselves comfortable." His gaze flicked from Tris to Zestine and back to Tris. "Okay?"

"Okay," said Zestine.

"Yes," answered Tris.

Lachlan inclined his head, untwined his hand from Dia's and placed it on her shoulder. Then the king and queen vanished.

CHAPTER 5

Zestine released a heavy sigh. The meeting was going better than she'd expected, which she attributed partly to their lack of surprise about the raptatawks' murderous conflict. Perhaps they'd already known about the troubling situation.

"That went pretty well," she said.

With his chin pressed to his sternum, Tris slowly twisted his neck to look at her. A storm raged within those ocean-blue depths. "Why do you say that?"

She raised her eyebrows. *Seriously?*

She meandered to the arced sofa and stretched out on the side to the left of Lachlan and Dia's seats, using her hands as a head-rest. "Well, they believed us. And they're not acting like we were foolish to come here."

Tris walked to opposite side of the couch and sat. He propped his elbows on his knees and shoved his hands through his hair.

The 'tawk's frosty mood was potent enough to give Zestine a shiver. She tried to reassure herself that he wasn't angry at her. Even so, she couldn't shake the disappointment souring her gut and chipping away her confidence. The barrier Tris had erected around himself from the get-go had gained massive layers since the start of the meeting.

When he'd pushed her against the wall outside the throne room, that barrier had vanished for an instant, during which erotic stirrings had inflamed her blood, the need to touch and taste him clawing at her with feverish vigor. Everything in her had pined for intimacy, for affection, for a connection beyond companionship. His looks weren't his only enticing quality, but something deeper that shook Zestine to her essence.

Perhaps his emotional wounds drew her, which were easy enough to discern given his unwillingness to stop whatever plagued his brethren. Denial could be a vicious monster.

Whatever the case, the intoxicating energy she'd tasted in that moment made her itch to erase the distance between them right then. She dug her nails into her palms instead.

"Can't trust 'em," he mumbled, cutting into her thoughts.

Zestine sat upright. "What did you say?"

"I said we can't trust them."

"We can't trust who?"

"Them." He pointed to where the king and queen had sat.

Her jaw dropped. How could he say such a thing under their roof? Eyeing the table of hyx between them, it reminded her the royals could monitor them from wherever they'd gone to have their discussion. "Are you crazy? Of course we can trust them." She flicked her gaze from him to the hyx several times consecutively, trying to tell him she and he might be under surveillance at that very moment, but he failed to understand or didn't care.

He shook his head. "Do you know anything about warlocks?"

Do you? That's what Zestine wanted to ask, but she bit back the words and tossed up her hands. "You need to stop talking." If he didn't, *she'd* have to silence him.

Tris raised his eyebrows. "Is that a no?"

She narrowed her eyes. "Ignorant b—… *man.*"

At that, he threw his head back and roared with laughter.

"What the fuck is so funny?" she inquired through her teeth, then lowered her voice. "You're going to get us in trouble."

A bitter smile remained on his face as his laughter died, the storm in his eyes still going strong. A moment later, King Lachlan and Queen Dia appeared in their seats.

Lachlan looked from Zestine to Tris. "Hello again. Dia and I spoke, and we agreed that we'd like for you, Tris, to help us. If you'd be so kind."

For several seconds, the raptatawk peered at the king with a blank look. "Okay."

"This strife between raptatawks is not news to us. We've known about it for some time and, obviously, kept it secret. But now the secrecy must end. The Pirmas deserve to know the unprecedented is happening." He paused as he and Dia shared a glance. "Not too long ago, we received troubling intel about your kin and a horde of demons."

Tris's eyes widened. "Demons?"

Lachlan closed his eyes and nodded. "We're uncertain there's any truth to it, but coupled with what we've seen and the information you and Zestine provided, Dia and I need to take action."

"What do demons have to do with it?" asked Zestine. Raptatawks were one thing. Demons, however, warranted careful consideration and a unique approach. Nobody marched into demon territory demanding answers, not even rulers of the First Tribe.

"We aren't sure, but we suspect demons and raptatawks are teaming up for war."

She gasped and looked at Tris, whose gaze was likewise on her before moving to his lap. "You had no reason to believe demons were involved?" she asked him.

"No." He gave a humorless chuckle. "But I guess I'm not surprised." He shook his head. "Of course it's the work of fucking demons."

King Lachlan frowned, his eyebrows pulling together as he released a heavy sigh. "Demons are the bane of the Pirmas. Not a day goes by when I wish they weren't my creators. But it's because of them I'm as powerful as I am, and I've no problem using my powers against them. If it's true they're planning war, I'll go after them with everything I have, but I need your help before that can happen." He held up a hand. "It won't be easy. You'll have to do bad things. Difficult things. Things that go against your nature."

Tris's Adam's apple bobbed as his face drained of color. He scrubbed his hands against his pants. Zestine appreciated he wasn't throwing a hissy, nor trying to trick his way out of it as he'd done with her.

Voice cracking, Tris asked, "What do you need from me?"

"We need you to go undercover as one of the changed raptatawks and find out what they and the demons are up to," Queen Dia said.

Tris took a moment to respond. "But... how? I've lost my telepathic connection with them. They'll know right away I'm not like them. Plus, their red eyes and teeth—"

"I'll take care of all that," Lachlan said. "They shouldn't discover you're a spy unless you tell them or severely mess up." He paused, allowing Tris a second to absorb everything. "Before I continue, I must know if you're game for this."

"I—how—" Tris pressed his lips together and pulled in a breath. "I have no experience with this type of work. How do you expect I won't fuck it up?"

The king inclined his head. "I need a raptatawk for this. None of your kind are spies, but you *are* warriors. Now, *can you do* this?"

Tris's gaze flicked to Zestine. A grimace marred his face, his skin bunched around haunted eyes. Breath catching, she broke eye contact. Circumstances beyond his control had backed him into a corner, and it wouldn't have happened if she hadn't saved his life. It'd never occurred to her at the time, but perhaps he hadn't wanted to live...

Nah. He'd wanted it.

Zestine refused to regret what she'd done, regardless of Tris's anguish. Considering what they'd just learned, this was bigger than them; selfishness was a luxury they couldn't afford.

Then she nearly fell out of her seat upon realizing the opportunity presented by the king and queen. She could partner with Tris. He was quite young, after all; Zestine and her fifteen hundred years could prove a vital asset. She'd already planned to request leaving Pyko, Kas, and Richelle and their futile search-and-rescue mission. Plenty human-hunting parties remained. One less Pirmas wouldn't make a difference.

This assignment with Tris would be dangerous, but if they succeeded, it'd *mean* something, not just to raptatawks, but to the entire Pirmas race. If they succeeded, she'd have finally done something worthwhile in her life. And if they didn't triumph, it'd be better than wondering what might have been, the thought of which almost made her shudder.

Zestine raised her hand. "Excuse me. Sorry to interrupt, but I'd like to help, if it's okay with you," she told the royals. *Please, please say it's okay.*

Lachlan nodded, put a finger to his chin, and glanced askance at Dia. The queen raised her eyebrows in response. Lachlan shifted his attention to Zestine. "We *could* use a partner for Tris. If it's okay with him, I'm fine giving you a chance."

Zestine smiled and her cheeks prickled with warmth. *Yes!* "It continues to be an honor serving the First Tribe." She pressed her lips together and bowed her head, trying to quash her smile.

"I look forward to it," said the king. Zestine lifted her head and nodded, unsuccessful at hiding her elation.

Lachlan looked at Tris. "What are you thinking? This is a lot to process."

The 'tawk snorted before dropping his face into his hands. "Fuck." He rubbed his brows, then raised his head. "Do I have a choice?"

No! she wanted to scream.

"You do," answered the king. "If you say no, I'll recruit someone else. But keep in mind if you work for me I will protect and provide for you. I can't give you those things if you walk away, but the choice is yours. I won't force you into something you're not ready for."

Tris's gaze moved to Zestine. "And Zestine? How does she fit into all this?" He glared at her through narrowed eyes, and flames of anger licked at her conscience, burning away the barrier that housed her beast. *If he ruins this chance for me…* Losing her smile, her canines lengthened and parted from her incisors to make room for her extra fangs, which punched through aching gums, her feral side the victor.

"Easy now." King Lachlan's silky smooth voice ribboned into her ears, quieting the beast to a lull. Just like that, her ire faded, replaced with a sense of peace. With a deep breath, she forced her gaze from Tris to Lachlan, then offered the warlock a smile once her fangs had shrunk and vanished.

To Tris, Lachlan continued, "She'll be there to help, directed by me and Dia. As a beast, she can switch forms as needed to thwart suspicion. She's also a lot older than you and, as such, will make better judgments. She can play messenger between us as well. Is there a specific reason you can't work with her?"

Tris's upper lip curled, but he shook his head.

Zestine leaned back in her seat, suddenly exhausted.

"Good," said the king. "I'll arrange for you two to have your own quarters here in Noctis, though once you've begun the mission there's no telling how safe or convenient it'll be to stay here. I suggest getting rest as soon as you can, however it is you do that. When Dia and I have everything in order, we'll notify you. In the meantime, try to relax."

CHAPTER 6

The royals gave Tris and Zestine small neighboring cabins on the shoreline of Noctis Sea. Each hut contained three rooms—a bedroom, a kitchen, and a bathroom.

Yuny and the unnamed blond elf led them to their temporary residences. Tris walked into one and slammed the door while Zestine parked her rear on the sand after a quick peek inside her cabin.

Though her body begged for a rest, her mind wouldn't shut up. The day's turn of events, and the male who'd come with them, gave her much to think about and lots to ache over.

Partnering with Tris for the mission vitalized her spirit for two crazy different reasons: life fulfillment and a zinging attraction to a raptatawk with a lousy attitude.

She was probably foolish for wanting Tris, who no doubt sulked mere yards away. But she couldn't deny the fierce hunger that had rushed to fruition when he'd lashed out at her. Some women would fear or resent such a response. Zestine was not most women. Between the two of them, she was by far more lethal. Besides, she'd hurt him when she'd grabbed his wrist. He hadn't hurt her.

A wicked throb settled between her thighs as she peered at Tris's hut. *That physique.* Pinpricks of heat raced over her shoulders to her chest and lingered on her breasts. *Those wings!* Physically, the man was as perfect as men came. *And he's... Right. Here.* So near, yet so out of reach.

What if she walked inside his hut and stripped naked? She sighed, imagining how it'd feel to have those dark-blue eyes devour every inch of her body. In the past, she'd always been forward with men, but she'd always known the object of her desire wanted her, which was not so with Tris.

Drawn shades lent only his silhouette to watch as he paced, his partly unfurled wings ruffling with each step. Zestine yearned to ease his strain, if only he'd let her.

Why wouldn't he? He was a man, and men rarely denied alluring women. With her fiery hair, sparkling indigo eyes, generous breasts, slim waist, and round bottom, she knew she was a temptress.

Nervous flitters danced within her belly as she stood and walked to his cabin.

~

Three knocks interrupted Tris's pacing. He crossed his arms and glared at the door to his hut. If only he could will the person on the other side to get lost...

Another knock sounded. "Open up!" Zestine called.

He didn't move. "Go away."

"Doing something important?"

He pulled his eyebrows into a frown. "I—yes. I'm busy."

Zestine's treble laugh trickled through the door, tightening his wings. "You're an atrocious liar, Tris. Come now and let me in."

Still frowning, he spun around and clenched his jaw. This woman persisted to a maddening degree. Why couldn't she understand he needed time alone? Yes, she'd saved his life, and he appreciated it. But he couldn't give her what she'd likely come over for. He was too fucked in the head, too blinded by sorrow, too furious at everyone.

"Hello?" she called.

Appease her with a simple gesture. Say hello, then good-bye.

With a low growl, Tris turned to face the door and used his mind to both flip the lock and swing the door open.

There Zestine stood, hands on her hips. Unlike him, she smiled as she met his gaze.

"What do you want?" He dropped his hands and turned away, then stretched his wings as far as the confined space allowed.

She gasped. "Wow."

He stilled his wings. "Wow, what?"

"Your wings," she said, voice breathy. "They're... phenomenal." Her soft footfalls got closer. "When I first saw you on Earth, I thought your pursuer had the more striking wings." And closer. "But I was mistaken."

Before he could turn around, she petted the top of his right wing. The touch was barely enough to ruffle a feather, but raptatawks' wings were ultra sensitive, and Tris bit back a moan as warm tingles spread through his body and blood flooded his loins.

Hands fisting, he whooshed out a breath as silently as possible.

Touching a raptatawk's wings could soothe or arouse—or both—and was a cherished act between lovers, or between parents and their infant. For Tris, doing it uninvited was borderline abusive.

His contemplation that Zestine didn't understand the significance of her action died with the rapture she'd set loose with her touch. Snapping his wings against his back, he whirled around and advanced on the she-cat.

She backpedaled to the still-open doorway, then halted, so he crowded her. Her chest rose and fell rapidly; her face was flushed crimson and her eyes radiated the glow of her beast—a warning despite her attraction to him. Even confronted with his anger, her gaze remained locked to his. She glided her hand along the front of her neck and swiped her tongue across her lower lip in unhurried strokes.

Then, he whiffed the scent that had disarmed him outside the First Tribal throne room. He darted back a step, unsure if the growl he stifled arose from aggravation or lust.

There was one thing Tris was certain of: with Zestine he was in oh-so-dangerous territory. His body wanted her, but his mind rebelled. Better to not cross that line, and not only because she irked him.

He couldn't deny she was breathtaking, a fact he'd confirmed the moment she'd revealed her female form in the woods. Truthfully, it seemed nature had sculpted Zestine to Tris's liking: long, silky hair to wind around his fist; a plentiful ass for his hands to explore; a toned belly to lick and full breasts to suckle; lips that'd look perfect wrapped around his cock. But one major detail hindered her perfection.

She was a beast.

Beasts repelled him, or they should have. Young raptatawks learned that beasts, as well as warlocks, were impure beings whose lives thrived on debauchery and other dark, unspeakable indecencies. As for his personal opinion, beasts weren't quite as anathema as warlocks because the former didn't need to ingest demon blood to survive, a fact that nigh guaranteed the everlasting existence of demonkind. Tris had always avoided both species.

Besides his prejudice, Zestine's assumption that they'd fuck—which meant she'd assumed other things about him, like his relationship status as well as the type of person he liked to fuck—irked him. Even though her latter two assumptions were correct, did she honestly think, considering the perilous circumstances surrounding him, he was emotionally sound for intimacy? Was she blind to his anguish?

Doubtful.

Her forwardness questioned her motives for saving his life. Worse than that, it made her look desperate.

Tris didn't do desperate.

Without breaking eye contact he shook his head and pointed over her shoulder. "Please leave."

Zestine slumped her shoulders and opened her mouth, only to slam it shut as regret flashed in her eyes. Guilt squeezed his chest for the space of a heartbeat, but she recovered posthaste, shooting him a cutting glare and resilient grin. "Too bad." Then she dealt him a naughty dose of payback.

As she walked toward the water, she pulled her shirt off and flung it on the sand. Without breaking stride, she reached back and unhooked her bra, letting the straps slide slowly down her arms and dangle from her fingertips a moment before it fell to the ground. Her slacks were next and for this she stopped and ever-so-slowly pulled them down, bending only at the waist until her hands reached her feet, then straightened and kicked them off.

Tris lost his breath as his gaze zeroed in on the minuscule white cloth serving as her panties. Her bum was completely exposed with only a thin strip of fabric wedged between her ass cheeks. When that strip slid free, he couldn't hold back a groan.

Infuriating woman. He scrubbed a hand over his face, then watched her through splayed fingers. *Tantalizing woman.*

Again, Zestine bent only at the waist and lazily pulled the flimsy garment to her feet.

She allowed him an eyeful of her bare pussy, making his dick swell for the second time in a matter of minutes, before righting herself and continuing her stroll to the water, not sparing him a single look.

Still he couldn't look away when she arrived at the water's edge, waded in a few steps, then dove under. As soon as the sea swallowed Zestine, the alluring spell she'd woven broke.

Tris slammed the door and killed the lights, wishing for the first time his kind were capable of sleep.

~

Zestine swam a short distance before floating on her back and surrendering to the sea's whim. For a time, she lost herself to the swoosh and trickle of the ocean's melody.

It wasn't that she'd fully expected to seduce Tris, but she'd believed he'd show *some* interest in her. His rejection stung more than she'd anticipated. Yet why was she surprised, especially considering he seemed to blame *her* for his turmoil?

So he didn't want her. Fine. It changed nothing. She'd still follow her conscience and accompany him to Underworld. Hopefully, he'd pull himself together and overcome his negativity by the time they left, as she was no babysitter.

Even as her eyelids grew heavy and the sea's cool caress eased her wounded pride, her itch for physical release refused to subside. Zestine went to shore and collected her clothes, noting Tris's windows were dark. She blushed recalling the feel of his warm gaze on her body, which she'd perceived thanks to her beast's special senses. Warm gazes pointed to lust, cold gazes signaled ill will, and angry gazes burned. As for loving gazes, she didn't know how they felt.

Inside her hut she showered, then snuggled under the covers of the massive bed, humming in pleasure as the satin sheets grazed her naked body. Since Tris had watched her strip, had he slaked himself afterward?

Suddenly feverish, Zestine pushed the sheets off and grabbed her tits, fondling the silken flesh and pinching her nipples. She gave a pleasurable sigh, then widened her legs and slid her hand over her belly and pelvis to the soft cleft between her thighs.

She moaned while pressing and rubbing her nether lips over her clit to create mind-numbing friction. Warm wetness blossomed, which she used to slick her swollen folds and stroke her clit.

Grabbing one breast, she worked herself wild with vigorous strokes. As she neared ecstasy, she imagined ocean-blue eyes, sculpted shoulders beneath her hands, and a long, rigid cock driving into her while soft wings wrapped her flush against velvety muscles... *Heaven.*

"Tris, you fucking bastard," she half-muttered, half-moaned just before her climax roared through her, launching a cry from her lungs.

Then, Zestine slept.

CHAPTER 7

Not long after the Noctis sun peeked over the sea's horizon a striking orange disc kissing royal blue waves, the king and queen summoned Zestine and Tris to the throne.

Zestine estimated their stay had lasted about eleven Earth days; the summons hadn't arrived soon enough.

The beginning of her stay had been nice, but once the night stretched longer than she liked and time had ceased having much meaning, she'd grown restless. No one, namely Tris, had been interested in friendship, much less getting to know her in any capacity.

Speaking of the grumpy raptatawk, he'd rarely left his hut during their stay, and she'd not the faintest clue how he'd spent his time. Raptatawks didn't sleep, so he must have repeatedly died of boredom only for the nuisance of immortality to reawaken him again and again.

The pair were silent as they followed two elf guards to the First Tribal throne quarters. Once in front of the king and queen, they knelt and bowed their heads.

Zestine counted five seconds before, as one, Lachlan and Dia said, "You may rise."

"We hope you've enjoyed your stay here in Noctis. Though I'm sure it was longer than you would have liked, it took a bit of time to get Tris's charms ready," Lachlan said.

"Charms for what?" asked Tris, and Zestine stiffened at his surly tone.

"Charms that will allow you to communicate telepathically with the changed raptatawks and match their red eyes and sharp teeth." Lachlan stood and dug into his pocket as he walked around the hyx-topped table, then presented Tris with several silver rings. Half were adorned with three red stones and the others with three purple stones. The king picked up a red-stoned ring. "This ring will both redden your eyes and sharpen your teeth for as long as you wear it." He dropped it and held up one with purple stones. "The rings with the purple gems will allow you to communicate telepathically with anyone and they with you. I spelled these charms to escape notice, so don't bother trying to hide them.

"As you can see, I've made several, and I'll make more. I want you to have plenty in case you lose any." His attention moved from the rings to Tris. "Always wear them and have extras on your person. If you can't carry extras, ensure Zestine has spares." He turned to Zestine. "There is no silver metal in these."

She nodded. Silver negated a beast's ability to shift.

The king offered a purple-gemmed ring to the raptatawk. "Try it on. It will fit any finger."

"It's huge," Tris said as he took the talisman, hesitated, then dropped it around his left ring finger. Once it landed, it tightened to a fit. Tris and Lachlan made eye contact and a few moments passed before the two men nodded at one another.

Tris's voice rang through her head. *Can you hear me? Answer in your mind.*

Yes, Zestine confirmed. How strange to share thoughts when not in beast form. Even stranger, she didn't need one of the charms to make it work. She couldn't imagine how powerful the magic in those tiny pieces of jewelry were.

"Does the telepathy charm have limits?" she asked.

"It doesn't work over long distances, but neither does telepathy," Lachlan said before handing Tris a red-stoned ring, which he put on his opposite ring finger. Like the other, it hugged his digit at the base.

The king beamed at Tris's morphed features, then reached up and shielded his mouth as he cleared his throat. When he dropped his hand, his face was as deadpan as ever.

Zestine held back an eye roll and fleetingly wondered if he'd been this strict on showing no emotion before he was crowned. Hopefully, for Dia's sake, the man let loose behind close doors.

"Good. Now, show me your teeth, look directly into my eyes and tell me if you look like the changed raptatawks," Lachlan directed just before his teal irises faded, followed by his pupils. In each eye, a silvery dot spiraled forth, growing larger until it coated the sclera and became reflective.

Tris bared his teeth and leaned toward Lachlan to inspect himself. Several seconds later Tris closed his mouth and stepped back. "I look like them," he said, voice barely above a whisper.

"Can I see, please?" Zestine asked, unable to quash her curiosity.

He turned to her with a phony smile. She winced, much preferring his deep blue eyes to sinister red ones. Those, paired with the needle-like teeth, made for a dismaying combination. Though she still found this villainous version of him beautiful, thus her sodding attraction to him wasn't going anywhere.

"How can I see the charms if they're spelled to deter notice?" asked Zestine.

The king, whose eyes were no longer mirrored, pursed his lips, briefly showing off his dimples. "You already know they're there."

She tilted her head back. "Ah."

"Just so you're clear on this, you must never remove these charms once you've gained the enemy's acceptance," said Lachlan.

"I understand." Tris dipped his head in acknowledgment. "And Zestine? What's her story?"

King Lachlan's gaze found Zestine's for a split-second before he spun around and returned to his seat.

Uh-oh.

Lachlan looked at Dia, and Dia at Tris. "The only believable explanation for her presence in your life is to say she's your mate."

Zestine refused to look at Tris as he said, in an incredulous tone, "Are you serious?"

Dia raised her eyebrows. "Very."

"B-but she's *not* my mate."

The queen shrugged. "Irrelevant. No one will notice as long as you play the part."

"Impossible," argued Tris, and Zestine couldn't hold back a giggle at his profound absurdity.

"If you can sell yourself as a Corrupted, surely pretending to fancy me shouldn't be too difficult," Zestine said, giving him a hard stare.

Tris spared her a glance. "Is there a charm for this task as well?" When neither the king nor queen humored him with an answer, he met her gaze through narrowed eyes, no longer red. "Neither will be easy," he fired back.

She narrowed her eyes right back at him, wishing she had the power to hurl his body across the room with her mind. It infuriated her that she was so drawn to him and he so obviously despised her, yet Zestine couldn't help what she wanted. His exterior pleased her greatly; his interior… needed work.

She'd at least try to instill a modicum of common sense into him. "Stop acting like a child, unless you like to embarrass yourself. You're not doing this for me, or even you. You're doing it to save your brethren. You'd be wise to keep that in mind. No one ever said this would be easy."

"Zestine's right," King Lachlan said, garnering their attention. He huffed out a short breath. "I thought we already went over this. If this is too much to handle, I need to know *now* so I can find someone else."

A moment later, Tris, whose face was bright red, shook his head. "That's not necessary. I apologize." He bowed his head.

Zestine almost wished he'd backed out. Almost.

Lachlan and Dia exchanged a look, communicating in their own mysterious way before returning their attention to Zestine and Tris.

"Are you ready to start the first task of your mission?" asked Dia.

This was a suicide mission. If not for Tris, definitely for Zestine. Chances the Corrupted would allow her privy to their plans were worse than slim, even if they were convincing as mates. *Love* was not something the Corrupted understood, let alone valued.

Tris didn't know if any of the changed 'tawks were mated. He couldn't imagine a mated brother self-Corrupting, unless their lover agreed to it. Although possible for a Pirmas to kill their beloved, Tris had never heard of it happening. A chill skittered up his spine, because if anyone was capable of such a depraved act, it was a Corrupted.

Pirmas could mate with whoever ignited their fancy. However, the occasion of romantic love gifted a remarkable asset to the couple who rendered it. Once two individuals fell in love, a protective force surrounded their union. Known as the "Pirmas bond" or "love energy," it had an innate agenda: keep its masters alive and together at any cost. This meant unnatural occurrences happened when the lovers' lives were in danger. If dire circumstances didn't trigger the Pirmas bond to act, which was preposterous to even consider, others would expect Tris to sacrifice himself for Zestine without hesitation.

Basically, he and Zestine wouldn't live long enough to help Mr. and Mrs. First Tribe.

He loosed a breath as defeat dug talons into his soul. Gaze rapt on the queen, he wondered how she and the king seemed oblivious to the sure death that lay ahead for their new spies.

Were they unaware? Was Zestine?

Now, Tris was stuck. Bringing it back up wasn't an option, not after they'd put him on the spot, so he folded his hands in front of him and listened to Queen Dia describe how his last moments alive would unfold.

"First, and this should come as no surprise, you will find 'the Corrupted,' as we're calling them, and establish yourselves as allies. Once you find someone to connect with, tell them you got separated from the bunch during a chase on Earth. This is not a lie per se, and it's important you stick to the truth as often as possible. Lying is a given, but doling out unnecessary lies will only endanger us.

"After you've gained their trust, we need you to contact us as soon as you're able." From under her thigh, Dia retrieved a flat, silver circular device about as wide as the palm of Tris's hand. Shaped like a saucer, she opened it to reveal two discs joined by a hinge.

"This is a hyx device infused with magic." She turned the item around to show that the scrying metal coated the upper disc. The lower disc was black, its circumference adorned with tiny golden dots. "Anyone can use this, not just warlocks and demons. The person who first activates it is the only person who can use it. To activate it, lick your finger and place it on a dot, then trace around the dots, ending on the exact spot you began." She demonstrated as she spoke. Each dot turned white once her finger passed it. After completing the circle, each speck intermittently flashed bright blue. "This will signal Lachlan's more complex device and one of our faces will appear on the hyx. Blue flashing lights means it's working. And as long as you use the one you activated, it'll work no matter what." Queen Dia snapped the gadget shut and set it on her lap.

"Like the rings, we will give you several of these," said Lachlan.

Tris and Zestine nodded.

"For now, only we four know what these devices are, so don't worry if you lose any. We must pick our battles wisely." He planted his pale, teal gaze on Tris. "Corrupted have been spotted in multiple Underworld towns. I doubt you'll have a problem finding them. Your first task is to find out if they're residing with demons and where."

Nervous sweat oozed from Tris's pores. "What if I see the brothers who were at the ambush? Won't they be suspicious? Like I said, they're not giving second chances. They'll wonder why I'm not dead."

The king stroked his chin. "Melvin's not here to counter your story. As long as the charms work, and they will, you shouldn't have to worry about this. Telling the truth when possible will help, but don't be afraid to make something up if needed."

Tris worried his bottom lip, his gut twisting with angst. *Am I any good at lying?* He'd never lied to any of his brothers.

They're no longer your brothers.

Tris inclined his head. "Okay."

The warlock nodded, his eyes flicking from Zestine to Tris several times. "That is all for now, I believe. Any questions?"

Zestine spoke. "What if we can't find a moment to contact you? How will you know we're still alive? How will you know we haven't sided with them and turned on you?"

Side with them? Breath catching, Tris pinned her with a glare, choking back the impulse to lambaste her for such an appalling question.

"Make time to contact us. As for the rest, I have my ways. Assume I'm always watching." Digging into another pocket, Lachlan took out two straight blades and two small glass vials secured with corks and placed them atop the hyx. "Which reminds me, I need blood."

Zestine stepped to the table without hesitation and uncorked a vial.

Tris tried to calm his jumpy muscles. "You're going to spy on us?" He eyed the beast as she sliced open her thumb and coaxed a drop of blood into the vial. She healed after two drops, then sliced her flesh a second time.

The king's pale gaze shot his way, ripe with authority. "Not something to worry about. You'd do the same in my situation. We're allies. My keeping tabs on you should reassure you, yes?"

He had a point. Tris nodded, approached the table, and grabbed the remaining vial and blade. He pressed the razor into the pad of his middle finger and dragged until a generous bead welled.

Lachlan checked on Zestine's progress. "A couple more drops," he told her.

After Zestine squeezed out two more drops, the king took her vial and swiped his thumb over the outside, turning the glass gold. Once Tris finished, Lachlan turned his vial silver before leaning back into his seat. "Any more questions?"

When neither Tris nor Zestine spoke, he offered a tight smile. "All right. Get started as soon as you leave here. I look forward to hearing from you once you've made contact with the Corrupted." He scattered the rest of the red- and purple-stoned rings across the hyx, and Dia retrieved several more compacts from in between the couch cushions and placed them next to the charms.

Tris grabbed the rings while Zestine took the compacts, then they knelt before royal couple.

"You're dismissed. May the High Lord protect you during your journey," said Lachlan.

CHAPTER 8

"So should we follow a script, or improvise?" Zestine asked as soon as they exited the king and queen's property. She and Tris were on their way to the nearest portal. When he didn't respond, she stopped and put her hands on her hips. "Hello? Did you hear me?"

Tris walked past her, but then turned around with a sigh. "Yes, I heard you, but I don't know the answer. I've never done anything like this. Lying to my brothers doesn't come natural, no matter what."

Zestine swallowed, nodding as she stared at the grass. "I'm sorry you're going through this wretched situation, but you must snap out of your stupor." She met his gaze. "Your horrible attitude will interfere with the mission, and it could kill us." Tris knew the Corrupted were *wrong*, but did he consider them an enemy? She wasn't sure. The last thing they needed was a misplaced sense of guilt acting as a deterrent, or worse—a dead giveaway—to their plans.

Tris bared his teeth. Scathing blue eyes whipped glacial fury at her. "Stop lying. You're not sorry."

Eyes wide, she looked down and dragged the toe of her boot against the ground. A full-fledged argument in front of royal guards would be a mistake, so she leashed any response besides, "Okay then. Improvisation it is."

They continued walking and soon arrived at the same portal that had deposited them in Noctis. "Do you have any idea what you'll say to them?" Zestine asked.

"Sort of," he answered, voice whisper-soft.

Ugh. Willing the tips of her claws forth, she scraped them along the back of her neck. This man's temperament made her itchy. The phrase "the calm before the storm" came to mind, only she nixed the word *calm* in favor of *defeated.*

The defeated before the storm… So not hopeful.

Zestine checked Tris's hands. The purple-stoned charm remained on the same finger he'd first donned it, but he hadn't replaced the red-stoned ring. "You need to put on the red charm now, Tris, before we use the portal." Even though she tried to sound gentle, it rang like an order. *Because it is.*

Jaw tightening, he fished a bunch of rings out of his pocket and selected one with red stones. After shoving the other charms into his pocket, he took a moment to regard the one he'd chosen, then finally slid it on his left middle finger.

This time when it tightened, she heard his teeth sharpen, mimicking the sound of crunching bones. Zestine shivered and focused on the portal.

Here we go. Whether successful or disastrous, we're on the verge of the unknown.

Side-eyeing him, she stepped aside. "You first." Since he'd previously tricked her into believing he'd be right behind her, she'd never again enter a portal before him.

Tris didn't argue, once again forgetting to state his destination as he walked zombie-like into the white, swirling mist.

"Dark Dimension!" Zestine yelled, rolling her eyes. The mission had barely begun, and he acted as if they'd already failed. Careless mistakes like the one he'd just made would get them killed in record time. Was that what he wanted?

As Zestine crossed into Underworld, she prepared for an ugly confrontation. Her raptatawk partner was stronger than this. And if he wasn't, she was so out of there.

~

Tris stumbled, but regained his balance before falling onto uneven dirt and rock, only to bend over and hack. Entering Underworld bombarded him with dizziness and delivered a gut-wrenching free-fall sensation, like something tried to suck out his stomach through his mouth. Even though he did his best to gird himself, it always got the better of him.

Then, the Darkness made itself known. After taking just a few steps, he clenched his jaw and braced his hands on weakened knees. The evil force smothered him, depleting his energy as it crawled along his skin, its touch like being stabbed with white-hot spears.

"Ah, err fuck!" Without thinking, he unfurled his wings and flapped them twice. Dust and debris lifted and danced to the wind brought forth by his rush to escape.

Several feet above the surface, however, Tris realized he was trapped. He couldn't turn his back on the mission, and escape from the Darkness was impossible in the Dark Dimension.

Focus. He closed his eyes and slowed his breathing. The uncomfortable sensations would subside as they always had when venturing into Dark territory. The Darkness had latched onto him in search of weakness. But he was a pure Light being with adequate and ready defenses, thus soon it would abandon him in favor of an easier target. The essence in his blood kicked out, the force behind it jolting his body in midair; a haunting whine pierced Tris's ears just before the sinister energy released him and he dropped to the ground.

With his bearings restored and his attacker slinking away to find a new victim, Tris assessed their location. He stood atop a hill. The lights of two towns—one to his left and one to his right—cut into the tenebrous air. No stars, moons, or clouds existed in Underworld. Other than what the towns' lights detailed, oppressive blackness swathed the realm.

He pivoted and caught sight of Zestine standing a few feet away, studying him. Head cocked to the side and eyes narrowed, she crossed toned arms over her chest, shielding her perky bosom.

Perky bosom? Where did that come from? Tris shook his head to knock away the unwelcome thought. Though he'd never admit it and had tried plenty of times to sweep it from his mind, her striptease on the beach still affected him. He'd lost count of how often the image of her bare pussy came to mind. It hardened his cock even now, which was messed up beyond comprehension.

He spun around, loosened the drawstring of his slacks, then secured his penis between his abdomen and waistband to hide his erection. Considering her demeanor, she was more apt to rip it off than fondle or lick it. With a deep breath, he turned back around and raised his hand in greeting. "Hi."

Zestine didn't speak or move, but her gaze stayed glued to him.

Tris furled his wings. When still she didn't respond, he gave in. "What?" he asked with a jut of his chin.

A smile played on her lips. "You *sure* you're up for this?"

Tris looked at his feet as his throat thickened with regret. Now that he was in Underworld, things were too real. The attack he shouldn't have survived was too real. He was tired of allowing emotions to best him. And though he'd not voice it, Zestine deserved better. "Uh, yeah. I'm here, aren't I?"

She snorted. "Physically."

He made a show of rolling his eyes. "You're being silly."

Zestine's eyes popped wide before she dropped her head forward, dragging the toe of her boot across the dirt. "No, I'm not." She met his gaze. "You and I didn't have the best start, but for this to work… in order for us to *stay alive,* we must trust each other, and that means being honest with each other, something I don't believe you're being with me."

Even though he knew she expected him to look away and prove her right, he did it anyway. Licking his lips, Tris tried to look anywhere but at her. "What do you want me to say, that I'm scared? Fine. I'm scared. I'm *really* fucking scared, because I'm positive we won't live past meeting the Corrupted down there." He pointed to the lights of the town to his right, which she gave a quick glance to before continuing to scrutinize him through haloed indigo lasers.

"Okay, what aren't you telling me? Why will we die down there?"

Tris frowned. "You honestly believe they'll welcome you, even as my mate?" He let out a discontented chuckle. "C'mon, you're smarter than that."

Zestine raised her eyebrows, the beginnings of a challenge evident as she crept forth in slow, purposeful strides. Resting an index finger against her chin, her brows scrunched into a frown. "Hmm. Perhaps my memory's wrong, so correct me if that's the case. But... I'm certain it was *your* job to inform the First Tribe of problems with their plan regarding things you know but no one else does!" Her voice rose with every syllable. "Why didn't you say anything?"

He had answers to that, but none that sufficed. "Look, I'm sorry, okay?" Tris looked at the town they were headed to. "Let's just get on with it." He unstrapped the bag from his back. It plopped on the ground and he dug through the contents, setting aside weapons. In his periphery, Zestine didn't move. He felt those laser eyes on him, but he was done quarreling. It didn't matter they were at odds, because soon they'd be dead and *nothing* would matter.

After arming himself, Tris poised to stand, but ceased movement when something thin and cool pressed against his throat.

CHAPTER 9

The instant Zestine's blade touched Tris's flesh, he dropped the bag and let out a lengthy exhale. Body roaring with tension, she cracked her neck and blinked hard, sweat beading her brow. Though she preferred her feline form during moments like this, against a raptatawk—in this specific position—she was better off humanoid.

Leash your emotion. "You must really hate me," she said, then gnashed her teeth and growled from the tears gathering in her eyes. She blinked them away and checked her hold on the dagger. Still steady. "I mean, you're happy leading me to my *death?*" Then she gasped, hit with an abhorrent possibility. "Is that what you wanted all along? What's wrong with you?" Despite wanting to hold back her aggression, she loosed a thundering snarl as her fangs emerged.

Tris began, "Zestine—"

"Shut up, *boy*," she said, drawing out the words meticulously so he could understand her through her fangs. "You know, if you don't want me to call you a boy, stop acting like one." She touched her lips to the shell of his ear and shouted, "Boy!"

He flinched, drawing her attention to the muscles of his shirtless upper body, jumping with tension. How badly she wanted to pet those steely planes while sliding her tongue along each groove…

No! Zestine shook her head hard. This was too important to allow lust to impede its payoff. Their lives depended on Tris flipping his shit, even if he hurt her in the process. She'd heal, and she didn't believe he had it in him to decapitate her.

Raptatawks were telekinetic, able to move inanimate objects, including the clothes she wore. But she was skeptical he'd use that power with a knife pressed to his throat. And if she was wrong, she wasn't worried. Desire him she did, his lack of acumen be damned, but if it turned into kill or be killed, she'd kill him so fast he'd never see it coming.

Time to bring out the viciousness she knew was inside of him.

"Listen here, child. Because compared to me, you *are* a child. I didn't come here to die, but it seems you did." She added slight pressure with the blade, stopping when it nicked his skin. Blood welled and trickled down his neck. The beast within whimpered; saliva filled her mouth. "Maybe I'll kill you now and get it over with."

Tris huffed. "Save my life just to kill me?"

"Saving you might have been a mistake. I mean, I *thought* I was saving someone who deserved it. Turns out you're nothing but a juvenile *coward—*"

Not a second later, Zestine was upside down and airborne. She felt the pull of her clothes as they fulfilled his demands, hauling her through the air before she landed hard on her back. "Oomph."

At least that didn't take long. As she tried to reclaim the air that'd deserted her upon impact, instinct made her raise the knife. The tip of the blade caught her gaze. It was the only part not coated in crimson. Beyond the blade loomed Tris, all red eyes and sharp teeth with blood bathing his neck.

Zestine sheathed the dagger, moved to a crouch, sprang back, and landed on four paws. Now a lioness, she circled him, a stratagem she'd adopted centuries ago to retake the upper hand during combat. People didn't like to be circled, especially by a species that could physically outmatch any Pirmas. She was no regular lioness, or panther, or jaguar, as the Pirmas blood running through her vessels made her far stronger and far more lethal.

Tris turned as she orbited him, never letting her out of his sight. Nostrils flaring and mouth set into a tight frown, those red eyes shone a desperate glint.

An immortal on the brink.

Making a tough decision, Zestine switched back into a woman and crossed her arms over her chest. "I wouldn't kill you."

He looked away, shaking his head and fisting his hands, then back at her. A frown marred his lovely face. "Then what the fuck are you doing? Threatening my life and insulting me won't make this easier."

"I won't let you lead me to my death! You're already defeated and we haven't even begun. That pisses me the fuck off. You should've told Lachlan you weren't the right 'tawk for this. You *deserve* my insults for not being up front with them, with me." Glaring at Tris, she marched over and stuck a finger in his face. "Where's that fire I've seen in you? Do you lack the will to survive?" At his inscrutable stare, Zestine's upper lip curled, her gaze drifting to his feet. "You're not even a child. You're an infant. A weak, sorry excuse for a man."

A split-second later she flipped head over heels. Her back smacked the ground with a thud. Then Tris was on top of her, his hand gripping hard the curves of her neck, as if he couldn't bring himself to choke her.

In her mind, she jumped for joy for finally getting this response, but pure rage burned in his red eyes. She hadn't anticipated Tris resorting to this level of violence, but she could handle it… couldn't she?

Maybe she'd gotten a bit overzealous with this tactic.

What am I doing? This isn't me. Tris saw his hands wrapped tightly around Zestine's shoulders, though initially he'd gone for her throat; he felt the effort of squeezing, but his brain short-circuited, unable to provide a reason for what his eyes perceived. Arms shaking and gaze locked on hers, he released a pent-up breath. This woman… wait no, she wasn't just a woman. This *insanely robust predator* was beyond capable of butchering him in a most gruesome manner, yet even as he held her life in his hands, she did nothing but *watch* him.

Tris couldn't look away from those indigo eyes. Then, as if a barrier crumbled between them, he had the fierce urge to drape her body with his and skim his mouth over her jaw to her lips… He'd lick the top one, then the bottom before coaxing them open with his tongue…

Gasping, he bit his own bottom lip to stop a groan. The aroma he hadn't smelled since the night he'd turned her away struck him with the power of a thousand men prying his hands free. Abruptly, he withdrew his punishing grip and stood, then tried to back away. Instead he landed on his ass as Zestine coughed and fought for breath.

Still she wanted him, despite everything? Now that he thought about it, it *had* seemed like she expected he'd attack. But why? How?

Then, it hit him: she'd worked a strategy. She'd wanted to get a rise out of him, had *known* he'd react in such a way, but not because she wanted to fuck. Desire was a mere side effect of her effort to bring his inner zeal to the surface.

Zestine got to her feet. The scent of her arousal made him lightheaded, so he stood and staggered backward. Once satisfied with the distance between them, he said, "We must settle this now."

She stroked the areas his hands had been, where angry red marks tainted otherwise flawless skin. *Shit.* Tris eyed the ground and clenched his hands. Upon looking up, the marks had faded to light pink. He relaxed his hands.

"Okay," she said, voice rough. Her intimidating fangs had receded, which went a long way in Tris allowing himself to drop his guard. Zestine cleared her throat, or tried to. "It's simple. I need to know you're game for this and willing to give as much of yourself as I am. I need to know you'll be honest with me."

Tris peered at their lit destination, his stomach souring at the reminder of the men he was to find there, what they'd done, and what they wished to do.

"You're letting your feelings and beliefs rule." Zestine sighed. "But you're too young for your conclusions to mean much."

Tris looked back at her, humbled by his inability to argue with her rationale. Many Pirmas measured wisdom by age, something he'd always considered worthwhile. When one used that logic on him, however, it was harder to accept, which only further accentuated his youth and Zestine's shrewdness.

Would it be so hard to ditch the negativity and uncertainty flourishing inside him? Maybe, but he'd try. Though he still carried resentment for her unexpected arrival into his life, she was his ally. Like it or not, they needed to work as a team, hence he owed her his respect and honesty. He pressed his lips together. "Okay. I promise to give my all."

"Good." She threw her hair in front of her shoulders and ran her fingers through it, combing out dirt and pebbles. After retrieving a thick black band from around her wrist, she piled her mane atop her head and secured it with the band. The result was messy, but cute. As she sauntered closer, Tris noticed the marks on her skin had thankfully disappeared.

Zestine offered her hand. "Friends?"

Although skeptical their relationship would ever fit the true meaning of friendship, they were in this together, had only each other, so he took her much smaller hand into his and shook it. "Sure. Friends."

A small smile touched her lips as they let go, then she turned toward the bright spot in the distance where they hoped to encounter the Corrupted.

"Let's make a plan." She removed a harness with intersected scabbards from her backpack and secured it to her back. After sheathing the swords, their hilts jutted from both curves of her neck.

Zestine and Tris each had two katanas and ten throwing knives. Not enough weaponry for Tris's liking, but their goal was to blend in, not stand out. Possessing a more impressive arsenal than the Corrupted risked provoking suspicion. Nevertheless, having a beast on his side was better than a thousand swords. The only rivals to Zestine's lethality were fire fae and other beasts, most notably wolves and hyenas.

Tris furrowed his brows. Still, she wasn't invincible. The more he thought about it, the more convinced he became that introducing her to the Corrupted as his mate would be a dire mistake. One she'd not come back from.

Zestine had just re-donned her pack when he said, "All right. Here's me being up front with you." He sucked in a breath and clapped before briefly rubbing his hands together. "We can't pretend to be mates."

Her attention snapped his way, but instead of opposing him, she nodded. "Okay. What should I do then?"

"You could stay here—"

"No. I'm not staying here. If something goes awry, I can't help you up here."

He pursed his lips. "Okay. We don't want to arrive together, so you go first and I'll follow a bit later. If they're there, find an inconspicuous spot to keep tabs on me. Sound good?"

Zestine frowned, then sighed and rubbed the back of her neck, but to his relief, nodded. "Assuming we find Corrupted, how will we know when to reconvene?"

Tris thought that over. Catching sight of the purple-stoned ring, he rotated it around his finger and raised his hand to show her what he was doing. "I'll do this with the purple charm when it's time to meet back up." He switched to his other hand and rotated the red ring. "If something goes wrong and it's not obvious, I'll twist the red ring."

"Then what?"

"Which form are you going to take?"

She shrugged. "Not sure, maybe both. And I can't promise I'll stay the same cat."

He wasn't sure that was the best idea, but no one should become suspicious of a beast changing forms, so he let it go. "Okay."

"Meet back here?" She pivoted to face the town.

"I guess. Then we'll contact Mr. and Mrs. Pirmas and go from there."

"All right." She took a few steps, stopped, and looked back at him. "When should I expect you to show? Will you fly or walk?"

The longer between their arrivals, the better. "Maybe an hour? And I'll probably fly most the way, but enter town on foot."

She squinted. "An hour? What will you do for an hour?"

His gaze moved beyond Zestine and latched on to the town. "Prepare myself."

"Hmm. Okay. Good luck, Tris." Then she transformed—clothes, weapons, and all—into her black panther and loped off into the night.

CHAPTER 10

Once Zestine's eyes adjusted to the terrain, she took off at a run, enjoying the breeze whizzing past her ears and relishing the way her paws devoured the distance as she pushed to maximum speed.

Ten minutes later she reached the edge of town, then ambled the perimeter to get a feel for the place before entering.

This small city consisted of four side-by-side roads, each bordered by a handful of buildings. As one would imagine, the locales gracing the streets of Underworld weren't for the virtuous. Most businesses dealt in the darkest and most carnal of pleasures.

One such place, aptly named Ride My Orgy, offered suitors every kind of sexual fantasy imaginable, and then some.

Bite and Binge, a blood bar that she assumed hosted constant orgies, also hopped with customers. Blood bars had opened recently, after demons performed horrific experiments on diseased vampires to develop a way for healthy Pirmas to experience bloodlust without turning their prey into mindless bloodsuckers. The substance yielded from the experiments provided users a "high" where they essentially became vampires temporarily without suffering the infection and consequential mental deterioration of actual vamps. Those they bit experienced the high as well without infection. This fad was one in which Zestine would never partake. Vampires were vile creatures and she had no desire to *be* one, even for a short time.

Other happenings included multiple individuals copulating in the middle of the street for everyone to see, a group of wind-, fire-, and earth-wielding fae performing together on the rooftops of several buildings; people bloodying each other up for the fun, and the not-so-fun, of it. At least it was difficult to stand out here unless one wanted to go above and beyond the most extreme of revelries.

Just before Zestine completed her lap, she spotted them. Four Corrupted sat outside an eatery called Swallow Madness, quietly watching the townsfolk. Two of the four dug between sharp teeth with pointy ends of fragile L-shaped bones. Passerby went out of their way to give the winged men a wide berth.

Zestine cut into town and stalked as close to the group as she dared, which was a lot closer than she'd risk in human form. In beast form, her gait was steady, her manner nonchalant. Under different circumstances, she'd have chanced eye contact with one or two, but giving the 'tawks reason to remember her would be inept.

When she was less than five feet from the Corrupted, an undeniable aura of hostility wriggled along her hide; a faux sense of anxiety spurred her pulse to a gallop. *No wonder people keep their distance.* For a split-second, she didn't know whether to continue a lazy pace or give in to the discomfort, only to dart away as fast as her legs could take her. That's what they expected, after all.

After failing to find a secluded nearby place above ground level, Zestine slunk back to the edge of town and changed to her human form. She returned to the Corrupted via a roundabout route and parked her rear in front of Licky Sticky, a venue located across the street and about a block and a half from them. Tris would no doubt see her, and the distance between her and them allowed Zestine to face the group without raising suspicion.

Sitting back and letting her gaze wander, Zestine drummed her nails against a black metal table and waited for the upcoming confrontation.

～

Tris stayed atop the deserted hill for a good half hour before disembarking toward the city lights. At the halfway point, he took flight, opting to check things out from the sky before heading in on foot. His altitude high enough to escape notice, he skirted the town's border.

It didn't take long to locate exactly who he'd gone there to find. Sitting in a semi-circle facing the street in front of a dive were four of his changed brothers. Easy enough to spot due to their wings, he descended for a closer look. It was their makeshift toothpicks that confirmed they were Corrupted. Tris recognized the slim white devices with handles and sharpened edges as raptatawk wing bones, which nobody from his side would ever fathom sticking between their teeth.

A low growl scraped the foul taste of malice up his throat as he studied their faces. Quinn was the only one he could identify, his black, spiky hair and ghostly pale complexion a dead giveaway.

Tris gulped breaths and cradled his stomach, which suddenly felt like it wanted out of his body. These guys would see right through him. He was a dead man.

Tris flew into the cover of darkness. *I can do this. It'll be fine. I look like them and can communicate telepathically.* As long as Lachlan's charms worked, all would be well. If they didn't work, he'd run for his life again.

He returned and after a quick scan of the area, didn't spot Zestine, so he finished his first lap around town and started a second. When he made it back to the Corrupted, there she was in humanoid physique, sitting a good distance away by her lonesome at a small table, nobody paying her mind.

Should he land right there or farther away? Though he considered the effort futile, he tried to see things from their perspective.

Tris thought it best if they assumed he'd sniffed them out beforehand and hadn't encountered them by accident. The Corrupted were a purposeful bunch, therefore he needed to appear purposeful. He also reminded himself that his lost brothers were calculated, monomaniacal, and never to be underestimated.

While eyeing the black abyss that stretched above him, Tris appealed to Father to keep him safe. He took a few deep breaths, turned his wings sideways, and drifted to the surface to connect with perverted versions of once-great men.

CHAPTER 11

As soon as Tris landed on the dusty street, the Corrupted, moving as one, turned to him. They regarded him for a few seconds before, moving as one again, they stood, their chairs crashing to the ground.

Tris willed his jackhammering heart calm as he studied each of them as they studied him. He knew them all. Besides Quinn, George had long, blond dreadlocks and red eyes, which used to be a rich golden color; Henrik, whose red hair, which almost matched his eyes, was a shade darker than Zestine's; and Konrad, who had no hair and towered above the others.

Before their change, Tris hadn't been close to any of them, but he'd have risked his life for theirs and they for him. Now, they'd risk their lives to *end* his, and though he still jeopardized his life for them, the reasons, compared to before, couldn't have been more different.

Why had they chosen the Darkness? Had the will to live won out? They'd rather be evil than dead?

Quinn, who Tris sensed led their small group, broke the silence. "Well, this is quite surprising. I thought you were dead." Then, via telepathy Quinn asked, *Are you dead?*

"I got lucky," Tris said. Mentally, he replied, *As you can see, I'm very much alive.*

Quinn snorted. "So I see. You know…" He looked to and fro, rubbing a thumb against his chin. "Melvin, uh, *reserved* you as his kill that day, and he's AWOL. Do you know where he is?"

Tris stiffened, feeling a twinge in his chest. *He reserved me?* "Fuck." Trying to hide his reaction, he dropped his head and shook it. Before he looked back up, he plastered a sheepish smile on his face. "Dumb bastard gave me a second chance, and on the way back to Otherworld, some fae bitch killed him." He held his hands out to the sides. "On Earth, of all places."

Quinn cocked his head. "Killed by a fae on Earth?" At Tris's nod, Quinn exchanged a look with the others. "What were you doing on Earth?"

"We portal-hopped before I changed my mind." Truth, he'd passed through portals; lie, he never changed his mind. "Earth is where he turned me." Lie. "Then, literally out of nowhere, this fae dropped a chunk of a mountain on Melvin." Truth. "Decapitated him on impact." Tris wasn't sure whether that was fact or fiction.

Quinn squinted, his red eyes like blazing coals. "Uh-huh, and what happened to this fae?"

"Dead. I ripped that bitch's head right off." Tris laughed, his conscience cringing at how sincere it sounded. "That was *after* I ravished her senseless." For good measure, he added, "Ferocious little vixen, that one."

The four brothers chuckled.

Quinn's eyes relaxed as he gave a slow nod. "It's good you recognized your mistake and found us." He exchanged another look with his companions. "You must meet our leader, the Ravager. He'll give you a proper introduction to our world."

Tris grinned. "Excellent. Where is he?"

"He's everywhere," said George.

"And nowhere," offered Konrad.

Tris bobbed his head once before realizing he had no clue what that meant. Clearing his throat, he continued nodding and hooked his thumbs in his pockets. "The Ravager, huh?" He snickered. "I like him already."

Quinn glanced at George and Konrad before approaching Tris and smacking him on the shoulder. "They're fucking with you. Our new father dwells at The Maw." Tris barked out a cough at the gag-worthy 'our new father' comment, then hastily disguised it as a laugh. "Come, Brother." Quinn guided him to the edge of town, where dusty terrain led to unforgiving mountains. "Let us take you home."

Tris inclined his head as he forced pooling saliva past the lump in this throat. Fighting the temptation to whirl around and seek a pair of reassuring indigo eyes, he allowed Quinn to escort him out of town and into the infinite darkness.

~

Zestine breathed a sigh of relief that the impromptu meeting hadn't hastened to violence. Based on her observation, things had gone as well as possible.

She waited until the group reached the edge of town to rise from her seat and transform into a cheetah before trotting after them. Upon reaching the border where the lights of the city gave way to boundless gloom, she hung back until her vision adjusted. Once she caught sight of them traveling via air, she followed at a careful distance.

Eventually, Tris and the Corrupted landed near an expanse of caves, walked a short way, and entered one. Zestine stopped outside the cave and shifted to a ten-pound, shorthaired brown-and-black domestic feline.

She entered the cave and hugged the wall as she caught up with the men. A couple of minutes later, she found them. Tris and the black-haired Corrupted strode side-by-side ahead of the other three, positioned single-file.

Before long they reached a fork. One way led to more pitch darkness and the other glowed hazy orange. The group took the lit course down a long corridor, then turned right into another corridor toward the pale, fiery glow. Voices, music, footfalls, and the sound of swishing fabric graced Zestine's sensitive ears.

Finally, after reaching the crest of a steep incline, she came upon a cavern spilling orange light through a wide archway. As the men breached the archway, she sprinted down the hill. Tris and the Corrupted halted on what could have been a platform or balcony, and Zestine bounded out of view, hugging the archway wall.

"Welcome home, Brother," one of them, not Tris, said.

Someone chuckled. *Tris?*

Uncertainty pricked at her psyche as she mulled over her next move. Even as a small cat people would notice her. If she went in, it'd have to be on two legs.

Zestine's ears twitched at the rumble of approaching footsteps. She changed her fur color to better blend with the reddish-brown rock, fell on her side and stretched her body to the max. Eyes closed, she tracked the proximity of those who neared by the strength and volume of their tread.

As they walked past, she opened one eye. The group comprised three females—two warlocks and a fae—and four Corrupted.

Once they were inside with Tris and the others, a woman said, "So this is where the fun begins?"

"This is where the fun never ends," responded an unknown male.

"Hey guys, look who's here. Someone got lucky!" declared another man.

Astonished mutters and enthusiastic profanity ensued. When the group quieted a Corrupted said, "Wait. If you're here, where's Melvin?"

"He got murdered by some fae bitch," replied Tris.

Zestine stood. His voice surged her pulse, giving her the crazy urge to see him. Slowly, she inched to the edge of the wall and peeked around the corner with one eye.

Tris faced her, claiming everyone's attention as he shared his miraculous survival story. At the same time he conversed with the group, he spoke into her mind. *If I see you, so can others.*

Zestine backed out of view. *Can I communicate with you whenever I need to and they won't hear me?*

They won't hear you unless you talk to them using your own telepathic ability.

What's happening in there?

Amazingly, he still spoke to the group without missing a beat talking to her. *I'm not sure. It looks like a social event.*

Really…- Her body vibrated with a purr. *More women are inside besides the three who just arrived?*

Many more, but—

Be there in a minute. Zestine dashed down the corridor and behind the nearest corner. After shifting to a woman, she stashed all but two knives inside her bag, leaving the katanas secured to her back. Most Pirmas, especially in Underworld, armed themselves, but she'd rather appear poorly armed than the other way around.

Once she turned the corner and headed for the entrance, Tris popped back into her head. *You shouldn't do this.*

She rolled her eyes. *Stop it. This is my job. I wouldn't have signed up if I wasn't willing to take risks.*

It's my job to inform you of things you're unaware of, remember? I'm telling you this is an awful idea.

Zestine halted, fingering the strap braced against her armpit. *What do you mean?*

"Hey there, sweetie. Comin' to the bash?" a male behind her said.

She swiveled on the heel of her boot, and her eyes widened at the Corrupted peering at her through red slits, his black Mohawk so short it resembled paint. Darkness dominated his aura. Coppery fumes stung Zestine's nostrils before she glimpsed sanguine coating his shoulders, neck, torso, arms, and hands.

Any shred of a coherent response got stuck in her throat. "Hu-um." She sealed her lips, swallowed. "I-I—"

He smiled, causing her to jerk back, then laugh like she didn't understand what she'd just done. This guy's energy was unnatural, turning her stomach and setting her body abuzz with the urge to flee. Even not covered in blood he'd have creeped her out, with sickly, pale skin stretched taut over mountains of jutting bones and valleys of sunken gray. Still giggling like an idiot, she shook her head and tried again. "It's, I—"

"It's right in here," he said, placing a hand against her back and nudging her forward.

She gave up on speech. *Looks like I have no choice,* she informed Tris.

Zestine and the Corrupted walked through the archway and she locked gazes with Tris for a moment before offering a smile to the others. The desire to cuddle close to him in this place, with these strangers, robbed her of breath.

"Hey bros, check out my sexy date," her unwanted escort said. He slung a bony arm around her and reached to give her breast a grope. Zestine clenched her jaw against aching gums, her muscles tightening as she ignored the impulse to chew the bastard's fingers off.

You're doing fine, Tris told her.

Zestine pursed her lips and looked at the floor. *It's harder than I thought to not act like myself.*

The black-haired Corrupted spoke, shifting the gathering's focus to him. "This one found the Dark," he told Mohawk while slapping Tris hard on the back.

"No shit," Mohawk said. Tris displayed a cocky smile and nodded, his gaze finding Zestine's before wandering away, but the sleaze hanging onto her must've noticed. "Congrats, my man. Here, you can have my date." He roughly shoved her toward Tris. Zestine yelped when her feet left the ground.

Then Tris's arm snaked around her waist and pulled her tightly against delicious, steely man. Zestine couldn't help but moan. In response, he gently squeezed her side, but before she could bask in his heady allure, something in her periphery snagged her gaze.

Immediately below the platform was a fissure, a crack in the realm's foundation that went down, down, *down*. She realized that if Tris hadn't caught her, the force with which she'd been flung would have propelled her over the railing and into the void. Zestine's stomach dropped to her groin; sweat coated her palms. The rift resembled two rows of jagged teeth.

Even more unsettling, it couldn't contain the Darkness within. Ghostly black fog brimmed both serrated lips, forming murky clouds above the crack. A high, whiny moan emerged from the pit's depths, followed by a wet growl and guttural clamor. In her mind's eye, Zestine saw a long black claw dig into her ear and scratch her eardrum. *Scrrr-ape, scrrr-ape, scrrr-ape. Scrrr-ape scrape scrape scrapescrapescrape—*

Chomping her bottom lip, she slammed her hands over her ears.

Scrapescrapescrape—

Zestine! Tris's voice cut through the digging rasp, shattering the frightening hallucination. Her gaze flicked from the swirling Dark chasm to Tris's red eyes, which widened briefly before he swiped a thumb over the lip she'd bitten. *What's wrong?* he asked, returning his attention to the group.

Th-I... Zestine closed her eyes. Best to bury it for the time being. They already had enough to worry about. *Nothing.*

Act the part, remember? You look terrified.

Right. Though she wasn't clear on what "part" Tris meant, she gave him a flirty smile that stole his regard from bystanders. She thought he focused on her lips as the corner of his mouth twitched, and she sighed. At least she didn't have to fake her attraction to him.

"Shall we?" said a turquoise-winged 'tawk, who gestured to the stairs leading down to the main level.

Before they descended, the black-haired Corrupted spoke. "We'll be back. I need to take Tris to meet the boss." He fixed his gaze on Zestine and lowered his voice. "I promise to return him as soon as I can."

Tris treated Zestine to a sexy grin and released her. "Don't disappear on me now."

Belly taking flight from that grin, she smiled and shook her head. "I won't."

He and the Corrupted ascended a set of stairs and disappeared into a tunnel while she reluctantly went to the main floor to mingle with dangerous strangers.

CHAPTER 12

Tris followed Quinn up to the next landing and directly into a tunnel. They traveled a series of tunnels, switching directions so many times he lost count. The last tunnel seemed to stretch for miles before they came to an abrupt stop.

Quinn knocked on a door Tris could barely see in the thick blackness.

"Watchword," uttered a deep voice.

"Seize new," replied Quinn.

"How many?"

"One."

The door unlatched, and Quinn pushed it open and walked into the room, Tris on his heels.

The chamber was small and lit by an unseen source. A few feet from the doorway sat a demon so ghastly, Tris's muscles locked from his concentrated effort to *not* cringe.

The Ravager's skin was shit-brown and severely wrinkled with scattered crevices and lumps. A black, gooey substance resembling string coated his body like a net and wriggled as if alive. His mouth was a misshapen, gaping hole, his nose marked by two tiny side-by-side orifices just above it. His eyes were his most unsettling facial feature. At least the size of tangerines, they comprised fleshy black spheres marred by five jagged, bright-red horizontal slices. Every time the ghoul blinked his rotting eyelids, foul-smelling, dark-gray smoke burst from the slices.

Atop the demon's head jutted four horns the same color as the red slashes across his eyes. Two horns grew on either side of the front of his head and stretched more than a foot straight back, ending in piercing spikes. The others sprouted just inside the lengths of the front two. Right above where the middle and front horns intersected, the middle horns flared out several inches before flaring back, then turned the opposite direction, ending in sharp points.

Though his face was mega hideous, his hands, if one could even call them hands, instilled fear into Tris's soul. Eight fingers per hand made for sixteen thick, bright-red claws at least ten inches long each. It wouldn't take much effort to decapitate with those things, not to mention other blood-splashing torment they were capable of.

"What's your name?" the demon asked.

Tris's gaze darted from the Ravager's ominous mitts to his freaky eyes. "Tris, my lord."

"Triiiiiiiiiiiissssssssssss," he replied. "I am the Ravager, your one and *only* ruler. Fall to my feet and renounce loyalty to the High Lord this instant, or face eternal suffering in the Pit of Teeth."

Tris fell to his knees before the Ravager finished speaking.

"Pledge your loyalty to me," the demon demanded.

He looked into the demon's nauseating eyes. "I pledge my loyalty to you, Ravager, and only you."

"Renounce the High Lord."

His gut heaved. *Forgive me, Father.* "I r-renounce all faith and lo-loyalty to the High Lord."

"Gooooood. Now, stand so I can have a look at you."

Tris stood, and the Ravager closed his eyes for several seconds. When he opened them, thick black smoke poured from the serrated carvings of his eyes into Tris's face, scorching his throat and snatching his sight. Rough coughs wracked his body as he threw up his arm to shield his eyes.

"Don't fight it," Quinn said just before Tris sunk into unconsciousness.

~

Zestine's gaze flitted over her surroundings, yet she saw nothing. Gnawing her lip, she studied her immaculate nails for the umpteenth time while trying to ignore her uneasy stomach.

Tris had been away much longer than anticipated. In addition to wondering if he still lived, without him she found it harder to 'act the part.'

Three Corrupted played haunting music using vocals, drums, wind instruments, and makeshift guitars atop a stage constructed with rock and bones and decorated with feathers of every color imaginable. Not long after Tris's departure, Zestine had settled at an abandoned table, watching people dance, drink intoxicants, bicker, brawl, fuck, and murder fellow Pirmas. She'd witnessed the demise of four unfortunate souls via the rift below the balcony, all non-Corrupted thrown in by Corrupted seemingly for entertainment.

She'd cursed her ears after hearing someone refer to the chasm as the 'Pit of Teeth.' Like she needed to know that.

She kept as far away from the Pit as possible and avoided eye contact with everyone. *This is where the fun never ends, indeed. Wow, this place is a rare nirvana. Why would I ever want to leave?* Covering her mouth as the corners lifted, she suppressed an incredulous giggle. The only positivity was no one seemed interested in her.

Zestine pondered leaving (while she could), but she couldn't make herself desert Tris. When he'd said not to leave before going off with the Corrupted, she'd thought he was acting, but it didn't matter if his request was sincere. Partners stuck together. If he went down, she'd join him in misery.

As she tried to still her tapping foot, two naked Corrupted slammed a raven-haired, golden-eyed female warlock on her back atop Zestine's table. One Corrupted had spiky blond hair and red wings with white stripes, and the other was bald with snow-white wings broken up by curvy purple and black expanses. Naked below the waist, the woman guffawed and propped her heels on the edge of the table. A second later she let her knees fall open.

"What are you manly men going to do to me?" the warlock asked once she'd stopped laughing.

Zestine's gaze moved to the raptatawks, who both smiled, though they weren't the kind of smiles she'd want to see if in the woman's position.

"We're going to do nasty things to you," said the bald one, his red gaze gleaming with promises of carnal torment. He grabbed his dick and stroked slowly up and down, claiming Zestine's attention. For whatever reason, she couldn't look away from the carefree display of masturbation.

"Hmm. Looks like someone wants to join this party."

Zestine's gaze whipped from the Corrupted's penis to the blond-haired, red-and-white-winged Corrupted. Her jaw descended, only to snap shut, teeth clacking. Hunching her shoulders, she folded her hands and pushed them between her thighs, hoping her body language would speak for itself.

The three Pirmas' gazes locked on her; six lust-glazed eyes roamed her physique. They may as well have wagged their tongues at her.

Zestine shook her head and dug her nails into her palms. *So much for staying under the radar.*

What to say? "I-I'm sorry." She offered a smile she hoped was convincing. "I'm here... *with* someone." She stopped shaking her head to give an enthusiastic nod. Zestine stood, but before she could take a step, the blond raptatawk snagged her wrist.

"Not so fast. You might be here with someone, but you're obviously interested in Konrad." He nodded toward the bald Corrupted.

Zestine tried to break away, but his grip was too fast. He tightened his hold, his fingers pressing into her bones so vigorously she emitted a squeak of pain. Normally she'd already be claws-deep in his flesh with her teeth in his neck, but she couldn't allow her temper sway. Though she was daring and lethal, those attributes wouldn't do her much good at the bottom of a chasm.

"No, I'm not interested in you," she said, looking at Konrad, who continued stroking his cock. "I'm sorry. You just caught me by surprise, and like I said—"

"We heard what you said, and I think you're lying," Blondie said. He pulled her against him and leaned in, the tip of his nose brushing her neck as he took a long sniff. Zestine's stomach squirmed, disgust rendering her near berserk with the need to revolt, and violently. Her gums throbbed as her fangs readied for bloodshed that she couldn't let happen.

I am so fucked.

The blond Corrupted withdrew, though not far enough, and displayed sharp teeth via a predatory grin, red eyes sparkling with lust and ferocity. "Lucky us. We have ourselves a beast, my friend." He slung Zestine to Konrad, who snatched her around the waist, then squeezed her ass none too gently.

Trembling from the force of her fury, the rush of blood roared in her ears. How dare these men think they could dominate and overpower her. Jaw throbbing from clenching it so hard, Zestine desperately tried to scheme an escape that wouldn't end in carnage.

She'd have to fight back with little chance of winning. Two Corrupted she could handle, maybe three. But a room packed with them? Not so much.

Konrad took her hand and placed it on his erection. A shudder rolled through her when the engorged flesh brushed her palm. Thoughts vanished as claws shot full-length from her fingertips. She raked into his dick. A couple slashes more and it dropped to the ground with a thud, the blood that followed smoking and bubbling where it hit the dusty rock.

Konrad's face blanched. He opened his mouth but emitted no sound. Eyes rolling back into his head, he fell backward, colliding with a chair that smashed underneath his weight.

Zestine looked on in horror, powerless to move. The blond Corrupted stared wide-eyed at his passed-out companion. The female warlock giggled. Zestine needed to act before Blondie broke from his stupor.

Forcing her body to move, she turned to flee, only to run smack into Tris.

CHAPTER 13

Things had certainly turned interesting during Tris's absence. He'd seen Konrad force Zestine's hand on his dick and everything that followed, but didn't know what had preceded the incident. She was damn fortunate he'd happened upon the scene, though given what he now had to do, she might not see it that way.

Secretly, Tris wanted to laugh and congratulate Zestine for mutilating the asshole Corrupted. Instead, he clenched his jaw and fisted his hands while making his head vibrate as if in a rage. *Play along if you want to live,* he told her, ensuring his telepathic tone was gentle, yet direct.

Zestine's bright indigo eyes shone with a myriad of emotions. *Okay.*

I'm sorry. As it turned out, he wasn't half-bad at acting like a deranged knave. What he needed to do next, however, deserved no pride.

Tris's chest pulled painfully taut as he wrapped a hand around Zestine's neck and yanked her to him while simultaneously pulling a knife from his belt and raising it to her throat, only for his gaze to settle on her luscious red lips. The urge to sample their flavor and find out how eagerly she'd part them for his tongue shattered his concentration.

Tris? Her voice resounded through his head, derailing his preoccupation.

He refocused on that pair of stunning bluish-purple irises. "Why the fuck did you castrate my brother, bitch?" he roared, using his hold to shake her, but not as hard as he could.

Luminescence spanned her eyes, her features surrendering to her beast as via their telepathic link Tris sensed it stir, bracing for the opportunity to sate its hunger. "Unwanted advances come with repercussions," Zestine said, tone deadpan. She peeled back her lips and gave a vicious snarl through two rows of nightmarish flesh-shredders. "It'll grow back, and maybe he'll have learned a lesson."

His own words to Zestine echoed through his head: *Play the part. Play the part.*

Tris feigned a diabolical smile, briefly wondering how differently she'd act if an actual Corrupted held her by the throat. "A lesson, huh?"

"Kill the bitch," Quinn said. Tris looked over and Quinn pointed to the crevice Zestine had been so fascinated with. "Toss her in there." The Corrupted's lips curled into a nasty grin.

Looking back at Zestine, Tris swallowed, then squinted at her. "I think she'd be good for a different purpose." He released her neck, but slid the blade around it as he circled her, staring her up and down and licking his lips. When he was back in front of her, he smirked.

Quinn chuckled. "Oh… yes."

Zestine's eyes tracked Tris's fist as he drew it back, then rammed it into her cheek. She fell backward, landing unconscious on top of likewise-unconscious

Konrad. Tris bent over and dragged her off the Corrupted by the ankles.

Be convincing!

Not wanting to, but knowing it'd look good to Quinn and the others, he hawked a wad of spit onto her forehead. "I'll teach you *many* lessons." He lifted and settled her over his shoulder. To Quinn he said, "Want to show me and her"—Tris slapped Zestine on the rump—"to our new home?"

Quinn, still wearing that icky grin, nodded. "Follow me."

~

Zestine awoke to an unfamiliar shiny-black ceiling. It took a few moments to realize she lay on a bed. When she tried to sit up, her heart sprang to her throat at the harsh clangs from above and behind her and the cool metal surrounding her wrists, restricting her range of motion. Gaze sliding to her feet, she gasped and shook her head in disbelief. Someone had chained her ankles together.

Closing her eyes, she inhaled deeply through her nose and let it out through O-shaped lips, then willed herself to beast form. When nothing happened she thrashed about; the scream that climbed her throat emerged a squeak as she tried to cover her mouth but only succeeded in jerking the restraints and producing more clangs.

This was new territory for Zestine, but she should've seen it coming. What had she thought would happen to her for slicing off a Corrupted's penis… they'd forgive her?

Numb hands quivering and sweat slicking her brow, she lay in stiffened angst, sinking into a silence that blared with dread.

The maddening quiet lasted long enough she eventually stopped expecting to hear anything. Her entire body jolted at the sound of a door opening and closing. Zestine didn't breathe, move, or blink as clunky footsteps approached. When she saw who those footsteps belonged to, she sagged against the mattress in bitter relief.

Tris entered the room through a doorless entry to her left. As soon as their gazes met, he removed the red-stoned ring and his features normalized.

"Just wanted you to know it's really me," he said before re-donning the ring.

Zestine stared at him, feeling her bottom lip tremble. Heated pressure developed behind her eyes when his lovely blue irises changed to the cruel red of a Corrupted. She looked away to hide her face. The transformation of his eyes wasn't by itself upsetting, but for some reason it triggered the weight of their plight to sink in with crushing enormity.

I'm okay. I'm okay, she told herself over and over again. *Things could be worse.* Though she tried not to think of how *much* worse.

"Hey," he said in a tone so gentle it warmed her insides.

"Yeah?" Before he could reply she said, "I'm okay." After taking a moment to gather herself, she tried to sit upright, scoffed, and slammed her back on the bed. "Why am I tied up? And why can't I turn?"

His gaze drifted over the room as he crossed his arms. "You're tied up because you'd be dead otherwise, and those chains are infused with silver."

She gasped. Why hadn't she concluded that herself? "Take them off. Right now."

Tris shook his head and tucked his chin against his sternum. "Can't."

"What?" she said, louder than intended. She softened her voice. "Yes, you can." She tugged the chains. "I'm not a prisoner."

That earned her Tris's frown. Zestine lost her breath as understanding dawned. "No," she whispered. Liquid seeped from her tear ducts and rolled down her cheeks. To wipe the tears away, she unconsciously yanked on the bonds, groaning at the resulting clang.

"I'm sorry, but this is the only viable way to keep you alive. Don't deny it. Tris the Corrupted wouldn't untie you. Tris the Corrupted *would* keep you prisoner."

Still whispering, Zestine replied, "But you're *not* Corrupted."

He cocked his head, then shook it as she blinked out more tears. She understood what he wasn't saying. It was written plainly across his face: *There's nothing I can do.*

She craned her neck to study the restraints and found it *was* possible to sit upright. Her ankles were shackled to each other, but not to the bed itself. Bending her knees, she pushed against the mattress with her heels, pulled on the vertical bars the chains were hooked to and rose to a sitting position. She rested her chin on her knees and stared at the stony black wall ahead. "Where are we?"

"My quarters. This is the bedroom, obviously, and there are a couple of other rooms…"

Zestine snorted, leering at the space. *His new home. How sweet.* "Raptatawks don't sleep," she said, mostly to herself.

Tris blew out a heavy sigh. "Other Pirmas can stay, and I think you know beds aren't just for sleep."

Attention snapping his way, Zestine didn't bother hiding a petulant laugh. "Oh, you changed your mind? *Now* you want to fuck me?" She canted her head forward and peered at him beneath her brow bones. "Stop teasing me, raptatawk."

Eyebrows lifting, he parted edible lips. "Zestine…"

Her insides jumbled. "What?"

"His dick *will* grow back. You said so yourself."

Zestine's blood grew frigid. "No," she breathed, then tugged as hard as she could on the shackles while groaning mounting frustration. How she detested the foreign emotions taking root. Helplessness was not a condition with which she had experience. "No. Please, Tris. Please." Was that a whine edging her voice? *Humiliating.* Here she'd thought she was something special, an asset to someone like Tris. Instead, she was a hindrance, a pathetic failure he'd have to babysit. She cowered from his penetrating gaze. "Please, get out."

Silence stretched for several heartbeats. "Konrad will be here as soon as he's fully regenerated." And with that horrific declaration, he exited the room, leaving Zestine closer to broken than ever before.

~

Tris didn't believe Zestine would forgive him, but that was tough. He didn't have a choice. Preventing the Corrupted from exposing them as frauds was top priority. To set her free would seal their deaths, not that he blamed her for demanding it.

Sure, she couldn't help him much posing as a prisoner, but that was on her. No one but Zestine had decided to mutilate Konrad, yet she *and Tris* faced repercussions. This didn't stop Tris from wanting to untie her, nor did it soothe the cramped throat or churning gut that'd arrived upon shackling her in silver.

Quinn had helped Tris bind Zestine. Right after he left Tris contacted the king and queen via the magical hyx device. He'd filled them in on most everything, and although Lachlan and Dia were less than happy Zestine needed to limit her role, they agreed Tris had done well to remain undiscovered. The good news was it pleased the royals he and Zestine had infiltrated the Corrupted's home base so quickly.

At least something is going right.

He'd imparted to the First Tribe his meeting with the Ravager, but not what had happened after the demon knocked him unconscious. The Ravager had put a spell on Tris that barred him from telling anyone what he'd experienced while in the clutches of the mind invasion. He couldn't even tell them there was information he couldn't tell them.

Tris rummaged through Zestine's backpack and removed a flask of water and a clear bag filled with dried meat before returning to the bedroom. He didn't care that she'd told him to leave. He'd take care of her as best he could whether she liked it or not.

The wet trails lining her cheeks caught his attention first. Her eyes were glassy, the skin around them red and puffy. Upon meeting his gaze she bared teeth that didn't sharpen.

He rubbed his chest, wishing time was reversible so she could've acted smarter with degenerate Konrad. A languished Zestine struck him as so… *wrong.*

Tris tossed the bag onto the bed. "Here."

She looked at it, then back at him and smiled, though it didn't reach her eyes. "Why thanks so much!" she gushed. "I was just thinking 'I wish I had some food to stare at.'"

Why did she insist on hassling him? Hadn't they moved beyond such behavior? "Do you want it or not?"

"Untie me?" she suggested in a sickly sweet voice.

Instead of obliging her, he grabbed the bag, ripped it open, and pulled out a hunk of dark-brown meat that felt moist, yet dry, and lent a rich, tangy aroma. "What is this?" he asked.

"Meat." She opened her mouth and he broke the piece apart before offering her a shred.

Tris snorted. "Yeah, I know. What kind of meat is it?" He waited while she chewed.

"Venison."

"What's that?"

"Deer meat." Zestine stuck out her tongue, atop of which he placed a chunk.

He fed her the rest in silence. Once she'd eaten the bag's contents, Tris unscrewed the flask and poured splashes of water into her mouth until she'd drunk it all.

"Thank you," she said as he screwed on the top of the flask.

Stiffening at the unexpected gratitude, he shook his head before meeting her gaze. "Don't thank me."

Zestine furrowed her brows as she wiped the corner of her mouth on her shoulder. "You didn't have to feed me."

Tris slid the empty flask in his pocket and clasped his hands in front of him. "Why wouldn't I?"

She licked her lips, an act that captured his gaze. Zestine's lips brought to mind spicy pleasures, and had since the moment he'd first seen her. "Tris *the Corrupted* wouldn't have," she told him.

His breath hitched. He looked from her lips to her eyes, parted his mouth to reply, but failed to conjure an adequate response. A knock came from the main door. Both their gazes whipped toward the sound, then back at each other.

Zestine's eyes widened and the color bled from her face. The churning in Tris's gut intensified.

Konrad and his revenge had arrived.

CHAPTER 14

Zestine's pulse raced as she fought sudden lightheadedness. Now she'd face the unthinkable, and fear like she'd never known iced her blood, numbing her bound limbs.

Tris turned toward the doorway.

"Wait!" she said in pure desperation. The chains clanged. "You-you d-don't *have* to answer the door." Her wrists flopped uselessly at her sides.

He frowned. "Yes, I do." Upon exiting the bedroom he projected into her mind, *I hope you can forgive me.*

As she stared blankly at the room's doorway, Zestine willed herself void of emotion, or she tried to. Sure, her sexual appetites sometimes ventured into rough territory, but she'd always been willing with her partners, not to mention capable of defending herself if things got out of control.

Being restrained and without the inability to shift were two huge strikes against her. Caustic dread lurched from her gut to her chest, where her heart thumped harder, up to her throat, where a lump formed, before flooding her system with overwhelming angst. Sweat seeped from her pores, causing her a chill and sprouting goosebumps across her flesh.

Calm down. Calm down. Calm down! I'll be okay. Tris won't let me suffer too much... will he?

Zestine took deep breath after deep breath and listened to Tris and Konrad's conversation as their heavy footsteps neared.

I'll survive this. I have no choice. Her eyes slid shut. *Breathe in, breathe out. Breathe in, breathe out. Breathe in...*

"Have fun, Brother. Try to leave her in one piece though, huh? I still need to attend to her," Tris said from just outside the room.

Breathe out.

"Hard to disfigure an immortal," said Konrad.

Breathe in...

Tris let out a laugh Zestine pegged as fake. "Right you are."

Breathe out.

Zestine didn't have to see Konrad to know he'd entered the room. Not wanting to be blind in his presence, she opened her eyes and refused to look at him.

"Hey there, little firecracker. Remember me?" In her periphery, he moved closer. When she didn't acknowledge him, he walked to the front of the bed. "Huh?"

She met his evil red gaze and cocked her head. Giving him a small smile, she furrowed her eyebrows. "No."

The smile he returned was anything but friendly. "That's okay, darling, because you're *going* to remember me." Attention shifting to her bound ankles, he opened the locks via telepathy before manually removing the chains. Interesting that no lock secured the shackles. As the links slid through his hands, he made eye contact and winked. "These might come in handy." Konrad set the chains at the end of the bed and proceeded to undress. He was ripped; a male she would've found sexy if not for his obvious shortcomings.

"First time I've ever had to grow my dick back," he said before grasping his erection and stroking using the same lazy motions he had when this whole mess had begun. It grew and hardened with minimal stimulation, making her wonder…

Did *she* arouse him or did forcing an unwilling female into sex turn him on? Now that she thought about it, the raven-haired warlock hadn't seemed in her right mind with the two raptatawks looming over her. Did Corrupted need to use drugs or force to get sex? Nothing would surprise her with these miscreants.

Konrad sat beside Zestine and undressed her. He pulled her pants off and tore the rest of her clothes from her body, including her bra, but removed her thong the regular way.

"This'll make a nice gag, don't you think?" He smirked.

Zestine clenched her teeth and sealed her lips, but he grabbed her chin and dug his fingers into her cheeks. This forced her lips open, but her jaw remained tightly locked. Konrad wound the garment around her head and situated an expanse of material against her teeth.

His lips touched the shell of her ear. She flinched, every inch of her body repulsed by his proximity. "Bitch, unless you want to experience unimaginable pain, I suggest opening your pretty little mouth."

Leashed fury jabbed at her from within like dull daggers. Having no choice, she unclenched her jaw and he re-applied the makeshift gag. The material stretched painfully against the corners of her mouth. Zestine growled, body shaking as she raked nails into her palms.

Konrad stood and surveyed his work, nostrils flaring and erection bobbing. Exposure to the cool air hardened Zestine's nipples into rigid peaks, but he didn't go for her breasts. Before she realized his intention, he was on his stomach with his head between her legs, pushing against her knees to keep them open.

Toxic rage dampened to make way for panic. Excess adrenaline hastened her pulse, acute dread causing her to jerk and bounce against the mattress. "Nmf, fmm!" With every bit of strength she had, Zestine tried to close her legs while bracing for the pain of his teeth, but the bite never came. Konrad's soft tongue glided over her folds and brushed the edge of her clit, coaxing from her a pleasant sigh.

The tension in her body melted. *What the...*

Zestine couldn't quite believe Konrad was eating her pussy and it felt *good*. Not that she could relax and enjoy. Distrust kept her head level and gaze rapt on the Corrupted's every lick, the intimacy of which she refused to entertain. She had other things worry about. Like what if she orgasmed and he took that moment to strike with his teeth?

The sounds of his tongue on her cunt filled her ears as she parted her mouth to cry out, then hastily sealed her lips. Yet the effort she expended to stifle proof of her sexual excitement was for naught. A few minutes later he circled her clit with his tongue, then licked the sensitive nub with breathtaking pressure only to circle around and lick hard, again and again. After several rounds of that, she fought to keep her gaze on him as she came, emanating a loud, muffled moan through the gag.

Once it was over, Konrad backed away and smiled, the sight of which made struck Zestine with a frigid sense of horror. Her juices coated his mouth. Disgust for enjoying what he'd done burned her face and roiled her gut—which, she suspected, was why he'd done it.

Rising from the bed, he stroked his shaft and moved toward her, using his free hand to undo the gag.

Oh no.

Konrad gave her a knowing look as he kneeled on the bed, cock level with her mouth, and pressed the head against her lips. "Open up."

She made a strangled noise as a potent wave of disgust slithered through her. He'd force it down her throat if she didn't capitulate. All she had were threats. "Not afraid I'll steal myself a snack?" she said with a snap of her teeth. And she'd *so* do it if she thought she could get away with it.

Konrad cupped and caressed her jaw with the gentle touch of a monster. "If you want to die, go ahead and try." He pushed against her lips harder.

Defeated, she sagged against the headboard, parted her lips, and welcomed his sex into her mouth. Up and down the length she slid her tongue. He groaned, and Zestine snapped her eyes shut while fighting the urge to retch. The meat Tris had fed her whisked in her gut. Dull daggers returned to prick away from beneath her skin, which was really the beast begging to deliver cutting retribution upon her sexual tormentor. A cocktail of emotions bombarded her so abruptly, tears leaked from her eyes before she even knew they were there.

Then an idea popped into existence, and she slowly convinced herself the man she pleasured wasn't an asshole Corrupted, but a sexy raptatawk whose mere presence got her hot and wet.

Imagining she was sucking Tris's cock caused her to put real effort into the task. Since she was unable to use her hands, she released his dick, only to drag her tongue to the base, then lower to lick his balls, eliciting from him a moan. She put his shaft back in her mouth, sealed her lips extra tightly around his girth, and worked her tongue every which way while bobbing her head. The moment after the tip of him entered her throat, he let out out a deep hum while his seed flowed into her mouth. Not having a choice, she swallowed. But upon opening her eyes, the proof of who she'd pleasured couldn't be denied. Zestine leaned over the side of the bed just in time to vomit his cum onto the grainy black floor.

Konrad stumbled off the bed, barely missing the puddle of vomit. He sneered at her, and she glared at him, not at all embarrassed. If she revolted him, maybe he'd not return. At least she could hope.

He lunged for her, got in her face, and grabbed her breasts, squeezing much too hard. Zestine yelped, then growled, digging her nails into the bed and willing herself a beast to no avail.

"This isn't over," he said, looking her over as if she were a pile of shit before releasing her bosom, snatching his clothes, and stalking from the room.

Gaze on the doorway, Zestine wished she could turn back time and never have gotten involved with the raptatawk she'd just, to retain her sanity, fantasized about.

CHAPTER 15

Tris waited in the kitchen while Konrad did his thing with Zestine. When she let out an elated sigh, his gaze shot to the bedroom. He'd expected screams, growls, thumps, and rips, so he tip-toed over and peeked into the room.

What he saw made his jaw drop and eyes bug out. Zestine wore not a stitch, her legs splayed wide as Konrad tongued the pink cleft at her center.

Not exactly what he thought he'd see.

Tris's gaze drifted over her body, starting at lovely round tits topped with stiff rosy nipples, then to her belly, an expanse of creamy light beige with a shiny white diamond nestled within her navel. Tris licked his lips as he envisioned playing with that ring using his tongue before sliding a wet trail to her loins. As his gaze fastened on her swollen pussy, he fantasized licking and sucking the needy flesh until she screamed his name and came on his tongue.

As he imagined the taste of her sex, its musky scent invaded his nostrils, and he concluded the flavor would be as good as, if not better than, the smell.

Zestine focused on Konrad the entire time he pleasured her.

Muscles bunching and skin heating to an uncomfortable temperature, Tris's gaze was rooted on the beast through her rapture. His cock begged for freedom. Begged for *her*. When the Corrupted brought Zestine to orgasm, an emotion Tris had never expected to feel concerning her propelled to the forefront of his mind.

Tris narrowed his eyes as he pinned Konrad with a glare so healthy the Corrupted probably felt its wrath. Baring clenched teeth, he spun around, returned to his seat in the kitchen, and fisted his hair.

That smell is for me. *That orgasm should be* mine. *That woman…*

He tried to slow his breathing. He couldn't understand how Zestine was turned on by the miscreant raping her, who'd also gotten to sample her gorgeous body *before* Tris, even though it'd been Tris who aroused her—with minimal touching—three times that he knew of.

Ridiculous. He didn't own her or the mouthwatering aroma of her pussy, but faced with this unexpected jealousy, perhaps he *did* want to own those things… and more.

He'd told himself the beast with fiery hair, spectacular eyes, and cherry-red lips was merely nice to look at while funneling his resentment for the horrific changes of his brothers toward her. *She* had made him confront a grisly reality before he was ready. So much had Tris begrudged this, he'd tried to convince himself of not one lie, but many lies.

She repulses me.
She's power-hungry.
She wants to play God, ravenous for control.
She's desperate, a smartass, annoying, and pushy.

While there may have been a smidgen of truth to the smartass and pushy assertions, he didn't know her well enough to draw such conclusions. Which pointed to another mistruth he'd tried to embrace: she wasn't worth getting to know.

Mixed emotions raged a war inside his head.

You could've lain with her in Noctis, but you sent her away.

She's a beast!

A gorgeous beast with a body made for fucking.

Digging nails into his scalp, he grasped his hair between his fingers and pulled. Wild innuendos promising to right this problem whispered from beyond the fringes of sanity, and he knew retreating from the premises was a must. When Konrad's moan broke through his mental chaos, Tris stood, armed himself, and left his lair to hunt for a distraction.

～

Tris found Quinn, George, and Henrik sitting at a round table in the main hall, where Zestine's troubles had begun. The men were focused on a sinister art project, sharpening delicate raptatawk wing bones into what Tris assumed were weapons.

The desecration of his *true* brothers' remains boiled Tris's blood. For a second he considered returning to his rooms, but the thought of hearing Zestine and Konrad enjoying each other yanked tighter the knot in his stomach. He'd rather deal with intense anger than the unfamiliar discomfort brought to him courtesy of the woman he'd all too easily rejected.

What an idiot he was, and now he had no choice but to keep her captive.

His sodding attraction to her aside, Tris had no problem admitting Zestine was a good soul. She exhibited selflessness, determination… and she *had* saved his life. She'd even defied her teammates' desires to ensure Melvin didn't hack him into pieces.

Tris squeezed his eyes closed. *There's nothing I can do. Stop thinking about her.*

He approached Quinn and the others. "What's going on?"

The men stopped filing bones and looked at him.

"Not much," said Henrik, who went back to sharpening the bone with outward strokes of his knife.

George set down his work and flipped back a few blond dreadlocks obscuring his face. "Shit. You look pissed."

"What's up?" asked Quinn.

Tris shrugged and looked around, trying to school his expression by studying the surrounding dull reddish-brown rock with feigned interest. "Bored."

"Why are you armed for battle?" George asked.

Not arming himself had never crossed his mind. "Um…" He shrugged again. "I—"

"Maybe he wants to hunt." Quinn dropped his bone and knife and stood. "I'll take you." He nodded. "It's time. If we're lucky, you'll get your first kill!"

"I want to go," said George, rising from his seat. "You coming?" he asked Henrik.

Without breaking focus on his project, he shook his head. "Nah." Then he stilled his blade and eyed Tris.

"Actually, I hoped to visit that redheaded whore of yours."

"Konrad's with her," Tris said, relieved he could use the bald Corrupted as an excuse.

Henrik's gaze shifted beyond Tris. "Not anymore."

Tris looked over his shoulder. A smirking Konrad headed toward them.

Fuck, fuck, fuck, fuck, fuck, fuck!

Tris quirked up one side of his mouth. "Eh…"

Play the part.

Chuckling, he turned back to Henrik. "Right you are." The urge to ask Henrik to wait until he himself fucked her popped into his head, but he swiftly quashed the idea. They'd point out he'd had plenty of time before Konrad's arrival, and what could he say to that?

Well, you see, she was too upset. Then she needed food and water…

No. Not an option.

Tris nodded at Henrik. "Go ahead. Don't kill her, and I'd prefer you don't make a huge mess." If he thought it safe, he'd instruct Henrik not to physically hurt her at all. "I'm in Cradle," he said, specifying the name of his quarters.

With an evil grin, Henrik set down his bone and knife and headed into the back tunnels. Tris watched him until he'd disappeared from view. His hands were shaking, and he could feel each pound of his heart, all because of Zestine. He found himself torn between two very different scenarios: he didn't want her to enjoy the Corrupted, nor did he want her to suffer. The best he could hope was for no one else to visit her during his absence.

George and Quinn went to their rooms to arm themselves, and upon their return the three of them departed the cave. Once out in the open, they soared into the black sky.

The breeze's cool caress against his wings provided a much-needed mental and physical boost. Tris took advantage of the flight to swoop, flip, and twist his body in the air. The other two laughed amid snide comments, but he didn't believe they'd question his Corruption status just because he liked to clown around in the sky. The Corrupted had shown they weren't emotionless, and they had a sense of humor—though it was dark, it existed.

Feeling part bold, part reckless, Tris flew over to Quinn and used telepathy to ask, *Where are we going?* They'd already passed the town where Tris had first intercepted them.

Quinn pointed to the nearest illuminated strip comprising the other town Tris and Zestine had seen when they'd crossed into Underworld. *I want to check that place out. Seems the city closest to The Maw has been raptatawk-free for a while.*

Does that mean survivors? Tris replied.

Quinn growled. *It appears so. That was once our hot spot. The first time raptatawk blood was spilled there it caused quite the ruckus.*

You were there? Tris tried to sound fascinated.

That's when I was turned.

Upon reaching the outskirts of town, they flew the perimeter looking for raptatawks. To Tris's disappointment, they soon spotted a group of five. Though he recognized their faces, he couldn't place their names. The thought of killing any of them tightened his chest and constricted his lungs, making him lightheaded as he inhaled without hyperventilating. It was difficult maintaining his Corrupted attitude when planning to murder innocent men.

Quinn, George, and Tris landed several blocks down from their prey, who sat outside a venue with 'Ample Flesh' written in pink lights above a black awning. Two of the five 'tawks were busy with a female, and the other three drank intoxicants while playing a card game involving lots of discussion and laughter. A samurai sword dangled from the belt of each warrior. Not enough weaponry for the likes of three heavily armed foes with the edge of surprise on their side.

"Fuck, this is going to be so easy," George said, matching Tris's thoughts exactly, minus the enthusiasm.

Too easy. No way could he allow Quinn and George to slay all five.

Maybe the 'tawks would agree to join the Dark side, but Tris wasn't counting on it. That he *hoped* for such an outcome was reprehensible, bringing to mind King Lachlan's warning: *you may have to do things that go against your nature.*

Killing an innocent raptatawk definitely fell into that category, but so did forcing a brother to turn on his very soul and join the Darkness. Either way, Tris lost. Sweat dribbled down the front of his neck. He neglected wiping the bloody drops away, distrusting himself to move without unsheathing his sword and beheading the men standing beside him.

"How do we do this?" Tris asked through clenched teeth.

119

"It's pretty simple. We confront them and if they don't know about us, they'll ask about our eyes and teeth, and we'll tell them they must join us or die. If they do know about us, they'll either try to bolt or fall to our feet in submission." Quinn met Tris's gaze. "I probably don't need to tell you, most choose to bolt."

A lump formed in his throat as a troubling possibility struck him. Tris couldn't Corrupt a 'tawk. If his prey chose Corruption, Tris would give himself away. The turning happened by way of bite, and a chemical in the Corrupteds' saliva paralyzed whoever they bit while sadistic forces invaded their blood, where their Light dwelled, and slew it before replacing it with Darkness. Tris could bite someone well enough, but that's where the charade would end.

If they want to turn, they deserve to die.

Tris closed his eyes. *But not by my hand.*

Worry about that when it happens. Strangely, Zestine's voice spoke this thought, sparking renewed determination. Opening his eyes, Tris wrapped a hand around the hilt of his sword and squeezed.

"Are we ready, fellas?" said Quinn, red eyes gleaming with perverted anticipation.

"Fuck, yes. Let's do this." George drew his samurai sword and strode toward the 'tawks.

Tris took a deep breath, hoping whatever happened, he'd be in one piece by the end.

CHAPTER 16

Don't think. Just do what you have to do.

Tris and the Corrupted approached the five raptatawks whose delightful time was about to become a nightmare.

The first 'tawk to notice them had shoulder-length brown hair and light-blue-and-white wings. His smile faded as he took them in.

He knows.

"Shit," the 'tawk said, rising so fast his chair teetered and collapsed. He unfurled his wings, but Quinn snatched the end of the nearest one and dragged him into the street. There, Quinn stepped on the innocent's back and ripped off his wings, the sound of each rip chafing Tris's eardrums like a demon's screech. The two woman shrieked and ran inside the establishment while patrons and pedestrians greedy for bloodshed distanced themselves to watch the barbaric slaughter.

The screams from Quinn's victim lanced Tris's soul, but he couldn't dwell, as the remaining 'tawks attempted their own escapes. Two of the four spread their wings, but George stopped one and Tris the other by grabbing his wing, then knocking him to the ground with a hard kick to the stomach.

"No. No!" his victim cried. He pried his sword from its scabbard and swiped, nicking Tris on the wrist. Without thought, Tris wrenched his prey's wing this way and that, causing him to squeal, and stepped on the hand holding the samurai. Bones crunched under his boot, and the 'tawk bellowed as Tris bent over and seized the weapon.

The tip of the sword vibrated thanks to Tris's quivery, white-knuckled grip. He pressed the razor-sharp edge to the 'tawk's neck. Malice radiated from the honey-brown eyes of the man he was to murder, coupled with a fear Tris knew all too well—fear for a fate he'd avoided by virtue of the woman suffering under his good grace.

Stop thinking!

The male under him curled his lips, then laughed hysterically before saying, "Filth." He hawked and spat a wad of phlegm, striking Tris on the cheek.

Tris gritted his teeth and scrubbed away the slimy gunk with his shoulder. Stepping off the 'tawk's mangled hand, he crouched, put his mouth next to his ear and whispered, "May the High Lord grant you eternal peace in Paradise." Just as the man's eyes widened, Tris stuck him with the blade, rupturing his voice box before slitting his throat to his spinal column. Blood spurted and gushed, rapidly sending the raptatawk into shock, then unconsciousness. Tris grabbed an arm and leg and tossed him onto his belly with little effort, the potent angst rushing through his system, maximizing his strength and stamina. With vicious yanks he tore off his brother's wings, officially ending his life.

He dropped his chin to his chest. Out from his conscience emerged a parasite of ravenous guilt. *Forgive me, Father.* Could He hear Tris from the Dark Dimension?

If He could, did He care to listen to the killer His son had become?

Woozy and dancing the edge of mania, Tris turned to locate Quinn and George, who'd taken care of the other 'tawks. Splashes of crimson painted them from head to toe, and Tris didn't need to look down to know raptatawk blood covered him as well.

"Bring those wings here," Quinn told Tris as he situated the wings of their kills into a neat stack.

Tris carried over purple-tipped flaxen wings. He plucked a few feathers from one before dropping both at Quinn's feet.

George, Quinn, and Tris twined the five sets of wings together, top to bottom. Once secure, George crafted slots for his shoulders and used the remaining twine to tether the slots to the winged bundle. After George strapped the heap to his back, Tris and Quinn checked the twine's hold and situated the load as to not trouble George during flight. As they worked, Tris nursed a desperate urge to rip off George's green-and-gold wings, then stand over him, grinning, as he bled out and perished.

I deserve a brutal death too. I killed an innocent.

Now that he'd forever sullied his hands, uneasy questions devoured his brain.

Would he be the same Tris when the mission concluded?

By living among the Corrupted, would he become brainwashed and eventually believe the same horrendous things they did?

Would a time come when he enjoyed killing his brothers?

123

Already, he needed to justify the execution he'd just committed, so how long before he no longer felt the need to rationalize his evil deeds?

What if someday his guilt turned to pride, his regret to satisfaction?

"Let's go," said Quinn, cutting into Tris's dreadful musings.

As they walked to the edge of town, Tris fought to match the easy pace of his Dark brethren. The intense stares of the townspeople slithered along his backside. He'd taken part in an unprovoked massacre, spilling raptatawk blood on Underworld soil, no less. Although they delighted in bloodshed, the witnesses wouldn't soon forget such a devastating ordeal.

The trio took off and upon reaching a steady altitude, Quinn sidled up to Tris and asked, *You okay?*

Tris knitted his brows and chuckled in his mind, reminding himself Quinn didn't ask out of kindness. *Yeah. Why do you ask?*

You seem almost... in shock. Accusation laced Quinn's telepathic tone, causing a thorn of apprehension to prickle Tris's insides as he willed himself to maintain composure. This was a test. Just because he'd proven himself Corrupted in a physiological sense didn't clear him of suspicion altogether.

Tris pursed his lips as he carefully considered his words. *Well... It hit me back there, you know... how lucky I am. I don't understand why Melvin took pity on me.* He shook his head. *I sure as fuck wouldn't have for him, but I feel... blessed.*

Quinn nodded, his eyes turning frosty while his mouth thinned into a tight frown. *Melvin's decision didn't go unanswered. The consequence was swift. It's no mistake he died when he did.*

So true, Tris replied. Though tucked deep in the back of his mind, he imagined Quinn's surprise and fury if he knew the truth. The thought brought a genuine smile to Tris's face.

Falling back to fly by his lonesome, Tris promised himself two things. He vowed to attempt to see the world as the Corrupted saw it, through a lens influenced by demons and tainted by Darkness. Reciprocal to that, he pledged to never lose touch with the Light, no matter how Dark things became.

~

Zestine had just gotten comfortable enough for a dose of shuteye when the main door to the lair creaked open and heavy footsteps approached.

Expecting Tris, she prepared to gush about her time with Konrad to see if it'd spark jealousy. But when the redheaded Corrupted she'd seen in town entered the room instead, it robbed her of speech.

His hair was a shade or two darker than hers and eerily close to the red of his eyes, which held a glint that lifted the hairs on the back of her neck. He scanned her nude body, then met her gaze and smiled a smile that stole her breath. Needle-like teeth accentuated his features, but not in a good way. Her intuition indicated Konrad was a newborn pup compared to this one.

Speaking of Konrad, he hadn't bothered re-binding her feet, so she crossed her legs to shield her genitals, even though her new visitor had already seen.

He tracked the movement, then made eye contact and cocked his head. "Aw, you think you can hide from me. That's adorable."

Against her best interests, Zestine jerked back when he stepped closer. "Wh-who are you?" she asked.

"Henrik, and you?"

She opened her mouth to answer, but no words came. Finally, she said, "I'm no one."

Henrik smirked. "Okay, No One. Let's get rid of these pesky lights." Before she could protest, he held out his hand, palm up, and made a fist as he looked at the light fixture above the bed. The bulb shattered, bathing the room in darkness. A faint glow from lights beyond the bedroom prevented absolute pitch-blackness, but Zestine's relief was short-lived.

He exited the room and doused every light in the place, leaving her blind. Without her beast's abilities, her sight wouldn't improve, but his would.

Icy fear frosted her vessels, chilling her blood as Henrik walked back into the room, then stopped, took a few more steps, stopped, took more steps and stopped. He repeated this pattern numerous times around the bedroom. She couldn't pinpoint his whereabouts, and trepidation sealed her lips. He must have been fortunate enough to avoid the puddle of vomited semen, or didn't care about soiling his feet in a pool of foul muck.

As Zestine waited for his next move, hell overtook her mind. She screamed as images detailing gruesome horrors plagued her like a waking nightmare. Dead raptatawk after dead raptatawk—decapitated, wingless, flayed, and dismembered—flashed across her mind's eye. In addition to countless corpses, live 'tawks suffering vivisection and other vile procedures bombarded her. Awful sounds accompanied the unwelcome slideshow: rough howls, cracking bones, ripping flesh, wet smacks, gurgling body cavities, and a horrendous *scratching* ring that dug searing claws into her psyche.

Zestine shrieked herself hoarse, beseeching the moving pictures to cease, but they continued playing, playing, playing. The misery of those dead and dying raptatawks seeped into her blood, her bones, her very soul. Eventually, she lost track of where her fear ended and theirs began.

Henrik hadn't come to fuck her body. He'd come to fuck her mind.

After what felt like hours, the vision faded to silent blackness. Zestine sagged against the headboard and breathed as quietly as possible. Sweat covered her neck, chest, and arms despite the chill sinking into her.

Eyes heavy, she took pains to keep them open but ultimately failed. Too strong was the draw to escape the terror and the cold, and as she teetered on the edge of sleep, and unconsciousness beckoned with warm and loving arms, a stabbing pain in her nether region launched a scream from her throat. Sharp, digging agony ripped at her core, accompanied by wet sucking noises.

"Stop, stop, stop," was all she said, all she could think to say. But it didn't stop, and when she thought she was sure to pass out from the excruciation, the pain subsided and a grating voice inches from her face declared, "Gotcha."

Zestine cried out and squinted into the darkness. There, mere inches away, she barely made out a white face displaying a wide smile filled with dozens of pointy teeth coated in blood. She screamed and gagged, screamed and gagged while trying to get her hands on her attacker despite her bound wrists.

"Leave me alone!" she bellowed. The shrill desperation lacing her voice only added to the terror. Surely she'd explode into gory chunks soon. Nothing could feel so frightening without leading to a brutal climax. Another scream ripped from her throat at realizing her terrorizer was sitting on her legs, making it impossible to use them against him. "Get out, you ugly fucking piece of shit!" Zestine snorted snot into her mouth and was just about to let it fly when he finally spoke.

"Thanks for the taste, love." He stood and left the room, the sound of his strides fading until she heard the door open and close.

Hot tears poured from her eyes. Was she shivering from coldness or fear? Where was Henrik? *Am I still alive?*

Not daring to believe the Corrupted had left, Zestine sat ramrod straight and didn't so much as blink. No way she'd fall asleep now, so she remained in that exact position until the door creaked open once again.

CHAPTER 17

When Tris returned to his lair, he paused at the threshold. The place was black. He stepped inside and gently shut the door, then waited for his vision to adjust before heading to the bedroom.

"Zestine?"

"Who is it?" Her panicky whisper sliced through the dark.

"Tris." *Does she not recognize my voice?* He entered the room. She sat on the bed with her knees beneath her chin, naked. Her wrists were still bound, but her ankles were free. "Why are the lights out?"

She didn't look at him or move, just stared straight ahead. "Henrik."

"Why...?" Tris flipped the switch on the wall, but nothing happened.

"He crushed all the lights."

"What?" Tris sighed and went to the kitchen, where he rummaged around in cupboards and drawers until he found spare bulbs, then replaced each bulb and disposed of the ruined ones.

As he worked, question arose. He was dying to know what had transpired while he'd been gone. What had Zestine and Henrik done together? Had it been the

Corrupted's idea to turn out the lights or hers? Had they made love? Had she had sex with Konrad? Why not when she'd enjoyed his tongue so much?

After taking care of Henrik's mess, he returned to the bedroom, only to immediately halt. Zestine studied her groin with a frown.

Tris averted his gaze to the floor, fisted his hands, and inhaled deeply against the fierce temptation to stride over and steal a gander at the focus of her attention. Not that a mere look would suffice. Once centered, he asked, "Everything okay?"

She looked up with wide peepers, cheeks aflame. "I—um, bled."

"Bled?" He stepped closer and glimpsed her lady flesh. She closed her legs, but not quickly enough to hide the thick coat of dark red and underneath, a splotch that had coagulated into a hard puddle. Muscles tensing to the point of pain, he thrust a shaky finger at her. "You—th-this is…" What was the term? It started with, "Mm, Mme-ssic?"

"Menses?"

"Yes, that." Tris dropped his hand.

"No," she whispered.

Their eyes locked before she looked down and pursed her lips. He grasped his hips and paced to the wall and back. Which evil fuck had cut her *there?*

Tris would rip off the assailant's head and ram it up his ass. No, too kind. He'd behead a different Corrupted and shove *his* head up the offender's ass, all the way to his stomach… or mouth. "Who did it?" Though his voice was level, inside he smoldered, the rush of blood in his ears singing a murderous tune. "They'll *wish* for the Pit of Teeth when—"

"Tris. Did you allow Henrik in here?"

He paused his pacing with his back to her, then spun around. "He did it?"

She raised her brows and shrugged. "Just answer the question, please."

To deny it would be easy, but he respected her too much to lie. "I had to. I can't say no to them, Zestine."

"Figure out how to tell *him* no… I mean, if this is to become my life. And you won't do *anything* to him. Not till this is over, understand?"

He pulled his brows into a frown. "Retaliation is okay for you but not me."

The chains clanged against the headboard as she raised her hands. "Of course not. Tris, look at where that decision got me." Her hands plopped to her sides.

With a growl, Tris swung around and launched a fist into the wall, then both fists. "Fuck this. Fuck, fuck, fuck, fu—"

"Stop." Zestine's tone packed the punch of a smack across the face.

Tris went rigid, his bloody knuckles pressed to cool black stone. After a heavy silence, he forced himself to ask, "What happened?"

Zestine sighed. "You don't want to know."

He turned to face her. "I wouldn't have asked if I—"

"Tris." Her frantic gaze paralyzed his tongue. "Don't."

Practically feverish with the need for violence, he could only look away and nod as a wave of rage-filled dizziness swept through him. He left the room to wet a rag with warm water. At the sink he lifted the lever and tried to focus on the jingle of the running tap. The roar of blood in his ears was replaced with pounding. His vision flickered black before the blood coating the backs of his hands captured his attention. Mouth watering, he wet his lips. He wanted to see more blood. Rivers of it.

Tris groaned and propped his elbows on the edge of the sink. He tried for calming breaths, determined to smother the frenetic inferno burning within. Then a disturbing realization punched into his awareness: these violent emotions were for Zestine's trauma, yet he'd just finished slaying his brother. He cared more about what'd happened to her. Denial peeked out from the shadows of his psyche, but he shoved it away.

Prior to returning to the bedroom, he doused his entire head in freezing water. Back by her side, he almost gave her the damp cloth before realizing she couldn't wash herself with tied wrists.

Upon seeing what he'd brought, she parted her lips and slowly raised her gaze from the cloth in his hands to his eyes. "You're going to clean me?"

Thinking of his hands so close to her sweet spot heated his blood in a most inappropriate way given the circumstances. "I—well…" He glanced at the floor and cleared his throat. "Only if you'll let me."

Zestine met his gaze with huge eyes, then opened her legs.

Lord Father. Could things become more unexpected? Tris didn't move and instead stared at the washcloth.

"Just do it, please. You won't harm me. I've healed." She turned her head away, as if she couldn't stand to watch.

Tris swallowed, sat on the edge of the bed, and cleaned the most sensitive and alluring area of her body. Gingerly, he scrubbed the thatch of hair covering her sex. A bit darker than the hair on her head, the red curls were fine enough to view her slit, and his mouth watered from the urge to part the seam with his tongue before flicking and suckling her clitoris. Tris nearly moaned, imagining her slick, cushy flesh against his mouth and nose, burying him in her scent and flavor. His cock strained for freedom. As he wiped the juncture of her thigh with a trembling hand, the side of his pinky grazed her lips, and Zestine sucked in a breath.

Tris instantly withdrew. "Sorry. Did I hurt—"

"No," she practically shouted, then softened her voice. "It's... nothing." Zestine looked down, seeming to evaluate his work before shutting her thighs. "Thank you."

Fighting the desire to re-open her legs and take a good long look, then taste, of her, Tris stood, tossing the rag into the corner.

She already enjoyed a male earlier. A male who's not *me.*

Thoughts of Zestine and Konrad's rendezvous soured his sexual appetite... slightly. He crossed his arms. "So." He sniffed. "Sounded like your time with Konrad wasn't too torturous after all."

At once, her eyes narrowed. "I didn't ask him to pleasure me and I sure as fuck didn't want to like it."

Tris snorted. "Yeah... well, you *did* like it."

Zestine's jaw fell. "Uh. My gods. You're jealous."

Feeling his face flush, he opened his mouth to deny it, but what was the point?

"You could have had me, Tris, multiple times. But you didn't—no, you *don't* want me. You've made that very clear, so it's a little late for regrets. I mean, you *spied* on us?"

"No. I just took a peek."

Zestine continued watching him with parted lips that looked good enough to eat. Then she changed the subject. "Will you please loosen my wrists? My hands are numb."

Tris uncrossed his arms and ran a hand through his hair. He didn't wish for Zestine to suffer, but untying her was an awful idea. "Odd that the old and wise Zestine wishes to do something foolish."

Her eyes widened briefly. "I'll tie you up when this is over and you can tell me how willing you'd be to take a risk."

Perhaps they could compromise. "I'll remove one, restrain it later, and then remove the other." He freed the wrist nearest him. Once loose, she rotated it, then clenched and unclenched her hand.

Gaze rooted on him, she said, "Did you see what happened *after* Konrad… did that thing to me?"

Did he want to know? "No…"

She flicked her head toward the other side of the bed. "Come over here."

Something told him he wouldn't like what he'd see. He tore into his inner cheek with his sharp teeth. "Why?"

Zestine rolled her eyes. "Just do it."

Tris relented and stopped short at spotting brown chunks swimming in a gooey white substance. "What does this—" but then he knew. The puddle was Konrad's semen, which, based on the meat Tris had fed Zestine and the acrid scent wafting from the goop, came from her stomach. Hands fisting of their own volition, a low growl crept up his throat. Henrik and Konrad were dead men, but before their demise he needed to figure out how to keep them away from Zestine.

She gave a cynical giggle. "Why are you mad? If you don't want to clean it up, unchain me and—"

"No. I'll take care of it." Tris got towels and wiped up the mess, then threw the soiled towels in the trash and sat at the kitchen table, cradling his head in his hands.

Konrad's mouth all over Zestine's pussy had fucked with him big time. Now knowing Zestine had sucked the Corrupted's dick, brought him to orgasm, *and* swallowed his cum really flayed.

You could have had me, Tris. Multiple times.

He'd rejected her with ease.

You could have had me.

Now he wanted all of her and more.

Multiple times.

"Tris!"

He slammed his hands on the table and looked up. What did she want now?

"What?" he said before breaching the room. Once inside, he leaned his back against the rock and crossed his arms.

Zestine lay on her side facing the opposite wall, and his gaze landed on the generous globes of her rump. How sweet it'd be to spoon her in that very position. He'd kiss her shoulders and nape while readying her with his fingers. Once she was nice and wet, he'd slide to the hilt with a single thrust, then pummel oh-so-deep while fondling her breasts and petting the nub right above their joined bodies.

Fuck. Tris's erection thrust against his zipper. The effect this woman had on his mind and body…

"How long will you leave me like this?" Zestine asked in a small voice.

Huh? Tris shook off the titillating daydream. "What do you mean?" Then it hit him. She was probably hungry and thirsty. She had to have lost at least half her meal by vomiting. "Hold on. Be right back." Tris left the room and found her backpack, dug around until he located another bag of meat, then refilled the flask with water. "I brought more food and water," he said upon returning.

After a moment, Zestine slowly rolled onto her back and sat upright.

"I guess you can feed yourself this time." Tris tossed the sealed food on the bed, but she pushed it away.

"No. I'd rather you do it." Those spectacular eyes met his. Tris lifted a hand to smooth out her mussed hair, but at the last second lost his courage and grabbed the meat instead.

~

Tris opened the bag and offered Zestine a chunk of meat, which she readily opened her mouth for and chewed with gusto. After swallowing, she asked for water and once she'd washed the bite down, questioned him about his time away.

"Where did you go?"

Pinching a shred of jerky, he hesitated before withdrawing his hand and extending it to her. She took it with her teeth and chewed while he, well, *didn't* answer.

"Tris?"

He flinched. "Corrupted stuff."

"Okay… I asked *where you went,* not what you did. What does 'Corrupted stuff' mean?"

He gave a brisk head shake. "Nothing big."

The second answer that didn't match the question earned him a tut-tut-laced scowl. "Don't fucking *lie,* Tris."

Mouth parted, he ran his tongue along the inside of his bottom lip. Glazed eyes suggested he'd gone somewhere else in his mind. Moments passed, and with a click of his tongue, he snapped to. "I, uh… I don't want to talk about it."

Of course he didn't. "Sorry, but that's too bad. We're partners. Even though I'm stuck here, we need to work together. Would you hide things from me if you hadn't made me your prisoner?" She cocked her head, hoping he perceived her hard stare and recognized her passive dig even though he was staring at his lap and might've not been listening. Maybe, if he hadn't refused to follow the king and queen's instructions to pose as mates, she'd still be a free woman.

Shaking his head again, he sighed. "I don't know." His fingers resembled claws as he curled them toward his palm slowly, clenched his hand for a few seconds, then just as slowly unclenched it. Tons of questions buzzed around her brain, but she let the silence breathe, opting to at least fill her belly before pissing him off too much.

Upon finishing the meat, she drank the water herself, stealing peeks of Tris while he ogled her body. A wanton thrill blossomed within her core and radiated to the surface of her flesh, unleashing a shiver of pure need. He *wanted* her, for real, though what had changed since he'd denied her in Noctis, she wasn't certain. Circumstances rendered her perpetually naked, and she *was* a woman—as far as she knew, Tris wasn't into guys. He had no friends here, and she doubted he'd ever been so vulnerable.

Though she'd quit pursuing him after his rejection, she remained dangerously attracted to the man. The possessive heat burning in his eyes when he looked at her was what rekindled the drive to captivate him. Though the raptatawk seemed more dutiful than before, she'd use a subtler approach to seduction than she had the first time.

Zestine drained the flask and handed it to him. Tris left the room and returned seconds later. Hands cupping his elbows, he rocked on his heels. "Are you cold?"

She raised her brows as an idea popped forth. Maybe she could take advantage of his unwillingness to divulge the details of his sinister adventure. "If you don't want to talk about Corrupted stuff, I'd like a bath."

"Hmm…" Eyes narrowing, he bit his pouty bottom lip and tapped his chin. "Fine, but be quick." Tris walked to the other side of the bed and released her wrist. Before she could swing her legs over the edge of the mattress, he wagged a finger at her. "And no turning."

Zestine clucked her tongue. "Why does it matter? If a Corrupted comes and finds I'm free, you'll have a lot to answer for anyway."

He closed his eyes and released a heavy breath. "Just, please don't, okay?"

It didn't matter because the beast detested getting wet, but she didn't feel like explaining. "Yeah, yeah." She walked passed him.

He followed, hovering like a mate would hover. "And keep your hair dry. I'm only allowing this because they won't tell the difference once you're through, but—"

"Got it." Zestine halted in the doorway and turned toward him. When he stopped, leaving scant inches between them, she swooned. Despite his contribution to her pitiful situation, she couldn't be mad at him, even after the terrifying encounter with Henrik. "Where's the bathroom?"

"Take a right and it's the first room on the right."

She stared at him out of the corners of her eyes. Tris stared back. Now that she knew the attraction was mutual, the space between them crackled with unspent lust. "You can join me if you'd like," she said with a wiggle of her eyebrows. "Could make a good excuse if anyone visits."

Then she strolled out the door and into the bathroom.

CHAPTER 18

Once he heard Zestine close the door, Tris exited the bedroom and halted just outside the bathroom.

Should he take her suggestion? His cock ached something wicked. If she touched him, he'd explode. Fuck, he'd explode if *he* touched *her*.

He stroked his erection through his slacks and let out a faint moan. Zestine *had* to know how turned on he was, and that's why she'd invited him to join her. It could be the reason she'd asked to bathe.

Tris had three choices: accept her invitation and surrender to a desire that, since its emergence had proven merciless; gratify himself while she bathed; wait until she finished, then pay a harlot to take care of him. He wasn't without funds…

Thinking of another woman slaking him brought to mind one word: *unsatisfactory*. Even if this nameless whore was sensational at her craft, he'd fantasize about Zestine and be tormented by the inkling that sex would be crazy better with her.

As long as the temptress in his bathroom was willing, why rely on himself to relieve his hankering, especially since she was responsible for it?

Heart galloping with sudden verve, Tris strode to his lair's front door and pressed his ear to it. Not hearing anything, he slid the sole lock in place. No one dwelled nearby, but at least three men knew where he stayed. The most the lock would do was give them warning.

He took a deep breath, then pivoted and approached the bathroom. Zestine had turned on the water while he'd stepped away. He knocked, but received no answer. When he went to knock again, the door crept inward before his fist hit the wood. He nudged it open and after closing it secured the lock for extra warning.

A dreamy white vapor wafted about and warmed his skin. As in every room of his lair, shiny black rock surrounded them—magnificent really, and magnificence was rare in the Dark Dimension. The sink, tub, and toilet were white marble, their contrast to the rock a treat for the eyes. The melodic rush of flowing water and its subsequent murmur against stone resounded through the space.

Zestine stood at the sink filling a bin with steamy water. As he beheld her pale form against the rock, Tris could think of no word fitting enough to describe the woman's beauty. His fingers twitched with the need to touch and explore. A curtain of red hair fell in front of one shoulder, reaching to just below her breast. Those cherry-red lips looked downright savory paired with her creamy flesh, which the steam had rendered slightly pink.

To the left of the sink stood a spacious clawfoot tub minus a faucet. Tris wondered how well it'd accommodate sex.

"Glad you took my suggestion," she said, causing Tris's gaze to snap to her face. In this light her irises were more blue than purple, perhaps even close to the blue of his own eyes.

141

Thoughts of his eye color pulled his attention from Zestine to the red ring he'd worn since their journey began. He started to remove it, then changed his mind and slid it back down his finger. Too risky given the chances they were already taking.

"Leave it on. It's okay."

Looking up, Zestine was near enough to snatch into his arms. His gaze dipped to her plump, heart-shaped mouth, then to her neck, and collarbones, finally lingering on her bosom. Her breasts were plentiful and would fit in his hands perfectly. Her nipples were dusky pink, and he licked his lips as he imagined their texture. Next, Tris eyed her toned belly, admiring the diamond nestled within her navel before descending to the enticing cleft between her thighs, which he ached to touch and taste. Upon concluding his perusal, he met her gaze.

With a sexy smile, she tilted her head back and reached up to pet her throat, tongue swiping the corner of her lips.

Tris stepped toward her, intent on sealing his mouth to hers, but she swayed back and held up her index finger before returning to the sink.

He frowned. *What's she doing?*

"Are you going to take your clothes off, or..." Zestine said as she continued filling the tub.

Tris didn't hesitate to undo his pants and shove them down, finally freeing his throbbing cock. He stepped out of them and, not knowing what else to do, stood there.

Though it seemed she was dreaming, she knew she wasn't. Tris was actually in the bathroom with her *unclothed*, and his body was a sinful prize. Golden-tan skin covered steely brawn, his sculpted chest narrowed to cut abs and slim hips, and the organ between there and his thighs dried her mouth and dampened her pussy. His dick was, well, as she liked to say, *purr-fect*. Zestine guessed its length a good ten inches, and the girth generous enough she knew he'd have no trouble hitting all the right places. Though hard to tell from where she stood, she thought it was slightly curved. While viewing the thick head of his cock, more wetness slicked her inner thighs as she predicted the thorough bruising of her G-spot with that part of his body.

"Um, I think the bucket's full," Tris said.

Zestine flinched at the sound of his voice, then checked to find the receptacle overflowing. When she looked back at Tris, he sported a playful grin.

Shaking her head, she poured out a small amount of water before dumping the rest in the tub. "That should be enough." She dropped the bucket to the rocky floor. Then she realized she'd forgotten soap, but skipped asking Tris to fetch it from her backpack as he came at her, his strides purposeful, expression determined. Her body sizzled with anticipation.

Who needs soap?

She gasped when he cupped the back of her neck and leaned in… for a kiss? *Wait!* Darting back, she put a hand on his chest. "Hang on."

Tris froze, brows furrowed.

"I just…" Zestine grabbed his hand and slowly pulled off the red-stoned ring, giving him ample time to

143

stop her before removing it. She heard the reshaping *crunch* of his teeth, and her knees weakened at the deep blue eyes staring at her, *rapt.* She lifted a finger and petted his bottom lip. "Show me."

Tris smiled, stealing her breath. *Oh, Lord.*

His lips captured hers so fast, she yelped in his mouth before melting into him with a whimper, their tongues colliding in feverish urgency. Tris caged her waist with one arm and pulled her close, pressing her breasts against warm muscle. He slid his other hand from her nape through her hair to cradle the back of her head.

Zestine twined her fingers in his hair while feeling for his cock. She moaned upon grasping it, then alternated fondling his balls and stroking the length. She was slippery between her thighs. Never had she been more primed to accept a male. Zestine didn't merely want to come; she needed *Tris* to make her come. And of course she'd return the favor.

He hummed in approval just before breaking for air. His gaze smoldered as it drifted across her face. The raptatawk gave off a fierce intensity *for her* that not only further aroused Zestine, but pierced her soul.

She tried to burn his eye color into her brain before finding his hand and sliding the ring on.

The charm activated, and Tris's features transformed at the same time his expression crumbled. "You don't mind?"

She knitted her brows. "Doesn't matter what I want. It's too risky." *Everything we're doing right now is too risky.* "And no, I don't mind."

He nodded, then gestured to the tub. "Better get in before it gets cold."

Zestine beamed, grabbed his hand and stepped into the tub. Once they were both in, she sat, moaning as the warm water engulfed her body.

Tris settled across from her, and that's when the romantic ambience of the situation hit her like a blow to the back of her head. If a Corrupted walked in…

"What's wrong?" he asked.

"Well… this," she waved her hand between them, "would *not* look good if someone caught us."

"Want to go back to the bed?" He pursed his lips, and Zestine practically heard his thoughts whirl. "I thought we wanted to take this chance. If you're not willing, why invite me in here?"

She opened her mouth, momentarily stripped of speech. "What? I-I didn't think you'd want to… join me. I wasn't even serious, really." The moment the words were out, she yearned to take them back.

Tris shot up and stepped out of the tub.

Zestine's stomach turned. Despite—or perhaps due to—the regret roaring inside her, she'd lost the ability to articulate. "No, Tris, wait. Th—I… Please."

He pulled a towel off the rack and wrapped it around his waist. His erection tented the fabric.

Tears threatened. Zestine opened her mouth to demand he get back in and finish what they'd started, but the words jammed in her throat.

Nicely done, moron.

Leaning back against the wall, he wouldn't even look at her. "Get cleaned up. I've got things to do."

"Tris, I—"

"Just…" He shook his head. "Don't."

145

Zestine's ribs strangled her lungs as she scrubbed her body with shaky hands and no soap. The water still steamed when she left the tub. After drying off with the remaining towel and hanging it back up, Tris opened the bathroom door and Zestine led the way back into her dungeon.

Neither of them spoke while he secured her wrists to the bedposts and bound her ankles. He left without saying good-bye, and upon the main door slamming shut, she allowed tears to flow.

CHAPTER 19

What a liar he was. Tris had nothing to do. The only thing he wanted to do was sink his cock deep into the enchantress chained to his bed.

He stalked the gloomy tunnels doing his best to ignore his aching balls and trying to forget how much Zestine disheartened him. The dynamics of their relationship had flipped 180 degrees. She had desired him, and he'd denied her; now he thirsted for her, and she'd managed to deny him.

Her words echoed through his mind: *I wasn't even serious, really.* At least he wasn't the only liar. That kiss had felt serious. The magnetic charge between them was real and therefore serious.

Love was a vicious monster. Not that he *loved* her, but he bore *something* for her, something different and exciting. Terrifying as well, if he was honest with himself. Tris wanted Zestine to trust him and know he'd protect her as best he could, that he *needed* to keep her safe. In their unique situation, he couldn't romance her properly or convey the extent of his affection, and these inabilities fucked with him *and* fucked him over.

The narrow walls made his wings itchy, so he headed out of the caves. Just prior to entering the commons, Tris had to make room for several Corrupted, including Konrad, carrying pipes and toolboxes into the maze.

"What's this for?" he asked no one in particular.

"Making more rooms. Gotta equip 'em with the basics," said a Corrupted with dark-gray wings.

Tris smiled and bobbed his head at the horrible news. *How often do they recruit 'tawks?*

Once the group passed, he entered the main gathering area and stifled both a cringe and an eye roll at spotting Henrik and George, who approached him straightaway. They were dressed for combat.

Tris's blood heated in Henrik's presence; he took a couple of deep breaths, slowly so they wouldn't notice he was trying to calm himself. Though Zestine hadn't said for certain, he believed the red-haired Corrupted had wounded the part of her body that, if given a chance, Tris would treasure with his mouth, his fingers, his cock.

"Tris," George said by way of greeting.

Play the part. I am brutish. I am despicable.

Tris nodded at the pair. "What's up?"

Henrik regarded him, a sinister grin stretching his mouth too wide. His pointy teeth weren't quite touching, and he held the grin long enough that icy pinpricks skittered up Tris's spine.

"We were coming for you," Henrik said. "Multiple gawks have arrived in the nearest town. They're trying for an offensive. The Ravager said all unoccupied brothers must fight." Though this was Tris's first time hearing 'gawks'—he didn't need clarification to understand Henrik was referring to Light raptatawks.

Tris looked at his attire. Having been too preoccupied with Zestine's cutting remark, he'd forgotten to arm himself before leaving his lair. "I need weapons…"

"Don't bother," said George, who pointed to a table on Tris's left topped with swords, knives, shields, and belts. As if on cue, Corrupted poured into the commons through multiple archways. Some were armed and some went straight to the table of weapons.

Tris ground his teeth as he approached the weaponry, George and Henrik on his heels. Henrik leaned forward extra close, his breath skating the back of Tris's neck. It took everything in him to keep from slamming his fist in the guy's face. Lord knew he wouldn't be able to stop there.

"We must fight as long as possible, come back to heal if necessary, then return until we've defeated or recruited every gawk," Henrik said.

At 'recruited,' Tris halted and turned to look at him. "How can we recruit if they've come to engage?"

"Word is some came to convert." Henrik's red eyes gleamed with bloodlust.

More horrible news. Tris continued toward the array of weapons and once there, donned a belt lined with throwing daggers. After sheathing a katana and scimitar, he faced the two Corrupted.

"All right. Let's do this," he said.

~

They landed on the outskirts of the same town where Tris had intercepted Quinn, Konrad, and his two companions. The streets were devoid of townsfolk, not a single venue open for business. A telltale sign something was wrong when Underworlders avoided witnessing bloodshed.

Blood on the ground bubbled and steamed. Circular humps of bloody mud interspersed the area, expanding and contracting. With every expansion, the soil swelled higher and higher until the mounds exploded, spurting crimson fountains and leaving behind round black holes the size of Tris's fist. The drops from the explosions coalesced, sliding toward one another as if on a mission before disappearing into the earth and giving birth to a new mound.

"The Ravager will be very happy," said George as they approached the fray.

A raptatawk dove through the air at George, sword posed, but the blonde dodged his pursuer's swing at the last second and snatched his ankle before he could fly away. In a blur, George slammed his opponent to the ground, straddled his backside and ripped his wings from his body. Blood jetted onto his neck and chest as he held up the wings and roared a battle cry which Henrik, then a reluctant Tris, raised their fists and answered.

Fuck. How many brothers will I kill this time?

Having tasted blood, a corybantic George sprinted into the chaos while Henrik and Tris skirted the fringes. Tris drew his swords. He planned to engage only when threatened. That way he hoped to slay as few innocents as possible.

Corrupted and raptatawks fought in the sky, but Tris had been there, done that, and almost lost his life. The ground was safer. Airborne, an opponent could attack from every direction imaginable. At least the ground eliminated a few vantage points.

Two arrows zipped by Tris's head, prompting him to duck. Someone jumped on his back, put him in a chokehold, and encircled black, silver-dusted wings around him, cutting his surroundings from view. Tris tried to throw the man off by spinning in place, but his assailant's grip tightened, crushing his windpipe. If Tris didn't escape, he'd go unconscious and be as good as dead.

Miraculously, he sheathed the katana and used both hands to swing the scimitar at the arms around his neck. The blade struck flesh and his attacker's hold loosened. Pointing his sword at the ground, Tris grabbed a breath, then threw his upper body forward, flipping the 'tawk's body over his own and throwing him to the ground. Without hesitation, Tris retrieved a dagger and chucked it at the man who'd become his victim. It landed in his throat. The 'tawk coughed up blood, watching Tris with wide brown eyes. Once he passed out, Tris rolled him over and tore off his wings with trembling hands.

After collecting his knives and dropping the wings by the corpse, he turned around to see two long blades arc toward him. With no time to defend himself, Tris closed his eyes to meet his end. But death never arrived, nor did the sting of honed metal. His head remained between his shoulders; his body was still in one piece. When he cracked open his eyes, two slain men who hadn't been there before lay at his feet as an unfamiliar Corrupted yanked the wings off one. Tris parted his mouth to… thank him? *Not going to happen.* He wrinkled his nose and spat. Though thankful for the rescue, the gratitude made him feel dirty, so he forbade himself to act on it.

Tris turned and didn't take more than a dozen steps before a knife landed in the back of his shoulder. He hissed through his teeth, spun, and braced for attack. A 'tawk sped for him, sword poised above his head like an axe. Tris stopped his assailant's swing with the katana and whipped the scimitar into his side. The blade sunk deep before meeting resistance, but the 'tawk didn't slow, snorting and growling as he swung twice more. Tris blocked both attempts.

Dropping his katana, Tris stepped on its steel, nabbed a dagger from his belt and flung it at his opponent. It zipped downward and stuck the guy in the crotch.

He let out a shrill squeal, his eyes wide with terror as he watched Tris, who swung the scimitar at his neck. The offender's head took to the air, lost among the madness as his body crumbled to the ground.

Tris was about to walk away when his victim's wings caught his eye. They were yellow and orange, reminding him of Melvin's wings. His stomach twisted.

Thoughts of Melvin vanished when a sharp, nigh-overwhelming pain registered just below his right armpit, sending him to his knees with a squeak. Crimson wings flashed in his periphery. He struggled to draw a breath, his vision wavering and the ground quaking as he glimpsed the long sword stuck in his side. His heart fluttered. Had the blade pierced it? A violent jerk of his body spouted blood from his mouth.

Tris sank to the mud and lay on his belly, then played dead and wondered why he wasn't *actually* dead. Why hadn't the guy who'd stabbed him finished the job?

Once the ground stopped teetering and his sight cleared, he carefully peeked around. No more than two feet away, a 'tawk with crimson wings battled a Corrupted. As Tris tried to discern who was winning, another Corrupted zoomed by, swinging his sword. The crimson-winged 'tawk's head clunked to blood-drenched soil with a wet smack, face-to-face with Tris. One bright-green eye blinked, followed by the other before both eyes lost their luster amid extinguished life.

Tris knew he should feel something — sorrow, frustration, rage—but he was numb save his determination to survive.

Time to move. Tris stood, only to stumble and fall. He rose to his knees, gritting his teeth as he thrust his katana out, then used his free hand to remove the sword sheathed inside his body.

Don't pass out. Need to live. Zestine dominated his mind. So many reasons to return to her. To think of the horrors she'd endure if left to Quinn and company… He shuddered, and it had nothing to do with his injury. He'd make it back to her simply because he *had* to, and when he returned, he was through with their *should we, shouldn't we* futility, no matter what rash words she threw at him.

A wild battle cry made Tris's sputtering heart leap. Ahead, a figure sped for him, murder ablaze in his piercing green eyes. Tris hastened his pace with the sword. Once he could no longer reach the hilt, he grasped the blade and pulled. Steel bit into his fingers and palm with gut-grating stings. As the man neared, Tris roared through the pain, his vision flashing black. When he finally dislodged the sword, he shakily got to his feet, wrapped the hilt in blood-soaked hands, and swung it at the 'tawk, whose eyes widened and jaw dropped as he abruptly skidded to a halt. But Tris's momentum was too strong, and he severed the man's head and part of his shoulder in a thick spray of scarlet.

On his follow-through, the weapon slipped from his slick hands and sailed end-over-end into the fray.

Why hadn't the 'tawk killed him? And why hadn't Tris stopped himself from taking his life? His throat ached and chest grew taut with guilt. *Can't go there.*

Tris retrieved his weapon and, trembling violently as blood from his wound accumulated at his feet, turned and staggered away, doing a face-plant into standing blood as he prepared to launch himself skyward. Thankfully, his wings weren't as unsteady as his legs, allowing him to escape almost certain death.

Not until he landed outside Corrupted headquarters did Tris notice he'd lost a finger. Upon carefully studying both hands, a bone-deep chill seized his breath. The red-stoned ring had been on that finger.

Smacked with sudden vulnerability, Tris crouched low to the ground even though he had nothing to hide behind. He searched his pockets for a spare ring. Came up empty.

He whispered a curse upon remembering that he wasn't wearing his own gear, which was stuffed with extra charms.

What could he do? Zestine couldn't help. His quarters was too far for telepathy to work. His only hope was to reach Cradle without being spotted. Given how much the return flight had taxed his blood-depleted body, he wasn't exactly optimistic.

Steeling himself, Tris didn't look back before entering the cave with his head down. Faulty equilibrium forced him to peek up every so often, which he did with one eye open.

The commons was quiet. He sensed Corrupted present, but his "buddies" must've not been there because no one approached him. His injury probably worked in his favor, as no one with an ounce of common sense would think he'd want to stop and chat. Once swallowed by the back tunnels, he sagged against the stone wall and checked his injury. Still an open wound. Still bleeding heavily. Considering how far the blade had reached, it'd remain open for a while. Every drop of blood he lost robbed him of energy. Rest lessened the flow; movement increased it. And with a dwindling blood supply, he couldn't count on his powers to work either.

The tunnel wasn't wide enough to allow flight, a fact he'd noticed his first time walking the tunnels en route to meet the Ravager. How could the Corrupted not see they were prisoners in their own home?

Commotion from the commons made Tris start. He gritted his teeth and attempted to run. Two strides later, he crashed to the ground.

Clunk clunk. Clunk clunk. Clunk clunk.

Footsteps behind him coated his neck and chest in icy sweat. His surroundings spun and his entire body pounded with every heartbeat. He slammed his eyes shut. *Can't give up. Don't stop.*

Clunk clunk. Clunk clunk.

Bolting onward, he took three strides before veering into the wall and scraping his arm against the rough rock. Despite the fact that someone neared, Tris didn't know if he'd make it another inch. The door to his lair dwelled mere feet ahead… didn't it?

Clunk clunk. Clunk clunk. Clunk clunk.

Tris's knees hit the ground just as the approaching individual closed in.

"Wish I could help," a man said. Tris thought he recognized the voice, but wasn't sure. The mystery male chuckled as he breezed past. Vision wavering, Tris got a glimpse of feet. A moment later, a door shut. His door?

He pressed his arm to his wound and traveled the rest of the way at an arduous crawl. Outside his quarters, he groaned as he forced himself to stand on quivering legs and open the door. Warm blood gushed through his fingers as he stumbled inside.

Tris would've collapsed there, but he had to make sure Zestine was okay. Telepathy wouldn't do. He needed to see her.

CHAPTER 20

Zestine was dreaming.

She was asleep on a luxurious bed topped with white silk sheets, fluffy pillows, and cushy blankets. Lying on her side in a flimsy white nightie, the length of her red locks rayed a perfect arc around her head.

The sound of footsteps awakened her. Moments later in walked a winged man with chin-length, chocolate-brown hair, ocean-blue eyes, and a mouth and physique promising untold sensual thrill. He wore tan denim slacks and nothing else, his upper body comprising defined muscles wrapped in golden-bronze skin.

She beamed at her guest and asked, "Can I see your wings?"

He spread them for her, and she marveled at their majesty, their beauty befitting the male who carried them.

The same blue as his eyes began at the base of his wings, stretched past the middle and ended in curvy edges. From there, a field of white flowed to the tips. Each wing resembled the sea meeting a shore of snowy-white sand.

Zestine beckoned the man closer. He knelt on the bed, allowing her to circle him while she explored his wings with her hands. When she touched them, he shuddered and his breath quickened. She reveled in the power she had over him as she caressed the silky feathers. He growled in approval when she nuzzled his wings with her nose and blew hot air on them with her lungs.

After finding her way back in front of him, his pants had mysteriously disappeared and his cock stood at proud attention, begging for her hands, mouth, and cunt.

With a naughty smile, she squeezed his scrotum extra gently while grasping his length and stroking up and down, up and down. Soon she grew greedy for more and lay belly-down, stuck out her tongue, and treated him to long licks, giving special attention to the head. She relished his salty flavor and smooth hardness. Before long, she fucked him with her throat and twirled her tongue round and round his girth. Upping the ante, she tightened her lips while fondling his balls, and he came, groaning long and loud. She moaned as she swallowed his seed, unable to get enough.

He didn't waste a second before sliding the straps of her nightie down and caressing her tits in between thumbing and pinching her nipples. Her pussy, wet and aching, was ready for him. She straddled his thigh and ground against the firm muscle while he licked and suckled her pebbled nipples. Then he grabbed her soaked thong and ripped it away.

She bucked her hips and cried out the moment his fingers breached her nether lips. His kisses traveled from her breasts to her neck...

BANG!

Zestine jerked upright, moaning from her throbbing wrists as well as from the incredible dream.

She expected Tris to walk into the room, but when Konrad entered instead, she scowled. "What the fuck are you doing here?"

He scanned her body, a mad gleam in his eyes she didn't recall having seen before. Off came his pants, his erection bouncing as he walked to the end of the bed. He unchained Zestine's ankles, then crawled on top of her and poised himself at her entrance.

She was about to scream *no,* but choked it back at the last second, determined to use this to her advantage.

Lubed from the erotic dream, Konrad had no problem sinking to the hilt. After thrusting a couple times, he sneered. "Wet for me, are we?"

She tried not to sneer but wasn't sure if she succeeded. If only she could tell him just *who* had aroused her. Instead, she replied as breathlessly as she could, "Yes. I was just dreaming about you."

That gave him pause. He stilled for a moment, giving Zestine the opportunity to say, "Don't stop," then give a pleasurable-sounding cry when he resumed fucking her.

In reality, and despite her heightened libido from the dream, she felt nothing from his intrusion—not pain, nor pleasure, only numbness. Hatred for the Corrupted crowded her spirit, yielding deranged fantasies courtesy of her—caged and livid—beast. But she cooed the enraged feline. Soon, she'd let it out to play.

Zestine let him continue for a few more minutes, during which she intermittently gasped and moaned so he'd believe her enjoying it, while waiting for the right moment. When that moment arrived, she made a sound of annoyance and with a whiny edge to her voice said, "I'm too uncomfortable like this. Can I turn around and put my butt up in the air?" She bit her lip in feigned arousal. "I'd like it *a lot.*" She was taking a chance by assuming he wanted her to enjoy sex with him just so she'd torment herself about it later.

Konrad cursed, but his hips slowed and eyes narrowed.

"I can't even feel it anymore," she added. "In my dream you were fucking me on all fours." Her pulse thundered in her ears so loud she wondered if he could hear it.

After several excruciating seconds, he withdrew. "Turn around."

Zestine really hadn't thought he'd be dumb enough to risk it. She pursed her lips both in mock disappointment and to camouflage a smile. "I would, but…" she wiggled her wrists and the chains rattled against the metal bars.

Thankfully, he didn't hesitate before he leaned over and unshackled her left wrist. While he worked on loosening her right wrist, he pinned her with a callous gaze. "If you try to escape, prepare for a beating. A bloody fucking beating. I'll rip off your pretty little head and squirt my cum down your neck."

At that, it took great effort to keep from laughing. *It's not* my *head you need to worry about.*

Too bad she couldn't remind him of their first encounter. Had he somehow forgotten about it? Although it boggled her mind, Konrad seemed to have no idea what he was in for, which almost made her pity him. Almost, but he was an evil loser who deserved to die. It was a shame she could only end him once.

When the silver-infused shackles no longer touched her flesh, her body buzzed with violent anticipation. She'd never been more ready to do what she did best.

Zestine stood and pretended to stumble backwards to give herself a little extra room, then waited until Konrad leaned back from the bed frame to spring for him, simultaneously morphing into a jaguar. Upon landing, she'd sheathed her claws in his chest and had his crushed skull between her teeth. Distributing her weight onto her front paws to keep his body immobile, she wrenched his head off, excising it completely after three pulls of her powerful jaws. Red ribbons streamed from the headless stump.

That's what he gets for fucking with a beast.

Her only regret was the swiftness of the kill: a mere second between life and death. Though necessary, he hadn't experienced enough pain. Enough despair.

Zestine whipped his ruined head from her jaws and it smacked against the wall with a crunchy splat before hitting the floor. She cleaned the blood and sinew from her claws and teeth as she ruminated what to do next. If she thought escape possible, she'd do it, but chances were slim she'd make it out the cave unnoticed. Taking out multiple Corrupted, even if they were unarmed, wasn't something she felt confident about. She envisioned the Pit of Teeth. That chasm would eat her alive if she wasn't careful.

She started, her ears rotating toward the main door at its creak, and couldn't decide whether to shift or not before Tris stumbled into the room, covered in blood.

Instantly, she shifted to a woman. Tris collapsed on the bed, putting his hand out at the last second as if to stop his descent, but failed.

"What happened?" Zestine rushed to the far side of the bed and grasped the dead Corrupted's arms to pull his body to the floor.

Tris pushed against the mattress to sit on his butt and leaned against the headboard. He breathed laboriously through his mouth; his face was pale and stricken, eyes glossy. "I g-wa... stabbed. Wha-what happened..."—he took a deep breath—"here? Y-you shouldn't... why...?"

Zestine let out a dark chuckle upon understanding what he wished to say. "Well, if I was chained, I couldn't have defended myself against this rapist asshole." She gestured to the bloodied corpse at her feet, then went to the wall, grabbed Konrad's ear, and held up his misshapen head.

Tris's gaze latched on it for a millisecond before drifting away as if he saw something that wasn't there, telling her he was in worse shape than she'd initially thought.

Adrenaline surged into her veins. Zestine dropped the demolished skull and hurried over to him. "Tris, show me your wound."

He shook his head and looked up, but didn't focus on her. "A 'tawk got... he got..."

Those were his last words before unconsciousness claimed him.

~

Tris's wound was nasty but healing, and since he wasn't awake to stop her, Zestine took care of the mess she'd made. She got a large garbage bag from the kitchen, surprised by how domestic the place was, and shoved Konrad's body—as well as those sodding silver-infused bonds—inside. With some crafty bending and rearranging of body parts, she managed to fasten the bag around the tremendous dead weight. Then she retrieved a hyx device followed by a red-stoned ring and slid it on her finger. Running her tongue over sharp teeth, she opened the hyx compact and used the shiny metal side to look herself over.

The teeth, though creepy, were nothing compared to the teeth she rocked in beast form. The eyes, however, were quite the sight paired with her fiery hair. As she observed herself, it shook her to realize how much the red eyes and hair made her resemble Henrik. Although she'd planned on contacting King Lachlan, she snapped the device shut instead and left.

The plan was to deposit Konrad's body somewhere so Tris would escape immediate suspicion.

Etched in scraggly writing on the outside of Tris's door was the word:

Cradle

To her right, the passageway declined steadily before veering in a different direction. To her left, it slanted upward so far she couldn't tell which way it led.

Blessed with a good sense of direction, she wasn't worried about becoming lost, but the chance of encountering Corrupted gave her a fierce sense of urgency. Zestine was a half-foot shorter than most raptatawks and lacked a huge set of wings. She'd considered severing Konrad's wings and arranging them onto her back, but without Tris's help it'd be too much trouble. And if someone recognized the dead Corrupted's wings… enough said.

Footsteps coming from her right made her jump. She had two options: hustle in the other direction or go inside Tris's quarters. Knowing she could shift influenced her decision, and she took off the opposite way from whoever approached, Konrad's remains in tow.

Not fast enough. Her hands shook as she stopped and put the top of the bag—which she'd knotted—between her teeth, then shifted to a jaguar and moved as fast as possible. When her jaw started to ache, she shifted into a woman, then switched to a beast when her arms tired. The sound of the load dragging against the ground muffled the footsteps, which she soon lost track of. She didn't stop to assess, however, and roughly thirty minutes later she reached a fork that split three ways.

Zestine changed to human form and tossed the cumbersome load into the middle path using all her strength. It landed about one hundred feet away. Tris could've thrown it much farther with his mind, *if* a corpse counted as an inanimate object. The location wasn't ideal for dumping a body, but it'd do for her goals.

On the walk back to Cradle, she spotted two people approaching from the opposite direction. She glimpsed their figures at the same time she heard them. Instantly, she turned into a three-pound, jet-black kitten. Curling into a ball where the tunnel floor curved into the wall, she closed her eyes and prayed for the High Lord to keep her unseen.

"Did you see that?" said a male whose voice she didn't recognize.

"See what?" a second unfamiliar man said. The duo halted several yards from where Zestine hid in plain sight. As much as she loathed the Darkness, at the moment it worked to her advantage.

"I just saw someone. A female, I think. She was coming toward us."

"Do you see her now?"

"She was right here." They walked closer and stopped feet away. She couldn't have been more grateful no silver touched her skin. No way would she allow Tris to restrain her with it again, no matter how much sense it made.

"There's no one here."

"What the fuck?" the Corrupted hollered, smacking his palm with a fist. If in woman form, Zestine would've needed to suppress a giggle. "That's fucking weird. I swear, I *swear* someone was here."

"Well, they're gone now, brother."

The pair loped off, the one who'd seen her grumbling that he wasn't crazy. Zestine half-considered killing the men, but disposing of two more bodies didn't sound like the slightest bit of fun.

She remained a kitten until she reached Tris's lair, then went straight to the bedroom. He was still out, but his color had improved and his bleeding stopped so she cleaned the mess from the Konrad ordeal. When done, she ate another bag of dried meat, chasing it with two flasks of water.

Armed with the soap she'd packed in Noctis, she took a hot bath. Although her beast loathed water, her human half reveled in a nice, long soak. Washing her hair and scrubbing away remnants of Konrad from her face, nails, and teeth lifted some of the gloom that'd emerged after becoming Tris's "prisoner."

After bathing, Zestine carefully stripped the soiled blanket from the bed while Tris recovered, and since sleep beckoned, she then snuggled, naked, under the sheets. Seconds after her head hit the pillow, she entered dreamland.

CHAPTER 21

Tris cracked open his eyes. At first, he didn't recognize his surroundings, but when his gaze landed on the redheaded beauty slumbering beside him, everything rushed back.

The brutal stabbing he'd suffered marked the first time his body had shut down to repair itself. Rousing from sleep when your body wasn't made for it was discombobulating. His head swam, gut cramped, and a hot, tingly sensation burned the tips of his fingers and toes.

When his mind cleared and stomach settled, Tris rose and made a beeline for the main door to slide the deadbolt in place before replacing the ring he'd lost onto his now-intact finger. Inside the bathroom, the mirror over the sink displayed a man caked in blood. His usual snowy-white feathers were dark red. He turned on the water, raised his right arm, and rinsed away the blood to reveal smooth skin.

Tris sighed and dropped his arm. What about this wound had resulted in his body submitting to unconsciousness? Had it been its depth or the fact he was sure it'd pierced his heart?

Since a Pirmas' magic dwelled in their blood, the heart was devastating to lose. As with other vital organs, the heart healed like other body parts, but didn't grow back if removed. Lacking a heart impacted the ability to heal, and the Pirmas succumbed to the aging process. Basically, heart loss led to a slow and abominable death.

He approached the tub and noticed a film of moisture coating the porcelain. The image of Zestine bathing slammed into his brain. Just like that, he was rock hard and raring to fuck.

Not covered in and reeking of blood.

Though a lot of work, Tris filled the tub and used the bar of soap Zestine must have brought from Noctis to clean himself of dirt and blood. He rinsed off, unfurled his wings and air-dried while emptying the tub with the bucket. Afterward, he shook out his wings and donned a fresh pair of black linen pants before returning to the bedroom.

Zestine hadn't moved an inch since he'd left, still fast asleep facing the doorway. He sat on the bed, then stretched out on his side to look at her. Strong was the desire to stroke her hair and skim her face with his lips, but he held back. Though he wished she'd wake, he didn't want to startle her awake.

Before long, his pulse spiked when she stirred and, moments later, opened her eyes. She furrowed her eyebrows upon seeing him, then smiled. "Hey."

"Hey."

Her cheeks took on a magenta hue. "Are you better?"

Damn, but waking up looked stunning on this woman. Smooth red lips, bluish-purple eyes dark and shiny, hair mussed—sexy beyond words.

Tris ached to drown in her, to discover and share in her passion, but he preferred Zestine initiated things. Knowing she needed him as much as he needed her would make it sweeter.

In a way, he'd known the moment she rose to two feet from the four of her fierce black panther she'd be his. He'd denied it as best and for as long as he could and made plenty of excuses along the way, by attempting to create distance between them and lashing out at her. And yet, here he was.

Unable to stop himself, he smoothed a hand over her bedhead. "Good as new."

She raised her eyebrows and looked away, pressing her lips together as if trying not to smile. "Do you remember what you walked into... before going unconscious?"

Tris pulled in his brows, gaze drifting. Then he noticed the top blanket was missing from the bed, and an image flashed in his mind of Zestine holding a bloody chunk of...

His gaze snapped to hers. "Who'd you kill?" he whispered.

"I had to. Konrad raped me again. I tricked him into removing the bonds." Her eyes pleaded for understanding. "It's nothing I wouldn't have done anyway, so no one—"

"Where's his body?" Tris asked, fisting his hands upon hearing she was violated yet again. He sat up and looked around the bed, but found no evidence of the Corrupted's demise.

Zestine's face paled. "I dumped it." She looked upward and tilted her head the same way as her gaze, toward the front door of his quarters. "In the tunnels."

"Did anyone see you? How long ago?" He eased back on to his side.

She shook her head. "No one saw me. I have no idea how long ago. I'm no good at keeping time here, especially when I've slept. I did it while you recovered." Biting her lip, her indigo eyes flickered with uncertainty, triggering a longing to banish the troubles from her mind.

"We'll figure it out," he said before joining her underneath the sheet. He scooted toward her and lifted his arm.

On a satisfied sigh, she snuggled into his embrace, then moaned. The flesh-to-flesh sensations stole his breath before he echoed her moan, and Tris's heart shifted as a new, exciting emotion wiggled forth from the crevices of his psyche.

Zestine plunged her fingers into his damp hair and caressed his scalp with her fingertips. "You're not mad?" she asked in a small voice.

He shook his head, then went in for a kiss.

If Zestine hadn't known better, she'd think she'd died and gone to Paradise. Tris kissed her with genuine passion, their tongues tangoing to a dance of carnal purpose. The man tasted perfect, like nirvana and sin. He smelled like earth and rain laced with spicy vanilla, and she knew he'd feel heavenly—he already did.

Though she'd go to extremes to deter an interruption, a nagging thought popped into her head, as if some part of her was hell-bent on ruining a sexual union with Tris a second time. She broke away. "What if someone comes? I don't know if Konrad—"

He silenced her with another mind-numbing lip-lock. They moaned as one before his hot mouth descended to her jaw, then her neck...

"Tris," she half-protested, half-moaned.

"Mmm, what?" His husky voice acted like an aphrodisiac, spiraling liquid heat around her body. He dragged his tongue and lips from her neck to her collarbone while his hand found her breast and circled her nipple with a callused thumb.

Zestine yipped, then forced herself to ask, "What if someone walks in?"

"The door's locked. It'll give us warning." Lowering himself so his face aligned with her breasts, he gave a long lick to the nipple not being stimulated by his fingers.

"Oh," she exclaimed, a delicious throb softening her pussy with a rush of wetness. In desperation, she wrapped her legs around Tris's torso, pushed her core hard against him and rocked her hips to ease the tremendous ache.

"Ah, yes." *So good.*

As Zestine rubbed her swollen sex against his abdomen and his mouth worked magic on her bosom, he cupped the globes of her ass, guiding her movements to help her achieve adequate friction.

It was all too much. Too much stimulation, too much rightness, that soon her pleasure peaked in a loud and lengthy groan, her mind reeling and body trembling in sweet rapture.

"Beautiful," Tris said once she'd come down. Wonder sparkled in the raptatawk's gaze; she was a treasure in his eyes. She could see it.

With a shiver, she unwound her legs, tugged loose the drawstring of his slacks and shoved them down. Hand automatically finding the tempting cock she'd gotten to touch once for far too short a time, she grasped and stroked. Zestine watched herself pleasure him while feeling him watch *her*, which heightened her arousal even more.

As she worked him with her hand, her cunt clenched and further dampened with a fresh ache. She had the nigh-uncontrollable urge to rub her clit against the head of his member. The thought made her moan.

Since Zestine had already gotten off, she didn't wish to be selfish. So she locked eyes with him, uncaring his were red, as the only thing that mattered was they belonged to Tris, and asked, "What do you want?"

CHAPTER 22

What do I want?

"Whatever you want."

With a naughty smile, she guided his cock to her pussy. Tris didn't breathe, bracing for the pleasure of being sheathed inside her, but instead of joining them, she touched the top of his penis to her clit and rubbed in slow circles. He gasped, amazed at how enjoyable it felt to have her nub glide across his most sensitive flesh. They maintained eye contact as she worked herself wild with the head of his cock. Only when Zestine orgasmed did she look away, her eyes rolling back into her head while curses fell from her lips. As she rode the waves of release, Tris couldn't wait any longer and pushed into her. She cried out and briefly shuddered.

He sunk to the hilt easily but didn't thrust—and wouldn't until she acknowledged their coupling and he knew she was with him as much as he was with her. He looked at where their bodies joined, astonished her petite frame fit every inch of him so easily, so perfectly. Sweat beaded his nape as he shook with the need to drive into her.

Wrapping her legs around him, she cupped his cheeks and gave him a soft kiss before meeting his gaze.

"What are you waiting for?" she asked, rocking her hips and sparking a delicious sensation in his loins.

Tris moaned and spanned a hand over the crack of her bum. "You."

"Oh, well…" she tightened around his shaft before he slowly withdrew almost all the way, then slammed back in.

Oh gods. She couldn't feel more exquisite.

With a rapturous sigh, Zestine wrapped her arms around his neck and brushed wet kisses along his throat, sending a pleasant tingle up from the base of his skull.

Still shaking, again he slowly withdrew and slammed back in. Zestine moaned and he paused.

"Well, what?" Tris prompted, anticipation making him near crazed.

"What more do you need?" Her voice softened to a whisper. "You don't have to wait for me, Tris. I'm right here." She smashed her lips to his. Unable to hold back another second, he thrust deep and hard into her slick, welcoming heat.

Tris parted his mouth and sought her tongue with his, already addicted to the woman's taste. Their kissing was as feisty as their fucking. At one point he tasted blood, but she didn't seem to notice he'd cut her with Corrupted teeth.

The tang of her blood only increased his fervor, and he upped his tempo. Tris needed to go deeper, get *closer* to her, mark her in some way as his—only his. Grabbing her ass cheeks, he thrust as hard as he could and sunk his tiny teeth into the flesh above her collarbone.

Zestine cried out her pleasure and dug her nails into his skin. After planting a gentle kiss over his bite, he trailed his lips to her throat, groaning at her muscles' rhythmic contractions urging him to spill his seed. "Oh yes. Oh… yes!" she screamed, then propelled Tris to his back and rode him, tits jiggling as she pogoed up and down, up and down.

With a growl, he dragged his hands from her rump and pinched her taut nipples. She slipped a finger into her mouth and lowered it to pet her clit, the sight of which practically liquified Tris's mind.

How did he ever believe this female was a turnoff? He'd never get enough of her.

Never.

Zestine reached down and laced her fingers through his. A drop of blood from the already-healed bite he'd delivered trickled and stopped just below her collarbone. "Ohhh. You're gonna make me come again," she said.

"Mmm, come for me, Beautiful." He rolled them over, putting himself on top and placed their locked hands next to her head.

Pound, pound, pound, pound. The headboard smacked against the wall. *Bang, bang, bang, bang.*

"Ahh. Feels so fucking *good*," Zestine exclaimed before giving another cry and clenching her hand around his.

Tris's own release chased him down. As her muscles gripped him with mind-scrambling strength, his wings shot out, hitting the stone walls. He couldn't stop from roaring when an orgasm ripped through him, his cock blasting waves of cum into her womb.

Once spent, he moaned in satisfaction and leaned down to give Zestine a sultry tongue-lashing, then reluctantly pulled out and fell on his side.

"Wow," she said, beaming. Her hair was messier than before, her cheeks red and lips swollen, looking to all the world well and properly fucked.

He couldn't have stopped himself from returning her smile if he'd wanted to.

Zestine turned thoughtful. "I love it when you smile. Wish you'd do it more often."

Tris opened his mouth to respond, but desisted, his heart skipping a beat over the words he'd almost spoken.

He couldn't actually *love* her, could he?

~

One second she and Tris basked in post-sex bliss, and the next second his demeanor changed, and it wasn't a welcome change. Smile becoming tight, he broke eye contact, suddenly captivated by the wall behind her.

So *not* okay after what they'd done.

Zestine frowned, a jolt of paranoia striking the pit of her stomach. "What's wrong?"

His cheeks flushed. "Nothing." He smiled again, but it appeared forced. When he leaned in for a kiss, she pulled back.

"Don't lie, especially after fucking me." Here she'd believed things were different. Having received potent vibes from him of late, she'd thought it worth letting down her guard. Seemed she'd been mistaken.

In the beginning, Zestine had wanted him for his body alone, but that was no longer the case. Tris had shown her affection, something which, despite a long life and thousands of notches on her bedpost, she wasn't used to. Now, immediately following a searing—and meaningful—physical connection, he was becoming detached?

Nope. Not okay.

Eyes widening from her refusal to lock lips, he parted his mouth as if to speak when a knock on the main door shattered the uncomfortable silence.

"Father, no," Tris said, and faster than Zestine could track, he was off the bed and donning his pants. "Where are the shackles?"

She pressed her lips together, flinching at another loud knock on the door.

He stepped toward her. "Where are they?"

She shook her head. "I won't put those back on."

Bang!

"What?" Then, in her mind he said, *You* have *to, Zestine.*

Still shaking her head, she replied, *Tell them when you got home there was blood everywhere but you weren't sure what happened, other than I wasn't here.* This was something she wouldn't budge on. It wasn't as if they'd made stellar progress while she'd been subdued. Thinking about it, she didn't know much about the Corrupted she hadn't already known.

Are you crazy? Tris's incredulous voice rang shrill through her head. *I can't* — but another thud sounded, and she turned into the same small black kitten she'd been when escaping notice of the Corrupted and ran to the kitchen. There, she opened a floor-level cupboard with her claws, jumped into a tall pot, curled her tiny body into a ball, and closed her eyes.

CHAPTER 23

Tris's jaw dropped when Zestine morphed into a rodent-sized cat and scurried out the bedroom. He followed and almost screamed her name, but choked back the impulse. In the kitchen, a floor-level cupboard was ajar, so he knelt and peeked inside.

Zestine, he projected. *Are you in here?*

I'm in the tall pot, she replied.

Look, just stay hidden, okay? With a huff of relief, Tris closed the cupboard. No sooner had he stood when the door to his lair burst open and Quinn stalked inside, George and Henrik on his heels.

As Tris gathered his thoughts, he swept his arms out to his sides and asked, "What the fuck is going on?"

Quinn advanced on him, prompting Tris to backpedal while Henrik checked the other rooms before returning to his place beside George.

"She's not here," the redhead said.

Tris backed up until he hit edge of the counter, then raised his hands in surrender, his wings loosening on pure instinct to escape danger. Quinn's nostrils flared as he got as close to Tris as possible without touching him. A grimace marred the Corrupted's face as he eyed him up and down. Tris took the perusal in silence, not trusting himself to speak unless spoken to. He needed to know what they knew or risk blowing his cover.

"Where's the woman?" asked Quinn, who took a long sniff. "It reeks of sex in here."

Tris rolled his eyes without thinking. "She's been fucked many times by many men, and I don't know where she is." He waved his hand toward the bedroom, hesitated, then whacked his palm against the countertop. "Bitch escaped when I was gone. I'm not sure how, but—" He paused and ground his teeth as if trying to keep his anger in check. "I returned to a lot of blood."

"Blood?" Quinn looked around before turning to Henrik, who shook his head. "I don't see any blood."

Tris couldn't help but sneer. "I cleaned it up."

Quinn relaxed the slightest bit, but Tris didn't trust it wasn't an act. "Konrad's dead. Men downstairs said he was coming here the last time they saw him. We found his body dumped in the middle of our home in a garbage bag." Red eyes widening, he spoke through bared teeth. "It was the work of a beast."

"Shit," said Tris. He shook his head, lowered his gaze, and put his hands on his hips. Would they punish him for losing a prisoner?

"How did she get away without someone seeing her?" Henrik said to no one in particular, but Tris felt obligated to answer.

Leaning forward, he leveled a healthy glare at the Corrupted he most craved to slaughter. "How the fuck would I know?" His tongue whipped the question with acidic flippancy.

Henrik raised his brows and shrugged. "For starters—"

"All right." Quinn, who kept a wary gaze on Tris, raised his hand to indicate the discussion was over. "You need to come with us." He turned and George and Henrik parted to let him through.

"Where?" Tris asked.

"The Ravager awaits," said George.

His stomach flipped. Did the demon know the truth? Was the Ravager awaiting him or all four of them?

Having no choice, Tris inclined his head. "Okay."

"Since Konrad can't make it, you're taking his place," Quinn said in a clipped tone on his way out the door. Tris fell in step behind him with Henrik and George at his rear.

They walked for a while, and like his first visit to the Ravager, the final tunnel shrank and darkened considerably before they reached the door.

Quinn knocked.

"Watchword."

"Emergence."

"How many?"

"Four."

The door clicked ajar seemingly of its own accord and Quinn pushed it open. Tris followed him inside and found the Ravager sitting in the same place as before.

Did the demon ever leave this room or his chair, and where were the other demons if not with the Ravager? Were they there, but invisible? That was a definite possibility. The hair on the back of Tris's neck sprang erect.

The men formed a semicircle in front of the Ravager, who said from his motionless mouth, "My sons. You're here to shed blood for the good of our kind. Once you open your vessels, you must bleed until I say to stop, or until your blood yields the Dark God."

Dark God? Tris dropped his head and massaged his throat as he schooled his expression. A Dark deity, a balance to his Father's Light, didn't exist… yet. To create the High Lord, bits of essence from every plane of existence had gathered and coalesced before gaining wisdom from the ever-seeing heavens, empathy from living creatures, and tenacity from the passage of time. The process had taken centuries. How could Tris's present company think to make an entity of equal caliber from the blood of four broken individuals?

The Ravager continued, "I believe he is due forth on this occasion, from the Dark elixir of the brothers who come to me at this hour. It will be glorious indeed." He cackled, the sound resembling the persistent crack of a whip. It seeped into Tris's bones, chilling his blood and sullying his spirit.

"If the Dark God emerges, you will bow to him and do whatever he wishes. He will rule with me, and together we will bring detriment upon those who seek to ruin us. We will build an unstoppable army, take the fight to the High Lord, and once we've won, render all the worlds *black*." Inside the demon's abysmal mouth appeared two rows of hideously long, yellow teeth. Dripping red and shaped like daggers, they curved into a crooked grin. Tris blinked hard, thinking he'd imagined it, but the grin remained when he opened his eyes. Frigid fingers crawled up his spine as he stared, unable to look away. Before disappearing, the teeth parted, then clacked together with a *pop* that made Tris nearly jump out of his skin.

"The world will soon be ours," the Ravager declared.

A whir sounded as a mirrored wall behind the Ravager, which Tris hadn't seen during his first visit, rose from the floor. On the other side dwelled a chamber of fire. Flames danced everywhere except the floor, in the middle of which stood a tall white circular dais topped with a large golden bowl.

The Ravager swiveled his chair to face the newly revealed room. "Go, my sons. Fulfill your destiny with the Dark nectar flowing through your veins."

As the men walked to the dish, dread squeezed Tris's windpipe. There was a good possibility his blood wouldn't function like Corrupted blood. It could botch the rite or alter whatever they were supposed to conjure. Underworld soil reacted the same to his blood as that of the actual Corrupted, but this wasn't soil he'd feed. He was to feed magic. Dark magic. Dark and Light didn't mix, period.

Consequences could be dire. It could destroy the mission, not to mention end his life. He considered fleeing, but the safer option was to oblige the Ravager's commands. If nothing came of it, running now would prove a huge mistake.

Upon reaching the dais, Tris saw the bowl was half full of bubbling, dark-red blood. Four black-bladed knives lay around the saucer, and each man stood in front of one.

The presence of the gurgling blood curled Tris's upper lip. Its aroma was foul, like rotten, smoky metal. Heat from the fire burned his flesh, the crackle of the flame tore into his eardrums, and its light burned his retinas. The acrid taste of regret and disgust coated his tongue. As the seconds ticked by, it became harder to snag a decent breath. Tris fought every muscle in his body as the urge to flee grew nigh unbearable.

It's all in my head. My blood's mixed with Corrupted blood during battle and nothing happened.

There was no magic on the battlefield… right?

Breathe in…

Suck it up.

Breathe out…

I can do this.

Breathe in…

I have no choice.

Breathe out…

After several moments during which Tris's skin rearranged itself, the Ravager announced, "Cut deep and true. Bleed, my sons, and bring forth the Father of Darkness."

In a blur, Quinn grabbed his knife and sliced the length of his forearm open, then faced the gaping wound toward the receptacle, which collected every squirt and stream. The other two copied Quinn and likewise filled the bowl.

Pressing the point of the blade against his wrist, Tris was about to cut himself open when he realized something: their wounds weren't healing.

"Triiiissss," the Ravager rasped.

Shaking, but determined not to provoke suspicion, Tris pushed the tip of the dagger into a prominent vein and dragged it all the way to his elbow. The breaking of skin caused no pain.

Oh fuck. Why doesn't it hurt? This just got weirder and weirder.

Ears ringing, it was as if someone else controlled his body as he twisted his arm and held it over the collection bowl. Limbs heavy, his feet felt like blocks of lead that were cemented to the floor. If something went wrong, he'd not go anywhere.

As with his Corrupted companions, Tris's gash didn't heal. The phenomenon was due to magic, or the black blades consisted of a substance he'd never heard of. Then it hit him how dangerous the knives were—preventing pain and the swift, automatic healing process. Pirmas died in very few ways. Complete drainage of blood was one way, though it wasn't known to have occurred given their super mending ability.

Tris's pulse gained momentum, making his vessels drain faster. Never had he lost so much blood. Would it kill him? If he couldn't heal, how would he stop it? After a little more thought, he sucked in a breath, every hair on his body jerking upright.

Was he to give his life for this Dark God?

～

In kitten form Zestine followed Tris and the Corrupted through the tunnels and into a hideous demon's lair. Shrinking as small as her beast allowed, she camouflaged against the black rock. Just beyond the confined area housing the demon's seat, the stone walls slanted outward, opening into a bigger space and forming walls parallel to the giant mirror. After the mirror lifted, Tris and the others headed toward the fiery chamber while she dashed to the wall on her right. She scooted her posterior against the rock and folded her paws underneath her to watch a noble raptatawk fulfill a Dark purpose.

The yawning slash on Tris's arm resembled the Pit of Teeth, causing a shudder to wrack her tiny body. Zestine had seen plenty of deranged shit in her long life, but this could be the most malformed affair she'd ever witnessed. The actions of the four males weren't as worrisome as the reason they committed them. Malevolence saturated the air, yielding a vibration of foreboding that strengthened with each passing second.

Tris was in trouble. Mixing Light blood with liters of Dark blood seemed something that would end in disaster, but nothing of consequence had occurred. Zestine sent a quick prayer to the High Lord.

Almighty High Lord: if You can hear me in this awful place, I ask that You please, please *keep Your son free from harm. He's a good man, too young to die.*

Sure, she had selfish reasons for her pleas, but she and Tris had come too far for the enemy to learn the truth. Whoever, or whatever, this Dark God was, its birth would be tremendously important to the First Tribe. And she couldn't help but shiver over what its existence would mean to the Pirmas.

The four men bled, bled, and bled before bleeding some more. The amount of blood they lost was astounding, though they never paled or signaled exhaustion. Zestine figured the blood replaced itself as they expended it. That was the only sensible explanation for why, at the end, they remained standing.

Tris had started the ceremony jittery as hell but now his posture slumped and his eyelids drooped, making her want to stomp over and shake him. He needed to stay on guard. Had he forgotten *why* he was shedding his blood?

Eventually, black smoke rose from the blood like steam rising from boiling water. Unlike steam, the smoke didn't dissipate but coalesced into masses before spinning into body parts. It formed a forearm, a hand, then fingers—eight per hand.

As Zestine watched an abomination come to life, a crude stench invaded her nostrils. It smelled of vomited raw onions mixed with rotten eggs and topped with decayed corpses. But a different odor she couldn't identify stung her sinuses with a brutal headache and brought tears to her eyes.

A moment later, she knew.

The scent was the olfactory manifestation of evil, of true Darkness. Its potency increased as smoke continued ascending from the blood and amassed into an entity unnatural to this world.

The entity floated above the collection bowl and appeared to be a primate. Its upper body, except for its head, had already formed. The smoke whirled into hips, thighs, knees, shins, feet and toes. Then, to her surprise, a long, thin shaft took shape between its legs.

It was apparently a he.

The final tendrils of black haze rose to form the head of the miserable being. Once the finishing touches were in place, Zestine wished she'd stayed at the bottom of that pot.

CHAPTER 24

The floating figure to Tris's right was not corporeal. His body comprised a see-through mass of blacks and grays, but the ghostly quality didn't make him any less real. He was very real, *too real,* and as he drifted down to hover at floor level, Tris was all too conscious of the Darkness he radiated. Darkness Tris yearned to forever snuff out. The amount of evil within the creature was epic. He wasn't merely filled with Darkness. He *was* Darkness.

Tris had kept an ultra-tight leash on his Light ever since using it against the Darkness upon arrival to the realm. So effectively had he buried it, he wasn't even sure it remained. And he was afraid to check. Afraid that if he sought it, it'd escape the deep corner into which he'd stuffed it and explode within him, bursting through his pores and baring him to the Dark servants about him. If that happened, Tris knew he'd be no match for the atrocity before him. It'd take the Light of many more raptatawks to measure up to the amount of Darkness this creature exuded.

The being's head solidified with a loud snick, and pitch-black eyes assessed the men whose blood had birthed him. He stood at least three feet taller than Tris.

A raven Mohawk fell to the middle of his back in a thick braid, visible through his translucent body. Between his legs hung a phantom penis, minus testes. Was the organ for reproduction or bodily function?

Don't go there.

No question this monster was exceedingly powerful, as no other Pirmas could shape-shift from intangible to tangible, let alone with part of their body. No Pirmas was born from a pool of blood.

Careful, Tris. Don't expose yourself, Zestine said in his mind.

He inhaled sharply, digging his nails into his palms to keep from looking for her. *You need to get out of here.*

Impossible.

Tris bit down so hard his jaw creaked. *One of us needs to make it out of here alive.*

Yes.

The Dark God's murky gaze fastened on Tris. "You." His deep voice vibrated the floor and walls. "There is something… *different* about you."

Could the abomination hear Tris's racing heart or discern the shock holding his spirit hostage? Swallowing his fear, Tris said, "Different isn't a bad thing."

A cold stare from soulless eyes was his only response.

Tris looked at the floor, throat narrowing and skin crawling by the despicable entity he'd helped create. Then the inside of his arm caught his attention. It'd healed and he hadn't even noticed.

"Honor the Dark God, my sons, by bending at the knee," the Ravager commanded.

Tris stiffened. *No. Fucking. Way.* Pledge loyalty to this monstrosity? Never. He wasn't even certain his body could complete such a task.

Not for the first time since this had begun, he felt like a puppet manipulated by two opposing forces, only now the polarity between those forces might be his downfall.

He felt his soul was slowly and consistently peeling away. How could it not be? He'd killed his Light brothers and allowed for the rape and torture of an innocent woman. Would honoring the embodiment of Darkness rip away his Light entirely?

Do it, Tris. You have to, or else everything you've done so far will have been for nothing.

He set his jaw. *I can't.*

Zestine's growl rumbled between his ears. *Yes, you can. And you will.*

No.

Quinn, George, and Henrik dropped to a knee and looked at him.

Do it! I can't lose you. I promise… Tris, I vow I won't let you fall to the Darkness. We have to survive this so we can inform the First Tribe. They need to know. Please.

The level of desperation put into that last word sent him over the edge. Tris forced himself to kneel, feeling as if the floor and his knee were the same poles of two magnets, one repelling the other. He got past it, ramming his knee down with all his might. His kneecap cracked on impact. His eyes watered, and he forced his grimace into a smile as he somehow kept silent through the pain.

The difficulty of such a simple action was no surprise. He'd pledged allegiance to an evil he feared may mean the undoing of everything good in the world. That was certainly the Dark God's purpose.

The High Lord finally had His match.

~

Zestine itched to scram. The sinister energy in the crypt—which had exploded upon the so-called 'God's' birth—poked at her with bony appendages while emitting a screeching buzz.

"Goooood," said the Ravager. "Now, you must leave the Dark God and me to ourselves, my sons. We have much to plan. Much, much, much to plan." The demon let out a laugh horrid enough to tense her muscles and raise her tail fur. An arctic chill slithered down her backside, and she shivered for the umpteenth time since arriving there.

Tris was the first to approach the exit, followed by Quinn, Henrik, and George, who Zestine—after ensuring the demon and Dark God were focused on each other—fell on the heels of. Once out of the room, she paused to shake the nasty crypt atmosphere from her coat. She waited for the men to get a decent head start before trotting the gloomy path alone. Every so often she peeked behind her to make sure no towering phantom deity followed.

The tunnel was empty upon reaching Tris's quarters. Not wanting to shift in case Corrupted were inside, she contacted him with her mind.

Tris, you there? I'm outside the door. Seconds later the door opened and she darted inside, halting inches away from Tris. Only as tall as his ankles, Zestine vibrated with a purr as, unable to help herself, she rubbed against his leg from her nose to her tail, then swiveled around to do the same with her other side. *Anyone else here?*

"No," he said. She shifted and he instantly snatched her into his arms. They met for an urgent kiss, and she moaned in protest when they broke apart. He fixed her with a wild red gaze. "We have to get out of here."

Zestine scrunched up her face and gave a rapid head shake. "What?" That kiss had clouded her mind. Lowering her gaze, she saw his forearms corded with tense muscle as he tapped his third and fourth fingers against his thigh. "We can't just leave."

"We have to."

"We won't make it out without being seen." Not that she didn't want to leave, but she wanted to live more, and attempting to flee—especially lacking a plan—equaled death, likely via the Pit of Teeth. Tris could exit the caves without raising suspicion, but not her. Unless they found a different way out, she was trapped. As a beast or woman, it didn't matter.

He huffed. "We'll die if we stay."

"What makes you say that?"

Tris held a finger to his lips, grabbed her hand and guided her into the bedroom. "We have to whisper or speak through our minds."

Telepathy it was. *Why are you so adamant we leave now?* she asked.

He planted his hands on his hips and paced. *My blood. I don't trust it didn't influence the ritual.*

Zestine parted her lips. *What do you mean? You saw him. I'm sure you felt the Darkness flowing from him in droves.* She shook her head. *There's nothing Light in him.*

There has to be. If not, what does that make me?

Suddenly dizzy, she took his hand and removed the red ring, letting out a breath when his features normalized. She slid the ring back on and grasped his hands.

Calm him, urged an inner voice.

Zestine smiled and caressed his cheek. He closed his eyes. "It's okay," she said, nudging Tris onto the bed, where she straddled him and looped her arms around his neck. "I'm afraid too. But it'd be a mistake to leave now. You told them I'm gone so if anyone sees me, even if I'm not with you... you know how bad that would be. I won't take that chance." As Tris often did during rough conversations, he dropped his head forward, but she pressed three fingers beneath his chin and tipped it back up. "We can contact King Lachlan and tell him everything. He'll know what to do."

Tris raised a defiant eyebrow, so she lifted a finger and petted the top of his left wing. He gasped straightaway and flattened a warm hand against the small of her back, then kneaded the area just below her rib cage. *What are you doing to me?* he asked.

Raising her brows, Zestine removed her touch from his wing. He gave a disappointed grunt.

You can *trust the king, but since you refuse, how about trust me instead?*

As he considered her words, she stroked the top of his right wing, making him moan softly and lean in for a kiss. She pressed her lips to his and opened for him, echoing his moan as his tongue swept in and met hers.

Never had anyone tasted so perfect, livening her mouth with salty-sweet amaretto tang. The raptatawk's passion for her continued to quench her every need. A warm sensation tingled in her chest as that ever-present void within her began to fill. Or maybe it'd started filling earlier, like when she'd first kissed him, and was now becoming full.

She pulled back. "Your wings. I want to feel them."

Tris hissed in a breath as he slowly unfurled his wings, baring the terrific, ultra-sensitive organs to her. He encircled her with them.

Zestine brushed the pads of her fingers over the midnight blue feathers. They were so soft she couldn't even hear them shift under her touch. Tris's pattern of breathing changed to lengthy exhales and hitched inhales. "What does it feel like?" She turned on his lap to caress the white feathers on the end of one wing.

"Goooooood," he said, making her giggle. When she turned back to face him, his eyes were closed, his expression as relaxed as she'd ever seen it. Upon removing her hands his eyes popped open. "It feels amazing."

"Mmm." With a bit more pressure she grazed fingertips over the meeting of his blue-and-white feathers, then very gently skimmed delicate circles along the skin underneath with her nails. "I want you to feel amazing."

His eyes were near closed again, and they abruptly sprang open before he grabbed the hem of her shirt and lifted it over her head. Face between her breasts, he kissed her chest while thumbing her nipples, which hardened under his touch.

"Oh," Zestine moaned. "T-Trisss…" He replaced his fingers with his mouth, closing his lips firmly around a tight peak and tugging with mild suction. "Ah!" When he let go, she arched her back, palmed the back of his head and pulled him to her other nipple. Zestine broke into a pant watching him suckle her, the ache between her thighs prompting her to wind her legs around him. "Harder," she demanded though a husky whisper. He groaned as he obliged by tightening his lips and sucking with more force. Soon his kisses ascended to her neck, jaw, and when he nibbled her earlobe, she whimpered and humped his abdomen, a fresh rush of arousal flooding her loins.

While suckling her earlobe Tris whispered, "You're ready for me, Sheyn. I scent it. I've always scented it. Remember, outside the throne room in Noctis during our quarrel? You wanted me—"

"I've always wanted you," she said, stunned by his use of *Sheyn*, which translated in the Ancient Language to 'my only one.' Zestine wasn't sure if she was more surprised Tris knew the word or that he'd used it for her.

Romantic tales abounded with that term of endearment. As a young girl, she and her girlfriends had swooned over stories of lost and found love and forbidden coupledom. Always the hero swept the heroine off her feet and made affectionate love to her while 'Sheyn' fell from his lips.

"I was an idiot for denying you," Tris said. After wrapping an arm around her middle, he rose and undid his pants.

Zestine wriggled from his hold and took off her slacks. Then, still surrounded by his magnificent wings, stood before him.

"Come here." Tris lay supine on the bed and scooted toward the center, causing his wings to nudge her forward. "I need to taste you."

He didn't have to tell her twice. She crawled onto the mattress and knelt over him, positioning her knees on either side of his face.

"Oh gods." He planted his hands on her hips and further spread her thighs when he pulled her pussy to his mouth. Then, he feasted. Zestine gasped at the tantalizing contact of his velvety tongue brushing her soft flesh. He began with long licks from the bottom of her slit up, barely grazing her clitoris. After about five of those in which he savored her every inch minus the perky bud at the apex, Zestine forced his tongue to hit it by rolling her hips.

"How dare you tease me," she said, tone jesting.

Tris growled, then peppered kisses along her nether lips while his hands slid from her hips to her ass cheeks, which he kneaded before finally focusing on that sweet spot. He wagged the tip of his tongue across her clit fast, as if racing to make her come.

She moaned, already teetering on the edge of a climax. Unable to keep upright, she slammed both hands on the mattress and undulated her pelvis in perfect synchrony to his licks. Tris's wings closed around Zestine, cradling her firmly as he lapped her to a mind-scrambling release. "Oh, don't stop. Fuck, I'm coming, Tris." She cried out, her mind blissfully blank as pleasure gripped her body. His hands and wings held her in place while she cruised the heights of physical ecstasy.

Once the intense ride faded to peaceful calm, she couldn't help but smile. For the first time in her life, Zestine was falling in love.

CHAPTER 25

Tris licked his lips, relishing Zestine's flavor as he freed her from his winged embrace, his gaze locked on her slick and swollen pussy until it was out of sight. She hummed a cheery tune as she stood. Before he could move an inch, the wet heat of her mouth surrounded his cock.

"Oh yes," he said. It felt incredible, and she hadn't even gotten started. "Th-this will be quick." Just seeing his dick buried between her lips shook his legs with impending release. When she slid those ruby lips up and down and bombarded him with her tongue, he couldn't keep from rocking his hips. Once they found a rhythm Zestine added her hands, stroking his shaft with one, fondling his balls with the other, successfully robbing him of all thought.

As predicted, Tris didn't last long, but he didn't care. At the same time he filled her mouth with seed, a searing pain struck his lower right abdomen. Gasping, his hand flew to the spot. "Ah. What—" The pain pulsed as it traveled up, not relocating but spreading.

"Ow," he exclaimed, lifting his head to view his stomach. What he saw took his breath away.

"Oh no. What is this?" Zestine asked, getting to her feet and leaning close to inspect the red, black, and purple mass bordering his pelvis. "Where did this come from? It wasn't there a couple minutes ago…"

Tris's insides lurched, but not from the pain. "I don't know." His breaths grew labored as he tried to keep quiet despite the agonizing sensations. It took only a few moments for the affliction to color his entire abdomen red with black spots and purple specs.

"No… no." Zestine threw on her shirt and left the room, returning seconds later with her backpack. She ripped it open and dumped the contents on the bed, snatching and activating a hyx device.

With tremendous effort, Tris forced himself to stand and don pants, then collapsed on the mattress and covered his face with his hands. Bloody sweat dampened his hair and slicked his skin. He rolled to his side and lifted his knees to his chest. It felt like millions of tiny acid-soaked machetes hacked at his cells. If this thing affected his entire body, or even three-fourths, he'd beg Zestine to kill him.

The pain switched direction, dispersing to his pelvis and claiming territory on his right thigh. Limbs shaking, he straightened and lifted his pants to observe the anomaly. It pounded like a heartbeat and flashed with red light. Whatever it was, it appeared alive, or at least agenda-driven.

He let his head fall back. "Father—"

"Tris, no," Zestine said right before a third voice spoke.

"Hello," King Lachlan said from the hyx.

She didn't mince words. "Something's horribly wrong with Tris." She twisted the compact around so Lachlan could see Tris, who closed his eyes and covered his face again.

Please Father, get us out of here. I'll pay for my atrocities however You wish. Just please make this go away.

His bodily invader reached his right knee. Then, within the area it'd claimed, the pain flared. Tris bellowed, muscles yanking taut as he fisted his hands against the impulse to claw at his flesh.

This was the Darkness. It had to be. Thanks to his unforgiving acts, it had come for him.

"Zestine. Y-y-you ha-have to kill me." He didn't recognize his own voice.

"No. Tris, it's okay. It'll be okay." To the king she said, "Do you know what this is?"

"Uh, no, I don't. Where are you?"

"Underworld. Where we've been since the beginning."

"Leave, *now*. Both of you. When you've gotten to a safe place, contact me and I'll come get you."

"But—shit!" Snapping the device shut, she hurled it across the room. It clattered when it hit the wall, then the floor. "Stay here," she said, as if he could go anywhere.

Horrific uncertainties plagued him. Would he die before the age of thirty? *Could* he die of whatever this was? Though he wanted to leave the caves for several reasons, after the Dark God's emergence something deep within him had advised his Light was in jeopardy. If this ailment was Darkness itself, leaving wouldn't help. If it was Darkness, he'd have even more reason to surrender to death. Did Zestine have the courage to take his life? If she asked the same of him, he'd have serious qualms with it.

As a raptatawk, taking his own life was not only forbidden, but impossible. The High Lord had created raptatawks to be the last and only resistance to Darkness;

He'd not allow His sons to perish by their own hand. Even suffering and useless, their Light served a purpose.

It was nothing less than he deserved, which he suspected Father would appreciate. What could be more fitting than being slain by the very force that, though you were created to destroy, you succumbed and gave life to?

Tris stabbed pointy teeth into his cheek against the pain, severing part of his cheek, which plopped onto his tongue. Blood clogged his throat as he tried expelling the spongy clump; a shower of scarlet sprayed from his mouth, followed by the offending hunk of flesh. Afterward, he whimpered and gnashed his teeth, grimacing. "Make it stop."

Zestine all but flew into the room. "We're leaving. I'm getting our stuff together."

"Leaving?" How would they swing that?

"Yes. That's what King Lachlan ordered." She moved about the room so fast it made him dizzy.

Closing his eyes, he considered telling her to go without him, but she'd never agree, even if she alone could avoid the Corrupteds' notice and gain freedom. "Am-am I…" Tris swallowed, then emitted a grunt as his body jerked without aid of his mind, as if trying to exit his skin and escape torment. "Going to die?"

It went quiet, telling him Zestine had stopped moving. "No. I won't let that happen." She resumed her task. "Stop talking. I'm almost done."

"It…" He gasped, then an ugly sound of misery fled his throat. "Hurts." A single tear trickled out the outer corners of each eye. Never had he cried.

"Shhhh." A moment later, Zestine gently stroked his forehead. Tris's eyes popped open as she slid her palm to his cheek before combing her fingers through his hair. "We'll make it, but you have to fly, Tris. I can't do this by myself."

"We shouldn't go," he replied, aware of how ludicrous that sounded when he'd wanted to flee a short time ago and now had every reason to. Yet considering what he'd just discovered…

Ahhh. So soothing were her fingertips across his scalp. His eyelids lowered.

"We have to," she said before moving away.

Eyes flying open, he cried out and careened upright. No longer beside him, Zestine paused stuffing things into a bag and looked at him.

"I need your touch." He flung a quivering arm toward her. "It kills the pain."

Zestine gasped. "Really?" In a heartbeat she was next to him, resting her hand on his head and twining her fingers through his. The relief was prompt and immense.

"Really," he said amid a contented sigh.

"That's… incredible."

Armed with her touch, Tris surmised he could fly—no problem. "My savior, my anodyne." He reached up and brushed the backs of his fingers along her cheek. "You *won't* do this alone."

She squeezed his hand. "We need to go."

He couldn't resist another praise. "You're incredible."

~

"We're both pretty incredible," Zestine said with a smile. Her heart swelled with fierce sentiment at the way he regarded her—like she was the most precious thing in the world.

Tris parted his lips as if to speak, only to nod and look away, brows furrowed. Her smile faltered. If they had more time, she'd press him to reveal what he'd planned to say, but the alarm she'd seen on King Lachlan's face kept her action-oriented.

He sat up. "How should we do this?"

Zestine cocked her head and pursed her lips. "At first I thought we should depart separately, but since that's not an option… we'll leave together and hope for the best."

Tris frowned. "But we can't let anyone see you."

"Any suggestions?" Silence fell. Every couple seconds she darted a nervous glance at Tris's body even though at the moment his pants hid the mobile part of the mass.

"I have an idea." He released her hand and gave a tortured groan before biting out, "Turn-ah. In-into your beast." Zestine rose and transformed into a black panther. He placed his hand on her back, letting out a breath the instant he made contact. "Maybe, if you're a kitten, I could put you in a backpack and cut a hole in the back so you can touch me."

Zestine shifted to human form. "Let's do it." She'd try just about anything to get him to safety. He'd stopped paying attention to the oddity ailing him. High Lord willing, they'd never learn what happened when it claimed his entire body.

Tris grabbed her hand and Zestine willed her fangs forth to tear a hole through the backpack. As they prepared, her ability to eliminate his pain dominated her thoughts. It pleased her to alleviate his suffering, though she was conflicted on how it was possible.

It's a sign. We belong together.

But another inner voice insisted she not get her hopes up. She'd lived for centuries and never heard of such a phenomenon. Unless…

Had *it* happened? Had they fallen in love with one another, the occasion of which bore an incessant force tasked with safeguarding their lives and their love?

Only by mutual love can we achieve the impossible. It was what every Pirmas learned during adolescence. Her feelings for Tris were strong, but she didn't *love* him… did she? Did *he* love her?

"Zestine, it's time."

Upon looking at him, the urge to see the *real* Tris, just once in case something happened, consumed her. "Okay, just…" She wiggled the red charm off his finger.

"I need to wear that," he whispered jokingly.

Gazing into those rich dark-blue eyes, she tumbled into them and became lost in their depths. Lost in *him*. Her heart swelled to near bursting. *And he feels the same.* At the profound realization, a longing to consummate their love yielded a fresh wave of arousal.

Tris's nostrils flared. "Zestine…"

Breathless and full of pep, she slid the ring back in place and kissed him. The moment his tongue swept into her mouth, a knee-weakening, tingly sensation raced shoulders to scalp. When he pulled her close and locked her in his unyielding embrace, she felt united with him, no lovemaking required.

Even the ravenous Darkness couldn't touch this slice of euphoria. Engulfed in perfect wholeness, she moaned through their kiss while joyful tears pricked her eyes. She loved him, really and truly. Zestine had found her forever in the arms of a raptatawk.

Zestine broke from their kiss with rosy cheeks and shiny eyes. After a brief smile and nod, she disappeared. The agony of flaming saws tearing through his abdomen, pelvis, and legs jolted his heart and deflated his lungs. Tris barked a curse and slammed his fist against the kitchen counter, cracking it down the middle.

A whiny meow sounded right before Zestine jumped onto the ruined countertop a tiny kitten. He shook as he reached for her, heaving a sigh upon touching her soft black fur.

With no way to hide his bizarre condition, as soon as he donned the backpack with Zestine in place they departed Cradle. An electric thrill danced through him knowing he'd never return.

En route to the commons, Tris couldn't help but wonder what he'd do in this situation without Zestine. He recalled his annoyance when he'd learned of their partnership. The answer was simple: with extreme pain rendering him incapacitated, the mysterious affliction would kill him or—he shuddered—turn him Dark. Hence, he'd be totally fucked if not for her.

Not that freedom from the pain equaled victory. The anomaly continued to spread, and he tried not to think about the outcome if it conquered his every square inch. Tris wasn't ready to die. He prayed King Lachlan would know what to do.

No event crowded the commons, but right away Tris had company. As if awaiting him, Quinn, George, and Henrik stood with their arms crossed facing the back tunnels. They approached at once. Tris didn't stop and chat like he would've before.

"What happened to you?" asked George.

"Don't know." Tris took sure steps and kept his gaze straight ahead.

"Looks painful," Quinn said.

Lifting a shoulder, Tris pursed his lips. "It's not bad." The trio accompanied him into the tunnel leading outside.

"Where are you going in such a hurry?" Quinn asked, cutting in front of him and pivoting to walk backward.

"Out."

"Oh yeah?" Quinn stopped and when Tris tried to go around him, George and Henrik blocked his path.

"Out of my way," Tris said, a menacing bite to his voice. His pulse accelerated; adrenaline saturated his blood, stoking a rabid rage that stretched thin the mental ropes Tris had used to leash it. Fighting was risky, but he'd do it. He almost hoped he'd have to.

Pop. The first rope split.

You can't fight without touching me and I can't fight touching you, Zestine warned.

"You're an imposter, according to the Dark God," Henrik said.

Tris chuckled and raised his eyebrows. "Really?" *Pop* to the second rope.

"Yes, really," said Quinn, clearly not amused.

Run, said Zestine.

I won't make it. The third rope snapped; two more to go. Tris bared his teeth, his throat gurgling with a low growl. *I need to kill them. They* need *to suffer.*

I'm sorry, my love. I have to intervene. Brace for the pain.

Tris stiffened. Had she called him 'my love'?

George's fist slammed into Tris's face, shattering his cheekbone with a deafening crack as he fell to the ground. A millisecond prior to landing, scalding agony shot through his body on a cellular level, launching from him a tortured roar.

The echo of his roar was smothered by an animalistic screech. Warm liquid splashed on his face and hair, while all he could do was succumb to the parasitic force ravaging his system. There was a hiss, followed by a chorus of vicious snaps before a man's howl ceased as soon as it'd come, giving way to wet crunches and slurps.

Then Tris realized he couldn't see.

CHAPTER 26

Zestine felt Tris fall right before she leapt from the backpack a kitten and hit the ground a full-grown jaguar. But unlike Earthbound jaguars, she was larger, faster, more robust, and thus a force to be reckoned with. When situations called for quick deaths, jaguar was Zestine's feline of choice, for the strength of their jaw surpassed that of any other cat.

Ears back, teeth bared, claws extended, and tail twitching low, she screeched, springing for Henrik first as all three Corrupted gaped at her. Hesitation never turned out well for her enemies.

Hooking her claws into the meat of his shoulders, she punched through Henrik's skull with all twelve fangs. The fucker didn't even have time to scream. After five furious shakes of her head, Henrik was headless.

Sharp twinges to her back, that from centuries of combat told Zestine she was being stabbed, caused her to hiss, jerk her head around, and clamp George's arm between her teeth, easily crushing the bones. The knife dropped from his hand as she whipped her head back and forth. Once she held the forearm but not the man, she ducked—just missing a dousing of Corrupted blood—spat out the limb, and sealed her jaw around his leg.

Pulverization of his kneecap forced him to her level, where he glimpsed the back of her throat as she struck. Her bottom fangs sunk through George's eyes with a gushing pop, expelling squishy material before she broke through to his eye sockets. Top fangs pushing into the top of his head, she bit down until his skull gave and a flood of brains and bone spilled into her mouth. She swallowed every bit, the beast relishing nourishment from the kill.

Zestine used her claws to sever George's gaping head, then turned around and spotted Quinn halfway to the common area, yelling for backup. Shifting to woman form, she knelt over Tris, who was oblivious and howling in pain, and pressed her palms to his chest. It took a couple of seconds before he focused on her.

"We have to go," she said.

He nodded, then leaned over just in time for blood to pour from his mouth, but they had no time to dwell on that development. To Zestine's relief he stood without a problem, grabbed her hand, and took off, seeming at full strength.

Three Corrupted—including Quinn—tailed them. But they were poorly armed, even half-assing their pursuit.

She grinned. *Must've seen what I did to their buddies.*

With the cave's exit in sight, Tris shrugged off the backpack as he ran. "Put this on and climb on my back."

Zestine obliged without slowing. Once on Tris's back, she looked back at their pursuers, extended her canines, and hissed. Knives whizzed at her, one of which pierced her arm, but she barely felt it in the heat of the moment. She plucked it from her flesh and slung it back right before she and Tris lifted off the ground. Zestine threw up a fist and whooped to the pure black sky as her beloved soared high into the atmosphere.

Peeking behind her, she rumbled a growl through bared fangs. Quinn and one other hadn't given up so easily.

"Still on us," she said.

"What do we do?"

"For now, fly as steady as possible."

He leveled off. "Zestine, what—"

"No time," she yelled as Quinn arrived within striking distance.

Zestine unsheathed her sabre and reached out to block a swing that would've cleaved through Tris's rib cage.

Clang, clang, ping, jangle. The clash of metal serenaded Underworld's fathomless gloom. Blow after blow they exchanged until—*clink clank!*—he struck with such force her wrist bent the wrong way.

"Watch out," she screamed. Distracted by the pain, it took a moment to realize she no longer held a sword.

Tris swerved away from Quinn, only to suffer a deep slash to his shoulder by the other Corrupted. But the newcomer flew close enough that Zestine lengthened her claws and carved red lines across his face—a canvas for beastly artwork.

He growled. "Fffucking twat."

The Corrupted fell back, though not far enough. Snatching his wing, she yanked him forward and—*schhhlip-bip*—thrust a claw into each eye, then—*gwowp*—extracted his eyeballs. He screeched and swung his sword. As the blade descended for her neck, she severed his arm below the elbow with ferocious swipes of her claws. The sword's sharp edge missed her and Tris before it and the forearm plummeted from sight. Wings flailing, her victim bellowed and pawed at his face. Those empty eye sockets, paired with the web of crimson trails left by her claws, displayed the most striking depiction of failure she'd ever seen.

Zestine had just flicked the eyeballs free with her thumb when she and Tris abruptly dropped several feet, sending her stomach into her throat.

I have to spin, Zestine. Hold on tight, Tris advised at the same time Quinn's blade bit her rib cage, unleashing from her a pained yelped. The next instant she was upside down, clinging to the top of Tris's wing with one hand with a leg wound around his thigh. Electric panic sliced from her shoulders to her hands, seeping sweat onto her palms. Gasping, she dug claws into his wing while reciting *sorry* in both their minds.

Right-side up, upside down, right-side up, upside down, faster and faster they spun. In the vast darkness, she quickly lost track of which way was which. She also didn't know Quinn's whereabouts. Keeping hold of Tris was top priority.

Mid-rotation, they abruptly veered right, then left, zig-zagging back and forth for a time until Zestine heard a deep tear, followed by a maniacal yell. Seconds later the rough ride ceased and they flew straight and steady.

"I-I got… him," Tris said amid heavy breaths.

Zestine shuttered her sight against a wave of dizziness. "Is he dead?"

"Unfortunately, no. Maimed but not dead. I nearly ripped off one of his wings."

She grinned, imagining Quinn flailing through the air, then wrapped her arms around Tris's chest and her legs around his waist. She rested her cheek against his nape. Appreciation of his strong, capable physique made her shiver with appreciation and, despite the circumstances, a dash of lust. *And this body is all mine.* "We made it, Tris."

"Only because of you."

"Oh stop. I'm not the one who flew us out of there."

"You killed more Corrupted than I did."

Zestine snorted, shaking her head. "All that matters is we're free from that place." With a sigh, she shut her eyes and basked in the feeling of gliding through the air, carried by the wings of the man she loved.

After several towns passed beneath them, Tris touched down outside a random village. "Let me have a look at you," Zestine said, only to frown at his multicolored body, though they'd both healed from their aerial injuries. "How do you feel?"

He pulled her close and palmed her neck while rubbing the small of her back. She couldn't help but whimper, proving that *his touch* was powerful as well. "Fine, as long as I'm with you. I went blind in the tunnel. You gave me back my sight."

Mouth parting and eyes widening, Zestine found herself lost for words. She patted the hand touching her neck. "Let me see." Tris obliged and she removed the red-stoned ring, smiling when his features normalized. "There you are." The red polka-dotted nightmare had reached his neck, but had yet to mar his face. The flashing part currently roamed his upper right arm, having already claimed the entire left one.

Tris cocked his head ear to shoulder. He dipped to her level and captured her gaze with his own. Fierce heartfelt vibes charged the air around them as she slid her fingers into his hair and brought his lips to hers. The wild taste of him struck Zestine with a sense of relief, like sucking air after being oxygen-deprived. He kissed her with a passion and tenderness she'd never known. A surreal feeling took hold, as if the world paused, as mesmerized by them as they were by each other. More than a mere kiss, it was a declaration as well as a dedication to each other. Zestine's sounds of pleasure, the enthusiasm of her lips and tongue, told him the depth of her feelings and how hot she burned for him.

So tempting was it to lose herself in Tris, she nearly forgot about contacting King Lachlan. She broke from him and caught her breath as she put a hand on his chest and slipped the backpack straps off one shoulder, then put her other hand on his chest and shrugged the pack off. "We have to notify the king."

Tris nodded, knelt to open the bag, and fished out a hyx apparatus while Zestine kept in direct skin-to-skin contact. When the device didn't respond to his saliva, he handed it over, wrapped an arm around her waist, and cuddled her close. The hyx liquified and swirled before King Lachlan appeared.

"Where are you?" he asked.

"Still in Underworld, but we're out of danger… for now," Tris replied.

Zestine said, "We're on the outskirts of a small town. There's a place called Constant Chaos, and… Wily Smite."

"Meet me at Wily Smite. I'll be glamoured and wearing all black. You'll know it's me." The screen cleared and the hyx hardened.

Zestine tossed the device into the backpack and strapped it to her back. "Let's go."

They walked hand-in-hand to town and upon arrival, Zestine spotted King Lachlan straightaway. The warlock paced under the deep-purple cursive lights spelling 'Wily Smite.' His hair was longer than his real hair and brown instead of dark blond. Golden irises replaced his true pale teals, but his mannerisms and commanding presence were the same. It couldn't have been more obviously Lachlan, but she wasn't certain she'd recognize him without knowledge of his disguise.

"Fuck," Lachlan said as he circled them, assessing the damage to Tris's body through narrowed eyes. "Does it hurt?"

"Worst pain I've ever felt." Tris beamed and eyed Zestine, squeezing her hand. "Only when she's not touching me."

She smiled. "He went blind too... and vomited blood. When I wasn't touching him." Her cheeks heated.

The king stopped, gaze flicking from Tris to Zestine several times. "That's... unexpected." He pointed at them and wagged his finger to and fro. "Are you two...?"

They looked at each other wearing huge smiles. "Yeah, something like that," said Tris.

Lachlan nodded and looked beyond them for a moment before abruptly shaking his head. "We must go." He approached and placed a hand on their shoulders. A second later they arrived in the royal throne room in Noctis.

Zestine gasped, her eyes widening as she looked Tris up and down. The polka-dotted nightmare was nowhere to be seen. "Tris. Oh, my Lord. It's gone."

Tris peered at himself. "What… How…?"

"I suspected this might happen," said Lachlan, ever unruffled. He propped an elbow on his fist and stroked his chin, squinting as he studied the 'tawk.

Zestine raised her brows. "You did?"

The king nodded. "The mission exposed you to too much Darkness, I believe," he told Tris. "Your Light must've weakened and the Darkness took advantage. Or, at least, the Darkness was winning."

Tris inhaled deeply, then released Zestine's hand. "No pain!" They immediately rejoined hands.

"Wow," she said. "What would've happened if…"

"Nothing good," Lachlan said.

"This has happened before, right?" said Tris.

The king dropped his arms and pursed his lips. "Don't know. It's definitely worth looking into."

"What do we do now?" Tris asked.

"You two can relax for a while. I know you need it and Dia is busy at the moment, so we'll convene later. Your huts are still available and we've stocked Zestine's with food and water." He gave a tight smile, then inclined his head. "Go on. My guards will retrieve you when it's time."

Tris scrubbed his forehead with the back of his hand. "So… They've raised a supposed Dark God."

Lachlan nodded. "Sounds like I made a good decision sending you there. I look forward to discussing this in more detail, but now isn't the time, unless it's realistic to take immediate action."

Zestine, wanting more than anything to be alone with her lover, tugged on his hand. "Let's go."

Tris hesitated, then instead of turning to leave, he knelt at the king's feet and bowed his head. "Thank you."

That, she hadn't anticipated. Considering his behavior prior to the mission, the simple act delivered a powerful statement. "Tris," she whispered with a note of wonder before glancing at Lachlan, whose unreadable gaze was on the raptatawk. Struck with deep admiration, her throat thickened as she took a knee beside him.

"Rise," Lachlan said. They stood and he put a hand on Tris's shoulder. "You're welcome. Now go."

They walked into the Noctis night toward the sea, balmy breezes and spicy floral scents intensifying the fresh feeling of safety. Though as Zestine admired the winking stars, her chest tightened. More battles awaited. She was sure of it.

CHAPTER 27

"You must be hungry," Tris said when they entered Zestine's cabin.

She turned to him and slung her arms around his neck. "I *am* starving… for you," she teased. They met for a tongue-twirling kiss that furthered hardened his already-engorged dick, though he wasn't the only one aching. The enticing scent of his woman's need filled his nostrils, driving him near mad. Unfortunately he also smelled blood. Zestine was covered in it from saving his ass… a second time.

"We should clean up," he whispered between kisses.

"Okay," she whispered back with a suggestive smile before take his hand and leading him to the bathroom. Inside dwelled a group shower equipped with six shower heads. A hexagonal space, the shower was bordered by three angled walls of turquoise tile on one side and three panes of glass mirroring the shape of the tile on the other side. Side-by-side sprayers stemmed from the center of the middle wall and ceiling, and higher-placed, single sprayers on the two other walls slanted toward the shower's center.

Zestine let go of his hand and shed her sullied garb en route to the shower. When she bent at the waist to remove her thong, as she'd done on the beach, he forgot

214

how to breathe. This time, she prolonged the show, allowing him an eyeful of the pretty pink folds between her thighs, slick with desire. Desire for *him.*

After righting herself, she opened the center glass pane comprising the shower door and faced him, flaunting the full package while making known with bright eyes, glowing skin, and pebbled nipples how much she craved him, this sexy woman who'd crash-landed into his life, saving it in the process. She undid her hair, shook her head, and thick red locks cascaded down her back and shoulders. Eyes on him, she swept her tongue over plump ruby lips, which morphed into a naughty grin the moment her gaze found the massive bulge in his pants.

Tris tugged the drawstring of his slacks and kicked them aside, then stalked after her as she entered the shower. After she spun the dials, warm water shot from all six shower heads. Zestine planted herself in the heart of the flow.

He circled her from outside the spray, watching the water rinse the blood from her body, forcing it past her ample rump, over her toned thighs and calves to her adorable feet before swirling the drain and escaping through its tiny holes.

Damn. How'd she make something as vile as Corrupted blood look sexy?

When she ran her hands through her wet hair and peeked at him with those uncanny blue and purple eyes, Tris was spellbound, done for, totally consumed… by her.

"What?" she asked with a meek smile.

Should he tell her? *Why not?* He was pretty sure it'd become obvious.

He stepped into the spray, scrubbed the blood from his face and hair, then placed a hand behind her ear and used the other to grasp the soaked hair at her back. "I need to say something I've never said to anyone." He closed his eyes for a few seconds and upon opening them—

"I love you too," she blurted, then pressed her lips together even as the corners rose.

Tris's eyes widened. *What?* His mouth moved to ask just that, once, twice, three times until he gave up and said, "I love you, Zestine. We started off rough, and it was my fault. I was a fucking idiot, telling myself I didn't want you, but I did, even in the beginning. The moment I first saw you, I wanted you."

"It's okay. You acted pathetic, but we made things right."

"I'm sorry. And I'm not saying that because you expect me to. I truly am sorry for my horrible attitude."

"I forgive you." Her gaze slid to his chest, then back up. A flirty glint shone in her eyes. "If you were trying to push me away, I don't think it worked."

He chuckled, but turned serious when she ran her hands all over his pecs and abs. A gentle tug of her hair tilted her lips up to his, and he kissed her with as much passion as he could muster.

She sighed, then wrapped her arms around his neck and legs around his waist before breaking from his lips and meeting his gaze. "Please, Tris. I need you inside me."

With a growl he strode from the spray, pinned her against the wall, swung his hips back, and plunged his cock into her welcoming flesh.

He grabbed her ass and thrust deep and fast and hard. Zestine sucked in a breath and exhaled a moan. It didn't take long before she scraped her nails up his back and came, Tris's mouth descending upon hers to swallow her screams.

He wanted this slice of heaven to last forever, to pump his aching cock into her, make her orgasm until she clung to him breathless, sweaty, and sated. Until he was all she felt and all she knew. Never could he slack his need for her. Never did he want to.

Zestine's kisses moved from his lips to his neck, then she broke away and cried out at the same time her pussy hugged his cock, causing him to groan and his balls to tighten. *Won't last much longer.*

"So good." She gently bit his shoulder, then clawed his nape and released a moan while consumed by a second orgasm.

So close. "Zestine," he called, shoving her back and forth over his length, faster and faster until he erupted, blasting semen into her fervent body. Unsurprisingly, even while in the throes of carnal bliss he pined for more of his female.

~

Zestine slipped off Tris's shaft and he pulled her into a crushing embrace. They held each other for a time under the spray before heading to the massive bed, his dick rock-hard when they crawled beneath the covers.

"Beautiful," she said, gliding a hand over his perfect phallus, trying to memorize its feel. Zestine lay sideways, propped her elbow on a pillow, and patted the mattress. "Kneel here."

Tris obliged, and she grasped his erection while fondling his scrotum. He groaned softly, then loosed a breath and rested a hand on her head.

She licked the head like a lollipop, then twirled a wet trail around the girth as she jerked him off. Closing her mouth around the head and sucking, she added the slightest scrape of teeth, unleashing from him a gasp, followed by a groan. When he thrust his hips, she allowed him to breach her throat, moving her tongue every which way and sealing her lips *tight*. She moaned, relishing his salty taste and silky texture. Already soaked from earlier, her core pulsed with need, so she dipped a hand to her clit and rubbed herself off with minimal stimulation, humming in ecstasy as the orgasm slicked her inner thighs.

After circling his glans with her tongue one last time, Zestine sat up. "Do you want more of that, or—?"

Tris moved toward her, his cock bobbing, the head purple and shaft bulging—in perfect condition to fuck her brains out. His glazed eyes raked her body. "I want *you*." He palmed her ass cheek and skimmed fingertips along her rib cage, making her breath hitch.

Once her voice returned she said, "Give it to me from behind." Zestine turned around, got on her hands and knees, arched her back down and stuck her ass up.

"Oh gods. You're so gorgeous. Perfect." He knelt behind her, rested his cock within the crevice of her bottom, and pressed a warm hand on her back. When he smacked her rump, she wiggled it in return, swaying and circling her hips in search for his wide head. After teasing her with a suspicious amount of unsuccessful prods, he surrendered and slid between her lips, sinking deep, filling her completely.

The pleasure in this position was a shock, his single thrust temporarily numbing Zestine from head to shoulders. A wild ride was to come. She fisted the comforter. "Give it to me as fast and brutal as you like. Go crazy."

"Fuck." His grip on her hips propelled his movements as he fucked her hard and fierce like she wanted.

Vision blurring from the extraordinary sensations, unbidden curses spilled from her lips. He reached beneath her and tended to her clit with firm strokes until she cried out a release that left her boneless. Tris leaned down and locked an arm around her middle until her strength returned, not once pausing his delicious assault as his cock rubbed all the right places and tore scream after scream from her lungs.

The raptatawk felt unbelievable. She never wanted him to stop. "Harder," she demanded, so he pummeled her harder, punishing her depths in the most delightful of ways. The smack of skin-against-skin filled the room.

His hands shook against her flesh, indicating he was ready to blow, but not before her. Another climax raced forth, holding Zestine hostage to a level of pleasure she'd never experienced before Tris.

"Right there, right there, right thererightthere," she chanted just before her muscles snuggled around his shaft and held. Moments later, she cried out as her womb contracted and her mind shot to the stars in a soul-wrenching orgasm.

"Oh, yes. Zestine!"

As warm cum bathed the depths of her cunt, Zestine felt exquisite. She was in love, had orgasmed too many times to count… simply suspended in bliss.

Tris withdrew, pulled her into his arms and claimed her lips for an ardent kiss. Right before they parted, a whimper broke free of her throat. His love surrounded her, moved her, strengthened her.

They stared at each other with silly grins until an unexpected visitor stole their attention. Translucent violet mist adorned with golden starlight materialized directly above them. It crackled as it spread and dispersed the scant space between them, then stretched thin arms around their torsos as if to hug them. Zestine yelped at the energy's cool, yet comforting, vibration against her flesh. After only a short time the entity withdrew, snapping and popping as it returned to the area where it'd first manifested, morphed into a rectangle, then danced wavelike while slowly dissipating.

Once it was gone, Tris's lips curved into a curious smile. "What was that? At first I wondered if I should try to kill it." He laughed.

Zestine's smile was so big her cheeks hurt. She raised her hand toward where the mist had been, wishing she'd touched it with her fingers. "I think it was… our love… manifested." Unexpected, but awesome.

Tris tugged her onto his lap and pressed his nose to her cheek, his eyelashes tickling her temple as he stroked the damp hair clinging to her nape. "Love you," he whispered.

Turning her head to face him, their lips were but a hairbreadth apart. They stilled. Even after their wild sex-capades, this moment—their breaths mingling, being rapt under his ocean-blue gaze that stripped her of weakness and shame—brimmed with heart-rattling intimacy. Several quiet seconds passed before they exchanged a tender kiss.

Zestine lay her head on his shoulder. "Love you more." Although her eyelids felt heavy, her blood hummed with exuberance. It was nice knowing that for the time being, she could rest easy knowing everything in the world she needed held her in his arms.

CHAPTER 28

Quinn knocked on the door to the Ravager's lair. This time, there was no request for a watchword, and when the door clicked open, he hesitated, wondering if he should hightail it to a portal while he still could.

"Enter!" roared a voice not belonging to the demon. With his heart pounding in his ears, Quinn pushed the door open and stepped inside.

The Ravager sat in his usual spot. Behind him loomed the nine-foot-tall Dark God, who was also called Mrakzlo. Black wisps of Darkness radiated from his translucent flesh, his abysmal eyes shrewd and oppressive. His lipless permanent smile stretched the length of his mandible, and when he parted it his pointy, mostly black teeth were visible only by their bright white tips and thin edges, the rest blending with black gums.

The Ravager was a newborn pup compared to the actual newborn Dark God.

"What happened to the imposter?" The Dark God asked, his voice's grating boom vibrating Quinn's eyeballs.

For a split second, he considered telling them they'd killed Tris, but hastily quashed the idea. Merciless death awaited if he was caught lying, and he'd rather not find

himself at the bottom of the Pit of Teeth anytime soon…
or ever.

Quinn bowed his head. "He got away."

"What of the beast?" asked the Ravager.

He winced. "She escaped too, my lord."

The Ravager hissed right before a dull thud
prompted Quinn to lift his gaze. The Dark God's hand,
thumbless, with eight twelve-inch-long fingers topped
with red-tipped black claws, grasped the demon's
shoulder. Those fingers drummed slowly against the
Ravager's robe, then Mrakzlo grasped the Ravager's other
shoulder and did the same. Helpless to look anywhere
else, Quinn's gaze moved from one hand to the other.
Tap, tap, tap, tap, tap tap… pat, pat, pat, pat, pat, pat…

"Did you know," Mrakzlo boomed, breaking
Quinn's daze and making his stomach leap, "Pirmas heal
only as well as mortals from damage delivered by me?"

A moment passed before understanding dawned.
His eyes widened. "That's—"

The Dark God's hand shot toward him. Quinn
yelped at a sharp pain accompanied by a meaty tear on
the left side of his head.

Mrakzlo twirled Quinn's left ear between his fingers.
Gasping, the Corrupted reached up and felt a crater
where his ear used to be. He looked at his shaky hand,
covered in blood.

"For the beast," Mrakzlo declared. He reached out
with his other arm, which stretched easily across the
several feet between them, dug a claw into his right eye
socket, and scooped his eyeball out. With a shriek,
Quinn turned around to flee, or tried to, only to get
whiplash. His body refused to follow his brain's

command. The Dark God showed Quinn his right eye. "For the imposter."

"Don't forget Henrik, Konrad, and George," the Ravager said.

Mrakzlo rested a claw against his slit of a mouth. "Yes…" A couple seconds later he reached unnaturally far a third time and sliced a jagged web into the Corrupted's face before grabbing his black hair and yanking his scalp free of his skull. Quinn bellowed. Blood poured, coating his neck, chest, back, and shoulders. The injuries were more than enough for shock to knock him unconscious, but someone's magic kept him awake.

Mrakzlo tapped his chin with three long fingers. "One more punishment. Any requests, Qu-Qu-Qu-innnnnn?"

Lying would've been a better route. He couldn't imagine the punishment being any worse. Though he could do nothing about what awaited him, he begged anyway. "I… P-please."

The Dark God turned the shell of his ear toward Quinn. "What was that?"

In answer, he screamed, gasped for breath, and screamed again. Terror was an emotion Quinn had never endured, yet now was all he knew. Slamming his teeth together, he clenched his jaw until his back teeth shattered, then clawed at his already demolished face, nicking the corner of his intact eye. Mrakzlo's hand came for him, and when he realized where it was headed he broke into sobs. "No! No. No, please." As the deity's hand inched closer, his pleas turned to maniacal squeals that abruptly ceased when the Dark God ripped off his penis and testes in a gush of blood. Quinn's top teeth dropped like a guillotine, half his tongue tumbling from his mouth before his head fell back, the pain robbing him of breath. Blood collected in his throat, then spewed from his lips when he gulped for air. After tilting his head forward, animalistic respirations scraped past his throat as he sagged against the magic keeping him upright.

The Ravager let out a cynical laugh. "We must burn his wounds to stop the bleeding." Behind the duo, the mirrored wall lifted to reveal bright dancing flames.

Quinn finally collapsed into a quivering heap, his shoulders smacking into a puddle of blood. Sharp points pinched his intact ear and wrenched his head around. With his remaining eye, he glimpsed the Dark God's fuzzy black-and-white profile.

"Now, Quinn, you will help me rectify your failure."

⸺

Their break from the chaotic and odious world of the Corrupted couldn't last forever, and after approximately two Earth days, the king and queen summoned Zestine and Tris to their royal quarters.

Elven guards arrived to escort them, and Zestine forced a smile after opening the door, despite their refusal to acknowledge her. Yuny was back, along with an elf sporting fluorescent yellow hair. Spiking her tone with artificial respect, she said, "What can I do for you?"

"The First Tribal King and Queen request the presence of Zestine Amolora and Tris, Son of the High Lord," said Yellow.

"Give us a minute." She slammed the door in their faces. "Fuckers," she muttered.

"It's time?" Tris asked from the kitchen.

She frowned as she turned to him. "Seems to be."

"Hey," he said, drawing out the word and lifting his arm in a gesture for her to come, which she readily answered, sighing once within the comfort of his embrace. "It'll be okay. We made it this far. Maybe they'll cut us loose after we tell them everything we know."

Zestine didn't think that'd happen but tried to match his optimism. "I hope so."

Finding love had changed her attitude about life. All of a sudden, Zestine pined with startling intensity for a life she'd never known. For fifteen hundred years she'd waited for something without even knowing it, which was scarier than living for centuries bereft of notable achievement. What else awaited her, and would it take millennia to find? Sure, she could live forever. She could also die tomorrow, and Tris was no different. If directed back into the fray against the Corrupted, their demon handlers, and the recondite Dark God, dying was too great a possibility. Death hovered over the Darkness like vultures circled the currents for carrion. She and Tris had been lucky to escape its clutches until now, but eventually their good fortune would run out. In her experience, luck was limited and never warned of its departure.

Tris tipped her chin up and warm blue eyes pierced her with heartfelt empathy. "Smile?"

She couldn't help but give him what he wanted. He returned the gesture—no more sharp teeth—and they kissed before joining hands and approaching the door.

The elves escorted them to the royal property and once they stood before the king and queen, she and Tris unclasped hands and knelt.

"You may rise," the First Tribal leaders said.

They stood and Lachlan gestured for them to sit on the sofa. Instead of sitting on opposite sides like they had previously, they sat next to each other on the side closer to Lachlan.

"Please begin whenever you're ready," said Dia.

Zestine and Tris looked at each other. "You want to go first?" asked Tris.

"Sure." She looked at the royal couple and smiled, then cleared her throat. "Um, well as you know, I got incapacitated rather early on."

"And how did that happen? I wasn't given specifics," said Lachlan.

"Oh." Zestine glanced at Tris. "I'm assuming Tris told you we didn't present ourselves as mates?" At the king and queen's answering nods, she continued, "So… while Tris met with the Ravager, two Corrupted tried to lure me to join an orgy. One named Konrad grabbed my ass and forced my hand on his penis. I… sliced it off with my claws." She mimicked with her clawless hand the sweeping motions she'd used to sever the organ.

The king's brows shot up. "Really?"

"That's awesome!" said Dia, her eyes bright with admiration.

Zestine shrugged. "It was satisfying, but had I known the consequences, I wouldn't have done it."

"So this forced Tris to take you prisoner," prompted Lachlan.

She nodded. "Right. It's why I couldn't be of more use."

"What else?" asked the queen.

"They've conjured what they're calling a Dark God. I had to help raise him," said Tris.

Lachlan's eyes narrowed. "How so?"

Gazing at the arm that had bled into the receptacle of bubbling blood, he said, "A blood ritual. Zestine was there." Tris explained the ritual and when it'd occurred. "I was afraid because I thought my Light blood would expose me."

Zestine jumped into the conversation. "We aren't sure if it did. During our escape, Henrik and Quinn accused Tris of being an imposter. They said the Dark God told them."

Lachlan nodded, taking a minute to process everything.

Dia spoke up, saying exactly what Zestine had wondered. "If this Dark God knows you were an imposter, what else is he aware of?" The queen frowned, looking to her mate, but he had something different on his mind.

"I'm certain your blood *did* impact the ritual," he told Tris, who leaned forward and rested his elbows on his knees.

"How?"

The king shook his head. "I wish I knew, but *something* has to affect him differently than if he'd arisen from Dark blood alone."

A comfortable silence ensued. After a few minutes, Queen Dia said, "Anything else before we explain how the mission continues from here?"

And there it was: what Zestine had *not* wanted to hear. Her heart sank. Tris squeezed her hand.

"The place we stayed is their headquarters. It's a deep cave with tons of back tunnels," said Tris. "Also, they've recruited enough 'tawks to warrant adding more rooms." He shrugged. "That kind of surprised me."

"The Pit of Teeth," Zestine blurted, and all gazes settled on her. "There's a chasm in the main chamber. They call it the Pit of Teeth and use it to murder people and dispose of bodies. Darkness froths over the edges. It might be, I don't know, *alive.* Or something... monstrous dwells at the bottom."

Although nowhere near it, her stomach somersaulted thinking of how the opening resembled a mouth with sharp teeth. Always open, always hungry. She shivered and Tris snaked an arm around her waist and pulled her close. She looked at him. "When the guy with the Mohawk pushed me toward you, if you hadn't been there to catch me I would've gone over the railing and into..."

His deep-blue eyes widened, flashing with horror.

"It's okay. You were there," she whispered.

"Anything else?" asked King Lachlan.

Zestine consulted her memory, and something she wished she could forget jumped to the forefront of her mind. "Yes!" she shouted, then her cheeks heated from her overenthusiastic response. She gave a sheepish smile and cleared her throat. "Um, yes. The Corrupted aren't just killing innocent raptatawks. They're also torturing them, possibly experimenting on them." Images of live 'tawks sliced down the middle assaulted her psyche, and she covered her face with shaky hands, slamming her eyes shut. Never would she rid herself of the horrors Henrik had shown her.

"How do you know this?" Tris asked.

She dropped her hands and met his gaze. "Henrik."

His mouth parted for a couple seconds before he replied, "What?"

"He showed me things. Terrible things. Dead raptatawks, but also live raptatawks suffering vivisection." *Among other atrocities…*

"You're sure this is taking place?" asked the king.

Zestine hesitated. "I—well no, I guess I don't know for sure, but what he showed me was real. I—I mean… I never considered they weren't his memories." She pondered what she'd seen, replaying every second of Henrik's visit. Raptatawks were proficient at relaying visual memories via telepathy. But they were also gifted at projecting thoughts as images. "Everything else he showed me, I—we," she swept her hand in a circle to indicate she meant the four of them, "Knew was happening. Excising wings and murder… some are dying brutally, and what they do to their bodies." She thought she might throw up. Her gut settled when Tris skimmed his fingertips across her back.

"You are safe here, Zestine," said Lachlan, enhancing his voice with *lokoke,* thus calming her fraying nerves. Not trusting her expression to be neutral, she averted her gaze to her lap. He'd also used *lokoke* on her prior to the mission when Tris had tempted her beast. Manipulative? Yes. Warlocks could be infuriating. But given who he was and all he'd done for them, she'd not complain.

Though the king's promise of safety wasn't necessarily true, upon looking up she managed a tight smile and a nod. "That's all I have."

"Did you witness anything like this?" the king asked Tris.

He shook his head. "We never brought the living or dead back with us, only their wings."

"Maybe someone comes along afterwards to gather corpses," mused the queen. "What are they doing with the wings?"

"From what I saw, desecrating them and removing the bones for making weapons or jewelry."

"Is this Dark God a demon?" asked King Lachlan.

Zestine and Tris exchanged a look, then shook their heads.

"You're sure?"

They nodded. "He has no horns, but he does have a penis," said Tris.

Lachlan's gaze moved between them, down to his lap, then back up for him to stare at nothing in particular. "I want to lure him away from the tunnels. See what he's all about."

"See if we can kill him," said Queen Dia.

"But he's not the one who created the Corrupted," Zestine pointed out, not wanting to outright shun their idea. An idea that sounded way too risky. The Dark God was too unknown. Who knew what kind of powers he wielded?

Lachlan's teal irises paled, making them nigh colorless. "We'll terminate the Ravager too."

"How?" Tris and Zestine said.

The king and queen locked gazes and smiled. Attention back on his guests, Lachlan said, "Plans are coming together."

Dia's golden-emerald eyes sparkled with gleeful anticipation. "Trust us."

CHAPTER 29

Trust them?

"Do you trust us?" asked Lachlan, his gaze on Tris.

Before the mission, his answer would've been a firm *no*, but since then, the warlock had proven himself again and again.

He'd provided charms which allowed Tris to blend in as a Corrupted, and they'd worked. No functionality problems, no guessing games.

The king had known Tris needed to flee the enemy's nest when the anomaly invaded his body, *and* he'd come right away to teleport him from the Dark Dimension, which had gotten rid of the affliction. He hadn't lied to or misled them, and if it wasn't for Lachlan, Tris, and possibly Zestine, would be dead.

"Yes," said Tris.

The king and queen looked at Zestine.

"Of course."

"We need you both," Dia said, more serious than usual.

"Tris will lure the Dark God to us," said Lachlan. "After you two returned here with me, I dispatched three raptatawks to masquerade as Corrupted. They'll tell us when to send you in the cave. I'll provide detailed

232

instructions, and you'll be heavily armed and equipped with a hyx compact."

"What if that… thing returns to attack his body?" Zestine asked. "He'd be helpless."

"If that happens, we'll get him out at once." To Tris he said, "Don't go to Underworld before we attack. It's important you detox from that environment to be at full strength when it's time." The king took a deep breath. "Questions?"

The thought of sharing space with the Dark God made Tris's skin crawl, and not for obvious reasons, as the mysterious mass had bedeviled him directly *after* the deity's emergence. But what choice did he have? He couldn't bow out now. The right option wasn't always the easy option, and though it was tempting to give in to fear, he refused to let it stand in his way.

Tris pursed his lips and inclined his head. "I'll do whatever you need me to. What of Zestine?" The worry he nursed for himself was nothing compared to his concern over the woman he loved. Without her, he'd be nothing. Without her, he wasn't even certain he *wanted to be.*

"You'll have an invisibility charm that will get you through the Corrupted caves unnoticed," the queen told Tris before directing her attention to Zestine. "You're a formidable opponent. We need you in the upcoming battle."

"I'll be there," she replied with a crisp nod.

"There's something you may want to know, as Lachlan contacted each Tribe to request their best fighters." She turned to the king. "Should you tell her or I?"

Zestine straightened, as if awaiting a blow.

"It's nothing bad," Dia assured her, flashing a brilliant smile that seemed to brighten the whole room.

"You can tell her," Lachlan answered, nonchalantly reaching for his love's hand and lacing their fingers.

"According to Lord and Lady Belua, you're quite the efficient force. When we asked who to contact for reinforcements, they named you first."

That didn't surprise Tris. He'd seen the remains of her kills, knew how quickly she'd rendered them corpses. Zestine was among the most lethal beings alive, and she was all his. At his side, her face grew red.

"Whatever you wear or carry shifts with you, correct?" asked King Lachlan.

"Yes."

"Amazing," said Queen Dia.

"Wow." Zestine laughed. "I had no idea..." Tris wanted to call bullshit on that. She knew how deadly she was, but he held his tongue. "So, when will everything take place?"

"Soon," Lachlan said. "Immediately after Tris does his part, our forces will attack the Corrupted stronghold. Unfortunately, we can't specify a time. My advice is to relax, just be prepared for action at any moment. These are dangerous times. We have to be smart, and that means always being ready."

At that, guilt took Tris by the gut, reminded of his inability to inform Lachlan and Dia of what he'd learned during the surreal conference with the demons. If they knew what he knew, would their plans be different?

If released of his compulsion, he worried over the repercussions of keeping relevant information from the First Tribe. The knowledge he couldn't share constantly ate at him. His efforts to bury it into the recesses of his mind had failed, as even when he pushed it to new depths, it always crept back to the surface of his consciousness. Like it just had.

King Lachlan dug into his pocket and revealed two brass keys. "Beneath the pantries in your huts are full arsenals. Use these keys to unlock the floor door. It doesn't matter which key because they work for both. When the time comes, arm yourself as best as you can." Zestine held out her hand and he dropped the keys onto her palm. Reaching into his other pocket, he fished out two grayish-white stone rings and handed one to Tris and one to Zestine. "Put these on. Like the charms I gave Tris, they'll fit to your finger." Tris put it on his right middle finger and Zestine donned hers around her right ring finger.

Tris rotated the ring. "What are these for?"

"They're to summon you. When it's time for duty, these charms will illuminate, vibrate, and grow warm. So you won't have to sit in your huts and wait. Feel free to explore Noctis. If either of you are day-lovers, I'm sorry to say the sun won't rise for a while."

Dia shook her head. "I don't think I'll ever get used to it."

"Thank you," Zestine said.

Lachlan clapped once. "All right. Anything else?"

Zestine looked at Tris and he shook his head. "Not right now," she said.

The king inclined his head. "You're dismissed."

~

"You never told me about Henrik," Tris said on their way to the beach.

"You okayed his visit. Remember? You cleaned the blood from me."

He fisted his hands, wishing he'd been able to assist in, or at the very least witness, that fucker's demise. "I remember. But why didn't you confide in me about what he showed you?"

Zestine shrugged. "I didn't see a point. What would you have done?"

Tris pulled in a deep breath. "I don't know." Then Zestine and Konrad's rendezvous sprung to mind, making him re-clench his hands and grind his teeth.

"Hey." She moved in front of him, pulling them to a stop. "What's wrong?"

"I fucking *hate* what happened to you there."

Propping a hand on her hip, she glanced away and snorted. "Me too."

He had to know. "Did you enjoy it with Konrad?"

"No." She canted her head and squinted at him.

Was she playing games? "He made you orgasm."

"Yeah…" She huffed. "That doesn't mean I enjoyed it." Zestine's indigo gaze ensnared him as she touched his arm and pressed her palm against his chest, directly over his heart. "Why does it matter? I'm with *you* now. I love *you*. I killed Konrad *and* Henrik." Her brows lifted. "And if I could, I'd do it all over again to relive the satisfaction I felt ending their putrid lives." Zestine wrapped her arms around his waist, and without thinking he drove his fingers into her thick mane and cradled her head. Fierce sentiment thickened the air. "You're going to have to get over the fact I've been with others. With Konrad I had no choice." Her gaze flicked down, then back at him. "I had to trick myself into thinking he was *you* just to get through it."

Tris's breath caught. "You imagined he was me?"

She nodded, then settled her arms around his neck and pulled him down until her lips grazed his ear, sending a tingle up his spine. "Fantasizing about you was the only way I bore it," she whispered.

Shoulders collapsing, Tris inhaled deeply and peered at the pink moons—the left a disc and its neighbor a sickle. "That's all I needed to hear." He sought her lovely face with those rosy cheeks, cherry lips, and wide, smiling eyes framed by sweeping dark lashes and lost his breath. This woman belonged to him. Nothing else mattered.

A moment later his lips and tongue moved against hers in deliberate, charged strokes. Zestine emitted a sensual hum and sighed his name when the kiss ended.

Tris unfurled his wings, moaning softly as his tight muscles were treated to a stretch. Blood raced through vessels now free of obstruction, warming the skin beneath his feathers and readying him for flight. He grinned at Zestine, who ogled him through wide eyes. "Want a ride?"

She chuckled and wiggled her brows. "What *kind* of ride?" she teased, making his cock stir, but he wanted to take her up before laying her down.

With a wink, he patted his shoulder. "Hop on."

CHAPTER 30

Zestine jumped on his back, wriggling with excitement as his strong hands cradled her thighs. Tris beat his wings once, twice, and they were airborne. Every flap thereafter propelled them several feet, and when she found the courage to look down, the throne building was a mere speck amid a vast landscape of ocean, forests, hills, and valleys. Sweat oozed from her palms, a swift sense of alarm prompting her to shut her eyes.

Tris's voice resounded through her head. *You doing okay?*

After bathing her lungs with balmy air, she opened her eyes and viewed the wispy clouds alongside them. She let her body sink against his. *Yes.*

Enjoying this more than our flight in Underworld?

She laughed. *This is incredible. It's so peaceful up here.*

Are you afraid of heights?

Zestine pressed her lips together and rested her cheek against his nape. *A little.*

Risking a peek below, a slice of regret niggled that it wasn't daytime, as the colors of multiple terrains would've been magnificent to see. Still, it was a tremendous sight, and seeing Noctis from this vantage point strengthened Zestine's appreciation for Tris's kind.

For a long time, I never imagined someone could fear heights, but most people do, he said.

She snickered. *What? You're not afraid of land? Or depths?*

His body shook with a chuckle. *Nah. But caves make me antsy. I don't know how the Corrupted tolerate living underground.*

Zestine's heart thrashed against her ribs upon remembering a venture she'd entertained following her and Tris's meeting on Earth. She gnawed on her bottom lip and fidgeted as much as the scant space atop her lover's physique allowed.

Zestine… Tris drawled. Lord, how she relished his sexy voice bouncing around her brain. *What's on your mind?*

She looked at her trembling hands, swallowed. *Would you, um, thrill me?* She felt them lose altitude. *What are you doing? Don't land yet!*

The vibration of his laugh tickled her belly. *I'm not. Only navigating a clear path. Thrill you how?*

Just tell him, she chided herself. *Dive toward the surface as fast as you can.*

They veered left, then right. *Are you sure?*

No. *Yes.*

He unhanded her thighs. *Drape your arms over my shoulders.* She did, though not without gasping in panic during the second he wasn't holding her and she wasn't holding on to him. He took her wrists and pinned her forearms to his chest. *Wrap your legs around me and cross your ankles.*

Zestine's tummy flipped as she obliged. Then she waited while Tris circled the air. Was he stalling in case she changed her mind? Right when she was prepared to say something, he beat her to it.

Ready?

Oh gods. She was really doing this. *You're sure you've got me? I won't slip off?*

I've got you, Sheyn. Always. Don't uncross your ankles. If you think you're going to fall or need me to stop for any reason, I'm keeping our mental lines open.

Her hands prickled with anticipation. *Okay. I'm ready. And, um… count down, from three.*

Maddening seconds crawled by as Tris flew higher. *Here we go. Three…* His wings snapped against the air. *Two…* She sucked in a breath. *One.* He tilted toward land, ceased flapping, folded his wings close to his sides, and they hurtled earthward.

Stomach ping-ponging throat to pelvis, a powerful jolt sliced from her fingers to her toes as a wild shriek pealed from her lungs. The wind roared past, swallowing Zestine's cheers while immersing her and Tris in the night sky. Once the initial shock faded, their swoop acquired an illusive quality. At times it felt they floated upward as they sped downward.

About twenty feet from the surface, Tris leveled off before spiraling his descent. Near the ground, he flipped himself vertical and landed. Heart galloping, she let go of him only to reel and fall on her ass. A guffaw sailed past her lips while Tris beat his wings a few times, then tucked them in and turned to her.

~

He grinned and offered his hand to Zestine. "So you enjoyed that?"

Taking his hand, she stood and flung herself at him. He crashed to the ground, straddled by a version of Zestine he hadn't until this moment gotten to savor. "I've never experienced anything like it!" Face radiant and eyes gleaming, she pressed a hand to her breastbone. "Thank you. Truly. It's the best gift anyone's ever given me."

Warmth saturated his chest. To know he'd given her a memory beyond compare, and to witness the joy it brought her, wasn't just rewarding. It was addicting.

He sat up and she cupped his cheeks before kissing him with eager lips and a thorough tongue. Upon parting he asked, "Want to do it again?"

After touching down following their fourth nosedive, she hopped off his back and he furled his wings and spun around, then grabbed her rump and claimed her mouth in a frenzied lip-lock. Zestine moaned first, smooshing her breasts against his pecs and scraping stiff nipples over his skin, to which he answered with his own hungry moan. Tris was about to rip off their clothes and take her right there when she abruptly withdrew and looked at the punchbowl waterfall mere yards away. Having been too wrapped up in her, he'd not noticed it.

The cascading water formed an isosceles triangle, dropping from a wide cliff and narrowing before exploding into white foam upon hitting the pool. Behind the falls stretched a slate-gray rock wall. From its cracks grew spongy vegetation of every color of the rainbow and then some, adding splashes of vibrancy to the otherwise-dull crag. To the wall's right, lush greenery offered scattered windows of Noctis Sea before expanding into dense woodland.

"Wow. Did you know this was here?" She pivoted to face the scene.

"No. Did you?"

Zestine shook her head and disrobed. "Bet you can't catch me." She ran to the pool and dove in.

⁓

The tranquility under the water—crystal-clear and silky against her skin—rivaled that of the sky. As she swam toward the bottom, the light of the pink moons lent enough illumination for a detailed view of alabaster sand along with dozens of colorful plants and fish.

When something grabbed her foot, she screamed and shook her leg furiously, but upon breaking the surface, laughed at coming face-to-face with Tris. "You scared me!" She slapped him on the shoulder, then briefly sunk underwater to smooth her hair back. "I wasn't sure you'd follow me."

A chunk of wet hair dangled over his forehead, ending between his eye and eyebrow, and when he tried to smooth it back to join the rest of his hair, it didn't comply and settled right back where it'd been. Zestine doubted she'd ever seen anything so sexy.

"Why?" Tris said.

Huh? Her lust from a few moments ago was back. She moved toward him. "What?"

He chuckled. "Why did you think I wouldn't follow you?" With raised eyebrows, his mouth parted and the corners of his lips lifted as if he couldn't decide whether or not to smile.

She yelped when he snatched her around the waist. Her legs automatically wound around him, putting his hard length against her slit. Dipping her hand underwater, she held his dick in place and gyrated her hips to achieve delicious friction against her clit. Once she found it, she threw her head back; warm tingles ascended her spine. Tris lowered his hands to clutch her bottom, his muscular arms shackling her so close she trembled. Never had a man held her so tightly, as if he'd never let her go. Head still thrown back, Zestine gasped when his tongue slid a titillating path from her collarbone to the tip of her chin. More tingles raced across her neck and scalp.

He did it again, starting from the other collarbone. "Mmm. Does that feel good?" His voice had taken on that familiar seductive tone and easy cadence that made her even wetter.

"Yes," she shouted. "Oh, fuck."

"I want you to feel good." One of his hands left her ass and cupped the back of her head, which he tilted upright before capturing her mouth. They kissed with brute urgency—biting lips, sucking tongues, and knocking teeth. Zestine whimpered, jabbing her nails into his shoulders as she scrubbed her clit from his balls to his glans, again and again, her breath catching when the stirrings of a climax arrived.

Tris moaned. *Never get enough,* he voiced via telepathy, and she exploded, breaking away from their kiss to vocalize the delicious sensations scrambling her mind while coming within the arms of the man she loved.

Once she quieted, she rested her head against his chest and clung to him.

"Zestine," he said after a few minutes.

"Mm. Yeah?" Sneaking a hand between them, she found his cock—

"Wait." He grabbed her hand and laid it against his sternum, holding it there. "I just need to get this out."

That sounded... not good. She raised her head and met his gaze. "Okay."

Tris looked down, then back at her. "Before that thing invaded my body, I believed the greatest defense against the Darkness was free will." He licked his lips, looked down, and back up. "Now we know that's not true." Against his chest, his fingers curled around hers. "If we hadn't returned to Noctis in time..."

Zestine's throat thickened. The need to provide him comfort squeezed her heart. She cupped his jaw with her free hand. "Go on."

Tris's Adam's apple bobbed. He dropped his chin again. "If anything happens to me—" He shook his head. "I mean, if I become Dark and no one else kills me, you have to." Mouth a grim line, he met her gaze with haunted eyes, his raw emotion clawing at her good mood. "Promise me," he added.

At the word *promise*, her bottom lip trembled. She looked away as tears threatened. "I... don't know if I can promise t-to *kill* you, Tris."

He released her hand and wrapped her in his arms. "Yes, you can. And you will, if it comes to that."

Zestine's heart twisted, leaking drops of horror into her soul. "This—you—I—" She couldn't hold back a sob.

Tris's eyes widened through a grimace before resting his forehead in the curve of her neck. "Please don't cry, Sheyn," he said, voice strained. "I need your promise because without it…" He lifted his head. "Without it I can never be sure that if the worst happens, you'll be safe. You know I wouldn't be the same Tris. I'd be a monster, one who needs to die. One who wouldn't think twice before killing you and other innocents. Between death and Darkness, I'll *always* choose death. Who knows what this Dark God is capable of, and—"

"Okay."

His eyes searched hers. "Yeah?"

"Yeah. If it comes to that, I promise I'll do it." Now *she* felt like a monster for only thinking of herself. "I'm sorry, it's just—"

"Don't feel bad. I understand why it's a hard promise to make." Tris gave a wistful smile. "I love you," he whispered, then kissed her before she could tell him the same. Soon their uncertain future became lost to them as they lost themselves in each other.

Chapter 31

The pink Noctis moons still lit the starry night when Tris and Zestine's summons charms activated.

"You feel that?" asked Tris. They stood at the shoreline ankle-deep in the waves, ready to go for a swim.

"Yeah." She shoved her feet into her shoes and slid the glowing ring off, tempted to crush it in her palm. Instead, she put it in her pocket, then removed one of the tiny brass keys King Lachlan had supplied from a chain around her neck and handed it to Tris.

Studying the key for a moment, he pursed his lips before giving her a killer smile. Zestine knew he was trying to keep his disappointment at bay, and she appreciated his attempt to impede the negativity threatening to blacken their moods. "I'll get ready and come to your place after. Okay?"

Zestine nodded and, following a quick kiss, watched him take off to his assigned hut, which he hadn't used since their initial stay in Noctis. Dazed, she plodded to her cabin and, once inside, changed into battle-friendly attire prior to unlocking the pantry.

While staring at the locked wooden door at her feet, strong was the need to chastise herself for her reluctance to participate in the oncoming battle. *This is my duty. If*

I was a tougher person, it would be an honor. She acknowledged the despicable truth—as easy for her as chugging melted silver—and filed it away for later, in case she needed sober perspective before her part in the conflict ended.

She unclasped the chain from her neck and knelt to unlock the door. Upon flinging it open, she descended a short staircase and lost her breath at what greeted her at the bottom.

"This is crazy." She walked to the center of the huge bunker and twirled to take it all in. The arsenal was circular and lined with row upon row of shelves stuffed with weapons. No way was the room restricted to the dimensions of the hut atop it, as it stretched a good fifty feet in diameter. Never had she seen such a large amount of weaponry, the collection so vast she didn't know where to start. What would she need?

Luckily, Tris didn't have the same problem. A couple minutes later he joined her, armed with swords, knives, a chain-link vest, sleeves of armor…

Zestine gaped at the brown objects strapped to his getup. "Grenades?"

His lips twitched as he puckered his brows. "Yeah. Why?"

She shrugged, her cheeks burning. "No reason."

"Looks like you need help."

"Uh, yeah."

Tris strolled around the arsenal, replicating his attire on Zestine before arming her with knives, swords, grenades, and spray poisons. He stepped back and analyzed his work. "Jump up and down."

She did as he said. "Have you ever noticed it's possible to jump up from one surface, but it's not possible to jump down? I can jump up and *land* down. Is that what you meant?"

Tris's face scrunched up. "Lame." But a second later he gave a hearty laugh and Zestine joined him, pleased with herself for allaying their nerves.

"Now wiggle your hips."

"Wiggle my hips?"

"Uh-huh." So she wiggled her hips. Nothing came loose.

"Good." He turned away and scanned the shelves, then retrieved a large pouch with straps and secured it to her waist below the weapons belt. "All right." He fingered the pouch. "Fill this with sustenance."

"Okay."

Tris gestured for her to ascend to the main floor, then watched while she rummaged through the kitchen, packing food and water. When she glanced at him, he'd tightened his eyebrows into a frown, his face stricken as he worried his bottom lip.

"What's wrong?" she asked.

He let out a heavy breath. "I hate that you're so vulnerable, requiring food and water."

Zestine couldn't help but laugh. "I've *required* food and water for fifteen hundred years. Honestly, it's the least of my concerns." Though she knew how he felt. She'd fret about him every second until the mission ended.

After filling the pouch and slamming thirty ounces of water, she rushed over to him. He held her tightly against him and took her mouth in a sweet and slow kiss.

This is where I want to be. Always. Zestine wrapped her arms around his torso and met his warm blue gaze. "I don't want to let you go."

Shutting his eyes, he nudged his nose against hers. "You don't have to. I'm with you always." He tapped her temple. "In here." He brushed two fingers between her breasts. "And in here."

For a moment they stared at each other, minds silent and hearts yearning for a future waiting beyond the Darkness. A sharp knock on the door shattered the silence.

Tris managed a smile as he ran the pad of his thumb along her bottom lip. "Sheyn." He pressed his lips to her forehead. "We're going to be okay."

Knees quivering, she smothered a ravenous sense of foreboding and returned his smile, hoping with everything in her he was right.

On the other side of the door stood Mr. and Mrs. First Tribe, dressed in black combat wear and loaded with weaponry. When Tris and Zestine started to kneel, Lachlan stopped them.

"No need for that." He scanned them, then nodded with a tight smile. "This is when you say good-bye. Tris comes with me and Zestine will accompany Dia."

Zestine and Tris nodded before facing each other. "I love you," she said, uncaring they had an audience.

He grinned, and she allowed herself to fall into his ocean-blue eyes one more time. "Love you more." He leaned down for a soft kiss.

Stepping over to Lachlan, his smile never wavered as the king rested a hand on his shoulder.

Then he was gone.

"How are you feeling?" King Lachlan asked after he and Tris arrived in Underworld. Once Tris's vision adjusted, he saw the terrain matched that which surrounded Corrupted headquarters.

To ease the tension gripping his insides, he took deep breaths. "Honestly, I'm nervous as fuck."

"Mmm. I can alleviate that, if you'd like."

Tris's gaze snapped to the king, who'd tweaked his appearance to match how he'd looked when rescuing him and Zestine from the Dark Dimension. At first, Tris wasn't sure what Lachlan meant, but then remembered the tremendous mind power wielded by warlocks. Many feared their unmatched ability to influence emotions, and while Tris didn't fear *lokoke*, he'd rather not receive artificial relief for natural feelings. He shook his head. "I need to be nervous. It'll help me make proper decisions." When Lachlan didn't respond, Tris continued, "So what's the plan?"

"You will lure the Ravager and Dark God here."

"Right. How will I do it? They'll want me dead as soon as they see me." Perhaps a stellar plan would ease Tris's anxiety better than *lokoke.*

"They won't see you. Invisibility charm, remember? As for how, tell them the truth: I want to meet with them."

"That's it?" *Please say that's not it.*

"Oh no. No, no, no." King Lachlan circled Tris. "They're not going to come without some convincing, so you'll show them this." Lachlan retrieved a hyx compact from his weapons belt and handed it to Tris. "Here. Anyone's saliva works on this. There's something you must show them on the hyx. Also, remember that as long as you're wearing the charm, the device won't be visible. So when you're with them you must set it down or allow them to hold it. If you can get it back, please do."

Tris activated the hyx, which liquified and rippled to the edges from the center a few times before displaying the king's face. Tris watched as Lachlan, in his un-glamoured appearance on the screen, spoke.

"You may think I'm your enemy." His smile turned into a glower. "And you're right, but that doesn't mean we can't compromise for mutual benefit. You have something I need and I have something you want.

"My father, King Soren, kept many things from me, including…" Lachlan pointed a claw-tipped forefinger at the screen while displaying a mouthful of serrated warlock teeth via a wolfish grin. He moved to the side, revealing a large globe perched atop a tall red dais. The right half of the globe glowed matte white. The other half shone a black so polished, it perfectly reflected Lachlan and, behind him, Queen Dia, holding what looked like a giant hyx compact with the scrying metal facing the king.

Seeing the globe made Tris's jaw drop. "No fucking way."

"Yes fucking way," King Lachlan said.

"Where did—"

"Shh, watch." Lachlan nodded toward the compact.

Tris pressed his lips together, fighting back dozens of questions.

On the hyx, Lachlan walked over to the sphere twice the size of his head and hovered a clawed hand over it. Tris held his breath as the warlock teased his viewers, coming extra close—too close—to touching it, but ultimately didn't lay a finger on the sacred, and extremely powerful, object. When Lachlan turned back to his intended audience, every one of his warlock features surfaced. Spiky, uneven black branches forked across his face and neck, and large ellipse-shaped pupils stretched the length of his eyes, teal irises gone. Nothing but frosty menace lurked in that gaze. To complete the transformation, two horns rose with twisting motions from his skull. The front one aligned with the space between his eyebrows and grew just inside his hairline. The other was a bit taller and jutted inches behind its companion.

"I'm guessing this needs no introduction," the king continued, referring to the globe before stepping in front of it again and creeping forth. "I might let you get your filthy hands on this." He shut his eyes and lifted his forefinger. "If, if, if ififififif," Lachlan pronounced the f sound for several seconds, ending with "fah," then opened his eyes and pointed forward briefly. "Firstly, you tell me how you're Darkening raptatawks. Secondly, *stop* Darkening raptatawks, and thirdly, come out of that cave and meet with me so we can attempt to strike a deal and carry out an exchange." Lachlan paused, then ended his spiel with, "If you choose to not abide by my terms, I'll just use the Nucleus myself… after we slay you, of course. Your decision. I do hope you make the right one."

The hyx blanked and hardened. Tris snapped the compact shut, heart racing and hair standing from King Lachlan's sinister poise. Beside him the king stood with his hands clasped behind his back.

"Where'd you find that?" Tris asked.

"My sister, Brynn, had it." His face contorted when he said her name, as if speaking it caused him pain. "After her and my father's death, I was in no hurry to go through their things, nor did I believe Soren would leave such a valuable item with *her*, so I found it only recently." He shook his head. "I thought it was lost to the world, only to find it inside her closet."

The sphere was an ancient relic called the Nucleus. Rumor held it'd formed simultaneously with the universe. It displayed accurate representation of the universal balance of good and evil, or Light and Dark, at any given moment. The white part represented Light and the black part represented Dark. Throughout history, there were a few times when the Nucleus was more white than black, but more often than not, it was more black than white. The First Tribe were the globe's primary possessors, and although it responded to touch (expanding the white half when touched by benevolent folk and vice versa), it had a mind of its own, one more complex than any Pirmas. According to history, all of Otherworld knew when someone worked the Nucleus because all kinds of insanity ensued. Realms overlapped. Land became sky and sky became land. Oceans soaked into the sand, burying water fae and other sea creatures. Forests conducted lightning. Clouds dried out and shed dirt, dumping mountains of soil that rain would never quench. Colors bled from nature, yielding gray worlds. Sometimes these horrific events reversed and sometimes not. The correct way to work the Nucleus—if one existed—remained a mystery, the consequences of attempting a catastrophe, but that didn't stop the mad from trying.

Demons seemed the perfect candidates to take such a chance. The Ravager *had* declared that with the Dark God they'd render the worlds black. Supposedly, the universe would achieve unshakable stability once the

Nucleus displayed equal white and black halves, though not everyone agreed. Some thought the world needed an entirely white sphere, while others believed only a sphere of pure black sufficed.

Tris took a deep breath. With his nerves fraying rapidly and adrenaline coasting into his bloodstream, he felt electrified.

Lachlan studied him through narrowed eyes. "Are you sure you don't want me to calm you?"

"No—I mean yes, I'm sure. I don't want to impair my judgment."

"I doubt that'd happen, but if you don't wish for me to intervene, I'll respect that." The king dug into his pocket and presented yet another ring, this one thin and gold. "This is an invisibility charm. It's the only one I have, but I'm working on more. They're exhausting to make, so please be careful with it." He offered the ring to Tris. "Put it on."

Tris took it and slid it on his finger. As soon as it tightened to a fit, he vanished. "Whoa. That's crazy. I can't see myself." Looking down, it reminded him of flying low to the ground.

"You should still feel your body. Try taking it off."

Tris felt for the ring and slid it off, and there he was again. He took another deep breath and nodded. "Okay. I know my part. What are the women going to do?"

"The plan is to attack once you've gotten the leaders out. I have a few moles inside and they will notify me when the time comes. When you're through luring them my way, you can join the battle, then go home. I will not ask any more of you than this. I know you and Zestine are eager to start your lives together, and though I don't believe either of you are interested, I'd be happy if you two worked for me."

Tris nodded. For him, home wasn't a specific place, but with a specific person. He'd join Zestine in battle and fight until the end. He hadn't thought much about what to do afterward, but as long as he was with her, his future looked bright.

The king came over and lay a hand on his shoulder. They teleported and landed elsewhere amid the same landscape. Lachlan pointed to Tris's right. "Do you see the rock about fifty yards out that's bigger than the others?"

"Yes."

"That's the entrance to the Corrupted's home base. When you exit there with the Ravager and Dark God, return here. You will find me." He turned slightly and pointed at a particular cave behind him. "Just so you know there's a portal in that cave." He twisted back around. "Questions?"

"What are you going to do when you meet with them? Will you actually hand over the Nucleus?"

"Have a conversation, and fuck no."

Clearly, the king wasn't going to elaborate, so Tris asked, "What if… I don't come back?"

"You're forgetting about the invisibility charm again. But if you don't come back, I'll assume you're not wearing the charm and we will search for you."

Tris nodded, an image of the craggy Pit of Teeth floating through in his mind. If he was fated for that chasm…

Stop it! I'm strong and smart. I'm capable. So what if Zestine can't save me this time if things go bad? It wasn't realistic or wise to count on others, something Tris needed to remember.

When Tris finished his mental pep talk, he bowed to the king. "I'll see you back here." *I hope.*

Lachlan inclined his head. "Good luck. May the High Lord guide you and keep you safe."

Tris slid the invisibility charm onto his finger, turned, and started toward the cave, and the Dark savages inhabiting its depths.

CHAPTER 32

The invisibility talisman was incredibly handy. He and Zestine could've used a couple during their stay inside the caves. Tris passed three unfamiliar Corrupted on his way to the main gathering area and once there, he stiffened despite being invisible.

Careful not to bump into anyone, he entered the network of back tunnels leading to the Ravager's lair, grateful he had no problem remembering how to get there. Even as the Darkness thickened and stole his sight, the door to the hideaway glowed like a beacon in his mind. He got there without incident and knew exactly when to stop.

No going back. Steeling himself, Tris rapped his knuckles against the door.

"Watchword," came the Ravager's strident reply.

Shit. He'd forgotten he needed a secret code word to get inside, and he couldn't remember what Quinn had used. Fiery pinpricks raced from his neck to the tips of his ears. *Think!*

"Watchword!" the demon thundered.

"I-I come… bearing an important message from the First Tribal King." He hoped his voice sounded strong and level. Frailty was just as dangerous to display to these monsters as fear.

There was no response for a time. Tris was about to knock again when the Ravager asked, "Who bears the message?"

Think! A vague truth would suffice. "A warrior loyal to the First Tribe."

Another drawn out silence. "What's the message?"

"I have to come in so I can show you, or else I can't deliver it." He closed his eyes and huffed. Maybe that hadn't been the best choice of words, but saying more could make it worse, so he held his tongue. With his heart pounding in his ears and sweat beading his neck, he waited. Moments later, the door clicked open.

Gathering himself and stuffing down his trepidation as best he could, he walked into the room.

Before him sat the Ravager, looking his usual hideous self. Directly behind him stood the Dark God. A jet-black fog radiated from him in waves, stinging Tris's eyes and digging into his skin like acid-coated needles. His muscles tightened as he fought to keep quiet through the pain. Only once Tris's Light reared up did the Darkness abate, and he slowly exhaled in relief.

The Dark God's ebony eyes narrowed and his slit of a mouth bunched. After removing the hyx device from his pocket, Tris fumbled to activate it, which was tricky because he couldn't see it. Behind him, the door whipped shut with a thud.

At length, the Ravager grated, "What is this, a ruse?"

Tris ground his teeth, invisible sweat slicking his invisible nape. "I intend to show you." A deep growl resounded, though he didn't know from whom it came.

After the fifth try, King Lachlan's voice played. With trembling hands, Tris placed the device on the floor. "Watch."

When it was over, the Ravager craned his rotting neck to peer up at his apprentice (or was the newly born god his boss?). Gray smoke poured from the Ravager's eyes into the Dark God's face, but it didn't seem to bother him.

Tris allowed the pair time to converse telepathically, knowing they were finished when the demon faced forward.

"We meet him here," the Ravager said.

Tris narrowed his eyes. "Here, as in…?"

The demon pointed a long-bladed claw at the floor. "Here."

"Those aren't the king's terms."

"He comes here or you die," the Ravager declared through his gaping maw.

A chuckle escaped Tris's throat, something he'd have stifled if he was visible, but he stopped short of mocking the demon. "Those aren't the king's terms either." After a painfully silent pause, he got an idea. "King Lachlan and his army already know you're here." He pointed at the ground even though they couldn't see him. "Right here, and if you choose to not abide by his terms, you're as good as dead, whether you kill me or not. Remember, he killed King Soren without putting a hand or weapon on him. He's giving you a chance to control the Nucleus, but you'd rather kill me and die yourself? Pft."

The pair consulted one another. Tris waited, tapping his foot with his lips pressed together in anticipation. It was nice not having to hide his natural behavior for once.

Finally, the Ravager stood to his full height of what must have been just over five feet and said, "Tell us where."

"Out the caves and to the right."

~

Even invisible, traversing those dark tunnels with two maniacal beings on his heels was an experience Tris could safely say he'd never want to repeat. His footsteps were audible. They knew he walked in front of them. With each step, he braced for something to happen, like being shoved, grabbed, stabbed, kicked, scratched, choked, decapitated, ripped apart, or de-winged—the possibilities were endless. When they reached the common area, he breathed a little easier. *Almost there.*

Upon exiting the cave, Tris's whole body loosened. He followed his own footprints back to where he'd left King Lachlan. The king was there, lacking glamour and flanked by an entourage of elves, warlocks, fae, and centaurs.

Tris stopped several feet away from the group. Lachlan inclined his head, which Tris assumed was for him, then he joined the Pirmas behind the king. He'd locate Zestine soon. First, he needed to see this unprecedented exchange. He kept himself invisible. As long as he stayed in the Dark God and demon's presence, the invisibility charm would stay on his finger.

"I don't suppose I'll receive a bow," said the king.

The Ravager hissed. The Dark God, towering behind the demon, remained stoic.

Lachlan nodded. "All right."

The Ravager extended his blade-tipped hand. "Hand over the Nucleus."

The king cocked his head. "Surely you don't believe I'll just give it to you. We must first reach a deal."

In his periphery, Tris caught sight of a large group of figures heading toward Corrupted headquarters. The Ravager and Dark God had their backs to the creeping warriors, none the wiser.

The demon looked up at his much taller companion. While he was distracted, Lachlan gave a signal and several individuals marched forward, led by a female warlock. The Ravager rose from the ground and floated over to them, putting him eye level with the elves.

The instant he was within striking distance, the Ravager roared and thrashed, severing an elf's arm and slicing open a fae from pelvis to neck. The fae gurgled, hands covering his throat as he collapsed to his knees. Blood jetted from both victims, painting the soil dark red.

Whoever used telekinesis on the Ravager released their hold. Before he could strike, a different elf strode forth and with two quick swipes of his sword, the Ravager's forearms dropped to the ground. The demon's unholy shriek cleaved the air. Tris winced and covered his ears.

King Lachlan traced his forefinger across his throat, and the elf struck again. A split-second later the demon's head landed next to his forearms with a clunk, his stocky body landing atop it.

Wow. For how feared the Ravager was, it'd been almost too easy to kill him.

The Dark God still hadn't moved, seeming to wait for the attention to turn to him, and when it did, he spread shiny black wings and took off.

CHAPTER 33

Tris, the only raptatawk of the bunch, ripped off the invisibility charm and unfurled his wings. "Do you want me to go after him, my king?" he asked even though he'd lost track of the Dark God almost immediately after he'd ascended. The fiend blended into Underworld's sky, fusing with the Darkness.

"Not unless you can see him," replied Lachlan.

"I can't."

"Then don't bother. He'll turn up somewhere. He's probably counting on us to follow him. Let's not give him what he wants."

"Fuck." Tris frowned as he turned to peer at the warriors in the distance who were now upon the cave's entrance. "I'm joining the fight."

"As are we." The king raised his voice. "Are we ready to annihilate these Corrupted ruffians?"

Except for the fae with his torso slashed open and the armless elf, the entourage crowed and cheered. Some thrust their weapons into the air.

The group breaching the cave answered with their own battle cries.

Lachlan approached the wounded guards. The fae, mending but in bad shape, lay a bloody mess on the ground; the elf was beside him, applying pressure with scraps of clothing that'd covered his severed arm. "Return home and recoup," the king said. "Healers are standing by to accelerate the process. When you're better, if we're still fighting, you can join us then." The elf nodded and used his intact arm to heft the fae onto his back before running into the cave housing the portal.

Everyone else started toward the oncoming battle. Tris wanted to search for Zestine, so he stopped to let the others pass, then spread his wings and took off. He circled the Corrupted's cave, where blood was about to muddy the soil. The beasts within the crowd included other large cats, hyenas, wolves as big as horses, enormous gorillas, rhinos, and bears.

No Zestine. Tris's heart sank. He suspected she'd be in jaguar form, but there were several jaguars, and he didn't want to risk confronting a stranger who might mistake him for a Corrupted.

The roar of combat emitted its initial howl as, several yards below Tris, multiple Corrupted flew from the cave, chopping at their opponents with long swords. Tris withdrew two swords and dropped altitude. Catching sight of a Corrupted who'd just exited the cave, he dove for him. The guy never saw him coming before Tris swung the blade at his neck, slicing his head clean off.

One down. Many, many more to go.

Tris flew high and slew Corrupted after Corrupted. Upon ensuring a target had red eyes, he struck, growing hungrier for blood with each kill.

While en route to slay another, a panicked raptatawk rushed him.

"Stop! He's one of us!"

Tris ceased his advance at once. *Father, no.* Not okay. Why hadn't he checked his eyes? Perhaps vengeance was making him sloppy.

"You have to be extra careful up here, mate," said the 'tawk who'd intercepted his attack.

"Are there others besides you two?" Tris asked.

"Just us up here," replied the one he'd almost killed. He had shaggy brown hair kind of like Tris's, only messier, and golden eyes. "But look." He pointed and Tris followed his finger. Several yards away, Queen Dia rose into the sky. When she was level with them she stopped, nodded to them, and gestured to the fray below.

"What's she doing?" asked Tris, but they needn't answer because out of the melee rose a Corrupted with blue, yellow, and white wings. He spun helplessly in the queen's whirlwind, his wings tight to his back as he kicked and bellowed like a madman. And as he drew nearer to Tris and his companions, understanding dawned.

Tris shook with the need to kill, to make the miscreant barbarians suffer as they'd made him and Zestine suffer. Fury made his body temperature rise as he flew to Dia's hand-picked victim, grabbed his right wing, and tore it off. The Corrupted gave an ear-splitting screech, so with calculating efficiency Tris unsheathed a dagger and stabbed him in the throat until his head dangled by a single chunk of muscle. The blue-eyed and blond-haired 'tawk who'd stopped Tris from killing Golden Eyes grasped the man's other wing and pulled it off. Looking to the queen, she nodded again before the wind tunnel vanished and the dead male and his wings dropped from the sky.

"Gods' puckered dirty assholes," said Golden Eyes.

Dia crafted a tornado with which she snatched another Corrupted from the crowd and guided him to them, weakening her winds just enough for Tris and the others to strike.

They slew dozens of enemies with the queen until two Corrupted attempted to interrupt their execution cycle by coming at them from opposite directions.

"I got this one," said Blondie, allowing the pursuer's speed to be his downfall by dropping altitude at the last second and sticking him with his sword. Stabbed to the hilt, he reached around the Corrupted's body and yanked his wings off. Blondie's victim roared, then screamed like a babe before the sword slid free of his midsection and, wingless, he fell to the earth.

Tris threw a knife at the other attacker. The blade landed in his forehead, causing his wings to flail before he dropped. Tris dove after him, landed next to his crumbled body, then ripped off his pink and blue wings.

After a quick look-around, he decided he'd had enough sky action, as he'd partly gone up there to look for the Dark God. On the ground, he plowed a grisly trail through his lost brethren like he'd been born for it.

The bad guys were so much easier to kill.

Machete in one hand and a sword in the other, he fought to the edge of the conflict. Ahead, two Corrupted stood back-to-back engaging opponents, who they slaughtered at the same time. The duo turned toward each other, then slid their attention to Tris, who stopped to assess them. The Corrupted on the left was missing an eye, an ear, and a scalp, his face a hideous web of black cuts. He bared his teeth right when Tris sprinted for him and his comrade.

Within feet of them, Tris fell to his knees, skidding across blood-soaked mud and throwing up his katana to block their blows while swinging the machete at the knee to his right, severing the leg. As the Corrupted collapsed, his bellow was cut short when his neck hit the blade of Tris's katana. His head struck the spongy maroon earth next to Tris with a splat.

On his knees, Tris hacked at the one-eyed guy with his machete and thrust at him with his sword, but his opponent blocked every approach while backing away and making Tris advance. They exchanged blow after blow, each sustaining minor wounds as Tris chased the backpedaling Corrupted. Soon, they were alone, the melee but a whisper of clashing swords in the distance.

Tris growled. "Just fucking *die* already!" It maddened him the Corrupted had vast space to dodge blows as Tris expended tons of energy. But then he darted back when the guy suddenly came at him, taking several strides before halting. The familiar swagger broke Tris's bloodlust, his eyes bugging out as he white-knuckled his weapons. His enemy's sword pinged through the air. Once. Twice. He withdrew, and Tris glanced down to see two red slashes forming a long, skinny X just above his navel.

You must pay.

The voice pierced Tris's brain, making him gasp. "Quinn?" Pointing the machete and katana at him, he stepped forward. The Corrupted backed up, not bothering to answer but again baring his teeth.

Tris didn't know why Quinn wasn't talking, as he'd never been shy. He chuckled through his shock. "You look great. Really, *really* handsome." A lumpy crust of reddish-brown had replaced his black hair, appearing hard as bone.

You will pay. Quinn emitted a wet growl. Mayhap his old friend had lost his tongue?

Tris shook his head, not caring in the least what Quinn thought he needed to *pay* for. It seemed the Corrupted was through engaging him, or maybe it was a trick. Tris still had four grenades, having not used any in the crowded battle to protect innocent lives. "Have a nice afterlife," he said, then lunged at Quinn with his sword, sheathed his machete and retrieved a grenade. Flipping the pin free with his thumb, he tossed the bomb at his Dark brother.

Tris turned and sprinted. Eight strides later the explosive detonated. Gory bits and slabs rained down, smacking into Tris. He frowned. Why hadn't Quinn tried to save himself? Why'd he state Tris needed to pay for something, yet failed to make him pay?

After shaking off pieces of corpse, he turned to the fracas. When the ramifications of the explosion quieted, it was near silent out there. The battle was dying down.

"Tris."

He jumped, a sense of dread slinking up his spine and hiking his shoulders. That voice... he'd hoped to never hear it speak his name. To find who'd spoken, he needn't look around, just up. There, facing the ground inches above him on black wings, hovered the Dark God.

CHAPTER 34

Zestine felt particularly bloodthirsty as she ran into the cave where she'd already spilled massive amounts of blood. She slaughtered three Corrupted before rounding the first corner, and ended four more by the time she reached the commons.

The place was stuffed with bodies both alive and dead. The floor was slick with blood, the sight and smell of which made her fangs drip.

The time had come to do what she did best.

Staying as far away from the Pit of Teeth as possible, she fought like the animal she was, killing Corrupted after Corrupted after Corrupted. If a target battled another, she attacked their legs to bring them down to her level. If they came for her, she'd go for either their neck, head, or legs, depending on their weapon and how they brandished it. She rapidly lost track of how many she'd slain, and although her body sustained multiple injuries, she healed quickly, barely felt the blows as they were inflicted upon her.

Attack, bite, crush, kill. Attack, bite, crush, kill was all she knew. Every Corrupted she terminated was another Konrad, another Henrik who deserved permanent disposal. Their Dark blood, which tasted like soot, filled her nostrils, coated her mouth, and stained her coat. Though the flavor repelled her, she couldn't get enough because the more crimson that paved the floor and splattered the walls, the more Corrupted were dead and gone.

After beheading a foe with a single joining of her teeth, she lifted her head and her muzzle brushed a male crotch. Zestine peeked up and upon spotting sadistic red eyes, snarled and sealed her devastating jaw around his junk, slamming her teeth together and listening with delight as the Corrupted screamed like a youngling.

Blood gushed into her mouth. With two ferocious jerks of her head, she ripped off her kill's genitalia. Letting the foul chunks spill from her mouth, she raked through his neck with her claws. Upon severing his head, she licked her chops furiously to both chase away and relish the acridity.

A cutting sting to Zestine's backside launched a yowl from her throat. She whirled around to fasten a wrist between her teeth while her claws shredded a forearm.

Something sharp got her just above the right eye. Blood descended, obscuring her vision.

With two Corrupted fast approaching and the injuries she'd given them quickly healing, she bared her fangs in a grisly gnashing of teeth; she knew the moment the sound of her teeth sneaked into their brains because their faces went white and their eyes just about popped out of their skulls.

None of these fools had been prepared for her speed thus far. She sprang for the one on her left and chewed more than halfway through his neck while clawing his chest until she breached his rib cage. He fell, and on the way down a blade sunk into her shoulder as she swiped at the other guy's neck with the fatal tips of her paws.

Drenched in their blood and hers, manic fury took over, and as the second guy dropped she was already going for his face, which seconds later she ripped off. The deep and continuous rumble of her voice box warded off would-be attackers while she ended the losers' lives for good.

Jaw tired of breaking skulls, Zestine switched to her woman form and fought with as much ferocity as her beast. While she couldn't match her beast form in speed, she remained faster than most others. She stuck to the same strategy as before, maiming her enemies low and when they dropped and quailed, delivering the fatal blow, one decapitation or de-winging at a time.

Soon, so many corpses littered the floor, finding room to stand became a problem. People had begun tossing bodies, both alive and dead, into the Pit of Teeth.

Zestine changed to her beast and left the cave. Outside, the battle still roared. She skirted the mayhem, killing when approached and relaxing into her role now that she wasn't near the Pit of Teeth. The Corrupted proved easy kills. Zestine anticipated their moves and even how they assumed *she'd* move, virtually seeing the deadly exchange in her head before coming out on top, time and again.

Once the action started to dwindle, she looked for Tris. When she didn't find him on land, she checked the sky. After failing to spot him there, she put her nose to the mud, but it was hard to track someone who could take flight, and all the spilled blood flooded her nostrils with thousands of unique scents. Farther and farther out she searched, finally scenting him in a tiny area leading nowhere.

A single dark-blue feather on the ground caught her eye. Zestine shifted and picked it up to sniff, concluding from its mouthwatering spice it belonged to Tris.

Though a bit too early to fret, panic knotted her gut and singed her nerves.

It's probably nothing. So what she couldn't scent him beyond this one spot? He had wings!

Then why do I feel like he's in peril?

Zestine pressed her lips together, willing her eyes to stay dry while scouring her surroundings. "Tris? Hello? Tris! If... if this is a trick, I'm *not* amused."

No answer.

She buried her head in the crook of her arm. Had he died in battle? Though her heart twisted at the thought, she was sure she'd know of such an occurrence intuitively. But if Tris wasn't dead or in trouble, where was he?

~

The Dark God drove the curved talons of his toes into the meaty sides of Tris's neck and flew him deep into the mountains. Tris, feeling the talons slice slowly through his flesh, growled throughout the flight in both pain and fury. When the sharp edges ripped all the way through skin and muscle, he plummeted, his stomach soaring to his throat in panic despite his ability to fly. Before he was able to spread his wings, he landed—surprisingly on two feet—on the edge of a cliff, his knees buckling and forcing him to crouch. Tris stood just as his captor joined him, the supposed god's impressive stature not a little intimidating.

Tris's blood burned with anger even as his chest tightened with dread. Some of that anger was for himself. He should've been more careful, more aware. Especially after discovering Quinn and his injuries.

Quinn. That bastard had better face eternal misery.

He glared at the Dark God and swept his arms to his sides. "This is a joke, right? What's stopping me from flying away?" As soon as the question hit the air, he regretted it. He didn't need to give his abductor reason to remove his wings.

"You can try," the Dark God said.

Tris dropped his trembling arms. "What are we doing here?"

"You killed him."

What? "Who?"

The Dark God's sable eyes smoldered with rage. "Ravager."

Ah. So he'd seen Tris remove the invisibility charm. "I didn't kill him. I didn't even touch him!" But Tris knew it didn't matter. Even though he hadn't literally killed the Ravager, he was partly responsible for his demise. "What's your business with me?"

He crowded Tris, who stood his ground lest he backpedal into open air. He couldn't decide if an escape attempt was worth it. Could he outfly the monster before him?

Only one way to find out.

"I'm going to make you better," the Dark God replied. He parted his lipless permanent smile to reveal dozens of pointy white-tipped teeth stark against black gums.

Tris gulped; his throat spasmed. As gingerly as possible, he started loosening the muscles that kept his wings furled, causing them to spread ever so slowly. "I…

I'm happy the way I am, but thanks, I guess." Maybe if the Dark God thought him daft, he'd lose interest.

The Dark God cocked his head this way and that, this way and that, again and again. Green orbs flashed to life within his murky eyes, formed a circle, and spun. Tris couldn't look away. He swore he heard a maniacal snarl, though the fiend's mouth remained shut. The circle of green lights widened, bordering his eyes before snapping teeth appeared in the center, one snap after the other. The snaps slithered into Tris's ears and echoed through his head. *Chomp. Chomp. Chomp. CHOMP!*

Tris gasped and jerked when an unbelievably sharp pain, coupled with a vicious blow of pressure, struck him just below his heart. Looking down, he saw the Dark God had buried eight claws to the hilt in the left upper quadrant of Tris's abdomen, the keen lengths woven in between his ribs. He could feel the icy-hot tips of each claw. Out from under the tips spread a skittering sensation, like thousands of spindly legged insects had been released inside him.

Tris's wings unfurled completely, but he wasn't able to move beyond that. Panic seized him as he envisioned Zestine's happy face crumbling, her luster blasted to pieces as Corrupted swarmed her.

No! Don't think like that. She'll be okay. The First Tribe will protect her. Ironic that that inkling of hope mirrored some of her first words to him: *King Lachlan and Queen Dia will protect you.* Of course she was also more than capable of defending herself. And she'd promised to kill him if he turned Dark. He'd never imagined how nice it'd be for his lover to be one of the most formidable predators alive. She'd make his death quick, wouldn't let him suffer.

He couldn't move his body, save his head. Before long the paralysis affected his wings, causing them to loll. The pain ebbed, but he still felt the sharp prods dispersing inside him and the freezing-hot sensation of his tormentor's claws.

Tris hung his head, worry for Zestine giving way to fear for himself. Though as he languished, that fear turned into a peculiar numbness.

"What h—ha-have you done to me?" Tris asked with great effort. His eyelids drooped.

"I've made you better."

Dark. Corrupted. That's what he was making him.

The back of his mind pricked with a clash of information regarding a certainty he'd relied on before this very moment. Something didn't make sense. He clenched his jaw against the lure of nothingness awaiting him. *Think, you imbecile!*

Like a shot of adrenaline, realization hit him with brutal clarity: transition from Light to Dark required willingness.

"No," Tris said, his voice pathetically lacking the bite he'd aimed for. "Y-you can't do this. I don't... *I don't want* this. You can't!"

"But I can." Malicious laughter. "I *am*." The Dark God leaned down to Tris's level, stopped inches from his ear, and whispered, "My name is Mrakzlo, and I am your maker."

The skittering inside his body sharpened and heated into countless searing pins. Tris choked on a cry at the same time rays of dazzling Light graced his mind's eye, each swallowed by the snapping maws he'd seen within the green orbs lining the Dark God's eyes. His burst of lucidity faded as quickly as it'd come.

Then, black oblivion sucked him under.

CHAPTER 35

When Tris awoke, he sat in a chair, his body draped in a silky black robe. An inky shadow framed his vision.

The next thing he noticed was how unlike himself he felt. In fact, thinking about his previous self made a burning rage gather in his chest, so he pushed it from his mind.

"Welcome back," rumbled a deep voice from behind him.

When he turned to see who'd spoken, Mrakzlo stepped into view, then came to stand before him.

"Who am I?" Tris asked.

"There's a mirror behind you. Have a look."

Tris stood and pivoted, catching his reflection in the huge mirror covering most of the back wall, a wall he'd seen before. A wall hiding a room lined with fire.

He closed in on his reflection, shed his robe, and studied his naked self from every angle. The differences from before included his eyes, which were now as black as Mrakzlo's; his wings, also as black as Mrakzlo's; his hands still had four fingers and a thumb each, but halfway up each digit his flesh became black and hard as bone, stretching past his fingertips into three-inch claws.

He bared his teeth to see them pointy and similar to those of the red-eyed Corrupted.

Tris stuck his tongue out. It was the same as before. He analyzed the rest of his body. His skin and hair hadn't changed and his feet still had regular nails, unlike his hands.

Mrakzlo approached and met his gaze through the mirror. "I expected more changes to your appearance, but as long as you're no longer a being of *Light*," he said, as if the word tasted horrible on his tongue, "I'm satisfied."

"What am I? A god, like you?"

"You're my creation. A demigod. You can walk between the worlds like I can. You're the same except your blood and spirit are now Dark. And you worship me. Not that filth called High Lord."

"But I thought raptatawks couldn't transform without the desire to."

His creator chuckled. "There are no rules where I am concerned."

He glanced at his reflection and huffed. "Why don't I have red eyes like the others?"

The Dark God walked back to the chair Tris awoke in. "They were the Ravager's brainchildren. You are my creation, and like the red-eyed men you can make others like yourself."

Tris donned the robe before returning to his seat. "Just raptatawks?"

Mrakzlo shaped his mouth as close to a frown as was possible, which turned it into a subtle smile. "That's right."

"Are there Corrupted still here?"

"Corrupted?"

"The Ravager's creations."

"Most perished during the battle. The few that remain will be glad to see you. You'll bring them hope."

"Can I turn them?"

"I wouldn't recommend it. They're already Dark-blooded, so there's no need."

Tris nodded and tapped the tip of his forefinger claw against his chin. "So, have I taken the Ravager's place? Where are the other demons?"

"No, no. *I've* taken the Ravager's place, and I plan to summon my demon friends very soon."

Tris's arms and legs twitched as he hiked his shoulders. Inside, his cells seemed to leap and twist, urging him to dive headlong into his new world and begin his Dark journey. Suddenly, he couldn't bear to sit for another moment. He stood. "I better go. If I find the others, I'll take them hunting. Hopefully, our numbers will rise, them and us."

The Dark God gestured to the door. "Go on then, lad. Report back to me when you return. There is much to do, and many to kill."

Knowing Mrakzlo expected it of him, Tris dropped to one knee, then rose and marched out into the Darkness, a once-repellant force that now called to his very essence.

~

Zestine didn't know how long it'd been since she'd last seen Tris. She guessed at least several Earth days, every second of which had been excruciating. Wondering where he was and if he was safe was nothing short of pure hell. His absence had ripped her soul in half, leaving her weak and starving for wholeness. She pined for him to the point of debilitating emotional turmoil and mental deterioration.

In efforts to locate Tris, King Lachlan had ordered search parties to the Dark Dimension multiple times since the battle against the Corrupted, which had been a victory for the First Tribe. So far, there'd been no sign of her beloved. She'd searched for him on her own time, which she had lots of, but always returned more disappointed and lost than when she'd left.

The king and queen had told her she could stay in Noctis for as long as she needed. Though she was grateful, her hut only reminded her of Tris and their time there together—making love, laughing, teasing, and sharing stories. Sometimes, Zestine fantasized sweet memories taking place right in front of her, experiencing their every detail—how she felt, safe and loved; how he looked, sexy and so completely taken by her. The place where she'd enjoyed unparalleled bliss now served as a brutal reminder of all she'd lost.

Finding joy had become futile. Everything reminded her of Tris. The ocean and the trees. Nighttime. Noctis itself.

Was he dead, trapped, or *changed?* Not knowing was perhaps the worst part. But Zestine didn't believe him dead; she continued to cling to the notion that if he'd died, she'd know it instinctively.

Zestine dug her claws into the mattress and groaned. Naked under the covers of her bed, she glared at the ceiling as she twirled the end of Tris's dark-blue feather between her thumb and index finger. She was a broken soul clinging to sanity. Emotion packed a way bigger punch in human form, but she'd resisted the call of her beast, afraid if she switched forms she may never change back.

Even though she couldn't imagine he'd submit to it, she worried he'd somehow become Dark. If Tris was Corrupted, would she not also feel it as if he were dead? Unlike the other possibilities, Corrupted Tris could come to her—if he cared to, that was. His motives would be sinister, and she'd have to fulfill her promise to kill him—a task she might certainly fail at—but at least she'd know.

No. He wouldn't do that to me, to himself. The only way he could turn Dark was by force, which was impossible unless that multi-colored anomaly had returned to devour his body and soul.

A cool breeze, accompanied by the words "Knock knock," drifted by Zestine, and a moment later, in walked Queen Dia in all her prepossessing glory.

The queen worried about her and visited often. Zestine would've liked to leave the hut and see where Dia lived, but she was forbidden to visit wherever she and Lachlan resided. The location was a secret no one knew about, not even their most-trusted guards.

Dia walked over and sat in a chair beside the bed. Zestine hadn't moved beyond turning her head toward the door, and she wondered if she'd been in the same position the last time the queen had visited.

"No luck," Zestine said. It wasn't a question.

Dia sighed and studied her folded hands in her lap before offering a sympathetic smile. "I'm sorry. We know there's been recent activity in the caves, and it's rumored there's a new leader, but we haven't dispatched more spies yet. The Corrupted's numbers are too low and Lachlan's afraid it'll raise suspicion if new men show up out of nowhere."

Zestine swiveled her head to continue gazing at the ceiling. "I've looked, you've looked." She wanted to search the caves herself, but the only way to without risking death was with an invisibility charm, the sole one of which had disappeared with Tris. The king was making more, though, and he'd promised Zestine she'd be the first to obtain a finished product.

"I'm so sorry," said Dia. "I feel helpless. I can't imagine what it's like for you. Even when Soren separated me and Lachlan, he made me forget about him, so I never knew what I was missing."

"I think I'm out of choices. This waiting is killing me. What am I even waiting for anymore?" The idea of giving up hope—what little of it she had left—set her nerves abuzz, but she was slowly dying inside. Accepting that he was gone was the first step toward healing, but if she accepted that, she'd give up on him. What if he needed her? How could she go on never knowing?

Zestine wasn't sure how much longer she could stand to stay in Noctis. If not for Dia, the chance to use the invisibility charm, and the fact she believed Tris would come here to find her, she'd be gone.

The queen sat beside her on the bed. "For what it's worth, I don't think he's dead." Dia smoothed a hand over Zestine's hair. "Neither does Lachlan. But please don't tell him I told you that. He doesn't want to have public opinions anymore because he's… king?" She shook her head. "I don't get it." Dia's fingertips continued caressing the crown of Zestine's head, causing her eyelids to fall. A tear leaked from one eye.

She knew the benevolent universal energy maintained by the High Lord worked in mysterious ways, and the love between her and Tris was something the cosmos valued and sought to keep intact, barring either of their deaths. So in her mind, Zestine sent a plea to Tris, to the gods, to anyone or anything capable of hearing it. It was a desperate attempt to connect with the man who'd entered her life out of nowhere. A man who loved and cherished her madly.

Tris, my love, this is Zestine. If you can hear this, I need you. Send me a signal. If you can, come back to me. I love you...

CHAPTER 36

Tris was airborne en route to meet with Mrakzlo when a voice from his past rang through his head.

Tris, I need you. If you can, come back to me. I love you...

He knew the owner of that voice right away: the blasted redhead his contemptible former self had fallen in love with. Memories of her remained, but his feelings for her were long gone, nothing but blown-away ashes. He'd simply dumped those memories into his brain's junk pile, which was heaping thanks to his transformation. And now she'd reminded him via an appeal? How laughably pathetic.

Tris chuckled and dove for land, the ground approaching at a terrific speed. Just before smashing into the surface, he leveled himself parallel with the earth, positioned his body upright, and dropped to the dirt.

He sped through the tunnels, stopped in the common area, which was packed with Corrupted—both Tris's brand and the Ravager's—and deposited four sets of wings from deceased raptatawks onto a brimming pile, then entered the back tunnels.

Outside the quarters marked "Cradle," Tris used telekinesis to bust open the door, which split free of the hinges and flew across the main living area and into the bathroom. He went straight to the bedroom. As soon as he entered, her scent hit him full-force, stopping him in his tracks.

It was apparent no one had been there since they'd left.

Tris grabbed a blanket from the bed, buried his nose in it, and inhaled deeply, moving the fabric through his fingers to smell every inch. When he hit a patch doused in the aroma of her sex, his dick, which had shown no signs of life since his change, hardened painfully. Memories of her luscious body sneaked into his awareness; his blood sizzled with feverish arousal.

Tris shoved his pants down in frantic movements. Using one hand to keep the blanket to his nose and the other to work his throbbing cock, he jerked himself off in vicious strokes. Just before climaxing, he threw the scent-saturated quilt onto the bed and squirted cum all over it.

Gaze on the streams of white goo, his mind swam, the face of the woman who'd caused the pathetic outburst planted in the forefront of his psyche. His ears pounded a beat of fierce hysteria.

Something within him detonated.

With a crazed bellow, he flipped the bed over, raced into the bathroom and shattered the mirror, then chucked the clawfoot tub against the wall, smashing it in two. In the kitchen, he pulled out the drawers, ripped the cupboards off the hinges, and hurled their contents across the room.

It didn't help.

When he stopped to catch his breath, he combed bloody hands through his hair and assessed the damage. The place looked like a tornado had whipped through. A glower twisted his face as he flounced out of Cradle, his spirit aflame with enmity for the woman responsible for his abrupt conniption.

Her message echoed through his mind.

Come back to me. If you can...

Tris ran his tongue against the tips of his teeth, his mind sharpening from the taste of blood. He'd return to her just as she'd requested, and afterward she'd never distract him again.

~

A loud noise broke Zestine out of peaceful slumber. She bolted upright and looked around, but saw nothing amiss. The shuffle of footsteps on the roof prompted her out of bed, and she wasted no time shifting into her jaguar.

The foot thumps traveled toward the only door of the hut. Then, silence. She bared her fangs, waiting.

Seconds later the door flew open and there stood...

She shifted to human form. "Tris!" She rushed to him, but took only two strides before stopping cold. "Tr-Tris?"

His face displayed no emotion. At his sides, he clenched and unclenched his hands.

Icy horror cinched her throat. He had *claws*. Wild emotion crushed her chest as her gaze drifted over the shiny black wings jutting from his back and shoulders. It wasn't just his physical appearance that was different, but something else that ripped the air from her lungs. Something not seen, but felt.

He'd been *Corrupted*.

Zestine stepped back, moving her mouth to speak but uttering no words. Tris was right in front of her, yet *not.* She lunged forward to slam the door but his mental hold on it prevented her from succeeding.

Well, at least now she knew. Her beloved was no more.

He cocked his head. "I got your message. You asked me to come back to you." He spread his arms. "Here I am."

"No. No." She took another step back.

He entered the cabin. "Yes. Yes."

"I'll kill you," she said, her fangs forming and claws lengthening. *The real Tris would beg it of me right now.*

His bottomless eyes and stony expression betrayed nothing. He was an empty shell, and her heart chose that exact moment to shatter, the pain of which brought her to her knees. She loosed a blood-curdling howl, uncaring of how weak it made her appear.

Gone. Tris was *gone* and there was nothing she could do to bring him back.

The forever in his eyes, gone.

The physical manifestation of their Pirmas bond, gone.

The completeness she'd tasted in his arms, gone.

Becoming one with him while making love, gone!

Zestine shrieked when he grabbed her by the hair and tossed her onto the bed. Instinct screamed at her to shift and fulfill her promise. Instead she scrambled backward.

He advanced, his hands fisted and inky eyes ablaze with maniacal barbarity.

"No!" The beast and woman fought internal, her heart fighting logic but hastily losing. A cry squeaked out of her as she gave in to the inevitable, jaw elongating into a muzzle…

I will *end this.* "I love you, Tris."

In her mind, she'd already struck. Her huge paws crept toward the edge of the bed, a deep growl saturating the air with impending death. A split-second before rendering him a bloody mess, he fell to his knees with a hiss, throwing a hand out to lean against the floor. At the same time, Zestine sensed his Darkness weaken.

Instantly, she shifted back, shaking so hard her bones rattled.

After slowly getting to his feet, he shook his head as if to clear it. Then to her surprise, he sat on the bed, facing away from her with his wings partly unfurled.

She stared at him, at a loss for words and about what to do. This was the prime opportunity to kill him, but the fact that some of his Darkness had abated gave her pause. How could she end him now when there was reason to believe the man she loved was still in there somewhere?

Hesitantly, she neared him. "Tris," she whispered.

He flinched.

Biting back fear and clinging to hope, she moved closer. Emotion dripped from her voice. "Come back to me. Please. I know you're still in there. I can... I can *feel* it." Biting her lip, she brushed a finger over his wing.

Faster than she could comprehend, he was on top of her with his hand around her throat, his wings tight to his back.

Pitch-black eyes barreled into her. To make things even more fucked up, his hard cock pressed against her core. She was naked, but it was as if he hadn't noticed until that moment. He rocked his hips and she cried out, not in protest but in pleasure. With his free hand, he undid his pants and shoved them down, then pushed inside her.

He grunted at the same time she gasped. A wave of intense pleasure flowed from her loins to the top of her head.

It was all so messed up. She wanted to weep at the rightness of it even while cursing its wrongness.

Like always, he felt heavenly. His thrusts came fast and hit deep, rubbing her in all the right places. Less than a minute had passed when an orgasm took root.

His hand stayed around her throat, squeezing, but not firmly enough to knock her out, and she couldn't be bothered by it because *Tris was inside her*. Part of him had to be in there. Needing him, the *real* him, to know she had no qualms about what they were doing, she wrapped her legs around him, crossing her ankles at his back. He hesitated a split-second, his mouth a grim line, and she wanted nothing more than to reach into his heart and pull to the surface the Tris she remembered, the man she loved. She yearned to feel his mouth against hers and his rough, sexy hands buried in her hair and sliding over her body.

On the verge of climax, she tightened around him, causing him to quicken his tempo.

"Oh, oh," she cried, then went silent as her eyes rolled back into her head and a powerful release surged waves of ecstasy throughout her body.

Before long, he reached his own orgasm and moaned through it, the sound at disturbing odds with his Corruption.

After expending his seed, he stood. Without a word, he fastened his pants before turning and heading for the door.

No, don't leave!

Zestine shot off the bed. "Wait!" she yelled, but he whirled around and gave her a look that froze her. She wasn't sure how long they stared at each other, but once he spread his wings and flew off, she vowed to herself she'd find a way to get him back for good.

CHAPTER 37

Tris had fucked up. He'd gone there to kill her and had fucked her instead. Good thing he hadn't informed Mrakzlo of his intention to do away with her. If the Dark God found out he'd had a chance to kill her and had not only failed, but not even tried... he shuddered at the potential consequences.

Injuries inflicted by Mrakzlo didn't heal in rapid Pirmas fashion, making the god nothing less than a nightmare to all Pirmas. Corrupted feared him more than the dreaded Pit of Teeth.

Keeping things from Mrakzlo was forbidden, but Tris had made the right decision concerning the redhead. It wasn't even his fault she was still alive. Not really.

Something had happened after he'd thrown her on the bed. He'd planned to twist her head off with his bare hands when something beyond his control crippled him, and at the same time he felt the ever-present Darkness inside him lessen, thus making room for feelings he'd thought long dead. Then the heat and aroma of her cunt had beckoned and nothing else mattered other than burying himself within her inviting flesh over and over again. She had felt so *fucking good*.

Now that he was away from her, however, the Darkness crept back in, and by the time he'd crossed into Underworld, he felt almost whole again, so he went on the hunt. If spilling Light blood couldn't repair the damage done by the female, what could?

Tris found two raptatawks having a good-ole nefarious time inside a sex club named Looky Nooky. So distracted by debauchery were they he didn't even have to incapacitate them. He simply walked up to their orgy and tore the wings off one. The female fae servicing him let out a shrill scream, so Tris punched her in the face and she hit the floor so quickly it made him look twice. He grabbed the other 'tawk by the very corner of his wing as he scrambled to get away, then pulled him close. Everyone in the vicinity scattered.

"You want to join our side, 'gawk?" Tris asked, flashing his new sinister smile.

In answer, the 'tawk spat a wad of phlegm between Tris's eyes.

Fury roared out of him as he palmed the back of the 'tawk's head and smashed it into a steel pole once, twice, three and then four times, again and again and again until most of his skull and brains had collected on the floor. He didn't have to worry about severing the heads of wingless raptatawks, so after collecting both sets of wings, he strode toward the exit, no one so much as risking a glance at him. He left a serious mess behind, but no one would complain unless they wanted to perish in a most brutal manner.

Out on the street, Tris strapped the severed wings to his back and flew to another strip of venues. He didn't find any raptatawks at the next stop so he flew to the next town, and the next. Luckily, small towns in the Dark Dimension were virtually endless, and he eventually found two more 'tawks.

They walked side-by-side down the street, stopping when Tris landed before them. Their eyes widened and wings loosened.

Tris grinned. "Want to go Dark? Feel the rush of sin through your veins?" Since his own transformation he'd only Corrupted one 'tawk. Out of dozens and dozens, *one* had agreed to join him. Most wanted nothing to do with the Darkness, which was strange, considering he'd always found them in the Dark Dimension.

Luckily Mrakzlo didn't have the same problem. He could turn them whether they wanted it or not. Thus their numbers rose.

"No?" Tris asked when they didn't respond. He stalked toward them.

Out fanned their wings as they turned and ran. Tris stopped one by grabbing the end of his wing and dragging him to the ground. Silly fools always spread their wings, making them even easier to capture.

"Please! Please don't do this. I-I have a family," the guy said, putting his hands up in submission.

Tris let out an eerie chuckle. "That makes this all the more sweet." He forced him to the ground by the neck and stepped on the top of his wing, then stomped his skull with the other foot, crushing it into a stew of blood and brains and bone.

The other 'tawk got away, so Tris took to the sky after collecting the wings. He'd killed three innocent raptatawks mercilessly, yet the void that'd opened while in the redhead's presence—though smaller than it'd been when he'd left her—remained. He wished he knew why.

According to Mrakzlo, Darkness was Tris's lifeblood. It sustained him, and without it he'd waste away. If true, he'd better stay away from that woman.

Upon arriving home, Tris had abandoned his plan to kill the female and scrapped her from his mind. No matter how tempting, he'd not go to her. And if she came for him, she'd have to go through the Dark God first.

~

"What does he look like?" King Lachlan asked Zestine.

"Instead of red eyes, they're black. No iris, no pupil, just black. His wings are black too, like the Dark God's. His teeth are the same as the Corrupted teeth we've already seen."

Lachlan put his index finger and thumb to his chin and pursed his lips. He, Zestine, and Dia were in the royal throne room. Zestine had gone straight to them after Tris's surprise visit. Excitement had bubbled over quickly, which proved just how much Tris (and not just his absence) affected her. It also revealed how much their love had warped her sense of duty; her visit to the royals was more about getting him back than informing them an enemy had entered their domain.

Despite her joy that his disappearance was a mystery no longer, a twisting throb in the pit of her stomach evinced her wariness. Tris had come to kill her. Just because he'd failed didn't mean he wouldn't try again.

"How can this be? I thought raptatawks had to want to change for it to work," said the queen, who'd paled upon hearing the news.

Zestine shook her head. "Either it's not true, or he…" She sighed, unable to say it aloud.

"I say we put guards outside your door," Dia said.

Zestine grimaced. "But then he might not come back."

"He was going to kill you," the queen replied, as if Zestine needed reminding.

"I was going to kill him too, until he changed his mind. Guards would just get in my way."

"She has a point. You saw her against the Corrupted," Lachlan told Dia.

Thinking about how messy her kills were, she unwittingly envisioned a black-winged Tris mutilated inside her hut, blood pooling the floor and streaming down the walls.

What if I have to kill him? How could I go on? Zestine imagined stepping over his broken form and running to sea, then losing herself, forever, among the waves.

"At least if there were guards someone besides her would know he was there," the queen argued. She looked at Zestine. "You could've died and we wouldn't have known. Please, give us a chance to help you."

The king narrowed his eyes, his gaze on the hyx table. "Truthfully, our opinion doesn't matter. This is your decision," he told Zestine. "I must caution, however, that I will not allow Tris into Noctis many more times before eliminating him."

Automatically, she shook her head. "If anyone is going to kill him, it'll be me." She laughed despite herself at how ridiculous she sounded.

Guilt for not keeping her promise to Tris ate at Zestine. Yet she'd never promised to take his life if she'd reason to believe he wasn't gone. If she got him back, would he forgive her for failing him?

Don't think about that now. Worry about getting him back first.

"What knowledge do you have of the Darkness?" Zestine asked.

Lachlan leaned back in his seat. "Honestly, not as much as I should. Dia and I are due for a visit to the Hall of Tomes, but showing our faces in the Dark Dimension so soon after battle, even under glamour, is dangerous."

She nodded. Warlocks and demons had ways to see beyond glamour.

"What I do know is, for Light beings, Darkness must exist in total capacity or else it won't function as it's meant to. In non-Light beings, it doesn't have to overtake to dwell within and the individual can control it. With Tris, this isn't the case. The Darkness controls him."

Zestine ruminated on that. So it really hadn't been Tris she'd encountered earlier, but the Darkness, which had weakened and given her a glimpse of the real Tris, *her* Tris. Had *she* caused the Darkness to lose control? If not, what had? "What could disrupt the Darkness in a Corrupted? Could it be me?"

"Before knowing you stopped Tris's pain, I would've said no, but clearly something special was going on there... something beyond just you. You've never been able to relieve another's pain before?"

"No."

"Wait," said Queen Dia, who turned to Lachlan. "What about the Pirmas bond? Maybe that's what's happening here." She looked at Zestine. "Do you love each other?"

"I love him, but… he may not love me anymore." Damn, that hurt to acknowledge. It was decidedly wretched knowing her man was physically reachable, yet crippled of heart and mind. Did Tris lurk inside that Dark body, powerless to express his true self but able to understand the happenings around him?

Oh Lord. That'd be nigh too much to bear.

The king chimed in. "It shouldn't matter if he's lost his love for you, especially considering if it's gone, it left during whatever he endured to become Dark. What matters is *before* his change he loved you and you loved him. When my father erased me from Dia's memory, he also erased the memory of her love for me. It was still there, but in a sort of limbo."

"And it wasn't just words… or infatuation. It was real," added Dia.

Remembering the misty violet manifestation of their love, Zestine's lips twitched even as tears threatened. She breathed a deep, cleansing breath and slowly nodded. "Okay. We love each other, or did." Suddenly, a grave realization wrenched her heart.

Upon partnering with Tris, she hadn't acknowledged the possibility of failing the mission. And when her feelings for him had deepened, she'd not considered the miserable downside of love: losing it. So hungry had she been for life fulfillment, consequences hadn't even been an afterthought.

Had her longing for meaningful adventure inevitably lead to despair?

The king and queen side-eyed one another. "She may very well be correct," Lachlan told Zestine as he reached over and laced his fingers through Dia's.

Zestine's eyes tracked the affectionate gesture. Her heart lurched with jealousy at witnessing their solid connection, a love not in danger of forever breaking. She deserved to enjoy that too, had waited eons for it. Was fate really so cruel, to dangle true love in front of her only to rip it away once she'd gotten a taste?

Sighing, she propped her elbows on her thighs, rested her fingers against her forehead, and closed her eyes. *Stop feeling sorry for yourself. If Dia's right, I have a powerful weapon on my side.* "So... you're saying it's our love threatening the Darkness?"

"Well, it's only a theory," the queen said.

"One that makes sense," Lachlan added.

Zestine lowered her hands, only to twiddle them in her lap while she gnawed her lower lip. Finally, she looked up, her gaze flicking between them. "All right, let's say it *is* our love threatening his Darkness. What do you suggest I do?"

"You must test it. Find out how much power your bond has over the Darkness. That's the only way you'll know if it's possible to break him free," the king said.

How did he make something so difficult sound so easy? "When's that invisibility charm going to be ready?"

Lachlan gave a quick smile, reached into his pocket and, to her utter shock and delight, withdrew a thin gold ring. Her heart banged madly against her ribs. *One step closer to getting my man back.*

Dia grinned, showing perfect white teeth. "We wanted to talk to you before telling you it was finished. Looks like it's ready just in time."

Lachlan held the ring over Zestine's outstretched hand. "As your king, I command you to arm yourself before setting off."

"Yes. And don't do anything stupid. That's also an order," said Dia.

Zestine smiled broadly, feeling elated even as a fresh supply of nerves wriggled her insides. "Aye, aye."

Lachlan dropped the ring onto her palm, then flicked his head toward the exit. "Get out of here. Go get your man back."

CHAPTER 38

Zestine rushed to her cabin, packed a bag, and armed herself before donning a purple-stoned charm to use telepathy in human form if the need arose. Tris had cleaned her out of red-stoned charms, so she—and he, High Lord willing—would have to do without them. She filled her belly with meaty, creamy soup and water, then sped to the nearest portal and crossed into Underworld.

Strangely enough, the portal deposited her atop the same hill where it'd deposited her and Tris at the onset of their mission. A good omen, perhaps?

Sure, why not? She'd take whatever she could get.

Gaze bypassing the town lights to focus on the blackness hiding her destination, she couldn't help but reflect on how greatly times had changed since then. He'd been ready to lie down and die, and it'd taken a knife to his throat, along with several scathing insults, to get him on the right track.

Now he was on the wrong track, standing on his head facing backward.

The words he'd spoken during his visit played in her mind: *You told me to come to you. Here I am.*

He'd received her message, so she sent another one.

Tris, I'm coming for you. Simple, yet effective. Something told her it was best to forewarn him of her visit.

Zestine changed into a jaguar and raced toward the caves. A surge of adrenaline soothed her knotted gut and made it seem as if she was flying instead of running. Yet it also seemed she couldn't move fast enough, which she attributed to ever-heightening anticipation skewing her sense of time.

Then came an unwelcome realization that slowed her to a walk. So desperate was she to save Tris, she hadn't made a plan. She growled and paced in a circle; the woman thought while the beast pouted.

Assuming he'd receive her message, he might await her arrival. If not, she'd check the room they'd stayed in during the mission, and if he wasn't there… she'd go to the Ravager's lair, a dicey option given that, dead or alive, no one would find her should she require aid.

This is insane! Was the situation so dire she needed to risk her life? Did she *have* a life without Tris? Yes. Did she want a life without him? That, she wasn't sure about.

I'm not going inside without assistance. She had weapons, her beast, and, perhaps the most significant resource of all, the love between her and Tris.

As if on cue, a bright, violet swath appeared before her, rippling before it thinned to a silky tendril and circled her neck. At the comforting electric vibrations, Zestine gave a whine, and as the energy rounded her neck and completed its caress, it shot into the distance, slicing through the Darkness and blazing a violet trail to her destination.

Heart hammering a wild tempo of hope, she zoomed toward her very own waking nightmare, to save the man who'd made her dreams come true.

~

Tris was on his way to the Ravager's crypt, which now belonged to Mrakzlo, when *her* voice resounded inside his mind.

Tris, I'm coming for you.

He stopped and let out a string of curses before roaring and slamming his fists repeatedly against the rock wall, rendering his knuckles a bloody mess.

What was wrong with this woman? Did she *want* to die? Tris consulted his memory and replayed his time with her. He nodded to himself upon encountering the one when he partook in raising the Dark God inside the very room he was headed to. She'd snuck in and seen everything, which meant she knew how to get there. He wasn't sure how she planned to get past the numerous men en route to Mrakzlo's lair. Her beast was no match for dozens of Corrupted, though something told him she'd find a way.

He started down the tunnel again. If the bitch expected he'd wait for her with open arms, she'd be harshly awakened. When she arrived, Mrakzlo would greet her, and eliminate her once and for all.

~

Outside the Corrupted's cave, Zestine switched forms and slid the invisibility charm onto her finger. Her body vanished as soon as it tightened to a fit. She entered

301

and made it to the common area, where the Pit of Teeth waited, gaping and primed to feed, without seeing Tris.

The space wasn't as crowded as it'd been when she'd stayed there, but now two kinds of Corrupted wandered about: the red-eyed ones who kept their unique wing characteristics, and the ones like Tris, black-eyed and black-winged. Even killing the Ravager hadn't hindered the continuation of these abominations, and now that a supposed god had taken the reins, they were back at square one.

Zestine didn't know if the Dark God was killable, as there was no being to compare him to except, in theory, the High Lord, and the circumstances of His existence had always been a mystery.

She curled her upper lip, thinking about what would become of the world should Darkness prosper. She'd not let *her male* be a victim of, nor any sort of commodity for the side of evil. No. Fucking. Way. If hell was what they wanted, she'd give them exactly that.

The door to Cradle had somehow been ripped from its hinges. With no time to be wary, she breezed inside and hastily made her way through. Someone had ransacked the place, and though her nose told her Tris had been there since his transformation, there was no other sign of him, so she left and marched to her final destination.

Upon breaching the final tunnel leading to the crypt, chills wracked her flesh, the prickles intensifying the darker—and Darker—her surroundings became. Her heart *boom boom boomed* like a wild drum, each beat upping her anxiety. Zestine ground her teeth and clenched her hands against the urge to quicken her pace.

The door was impossible to see, hence she needed to keep her steps measured. If she didn't reach out and feel it first, she'd run smack into it.

Just when she thought she'd shatter from suspense, her fingertips brushed the cool wood of the door. Then, an irksome realization dawned. How would she get inside? She believed Tris was inside, but that didn't mean he was. She assumed he'd let her in if he was there, but the Darkness possessing him might not allow it. It was important she remember she wouldn't deal with *her* Tris, at least not right away.

Just do it. There was no going back, so after taking a deep breath, Zestine removed the invisibility charm, tucked it in her pocket, and knocked.

"Watchword," said a deep, raspy voice.

She rolled her eyes and glared into the blackness. "My fist up your asshole. Now let me the fuck in."

When the door immediately cracked open, she hesitated at the prompt welcome. After giving her body a shake to ease her angst, she squared her shoulders, ready. Instead of walking in and shutting the door like the others had done when she'd snuck inside, she kicked it open and stood at the threshold, hands resting on the hilts of her swords.

Sitting in the same place the Ravager had sat was the Dark God. Black mist hovered around him. The color of his hair was so dark and his skin so pale, the middle of his head looked missing.

His eerie smile widened. "Don't just stand there, sweeting. Come in. I don't believe we've met. I'm Mrakzlo, and you are…?"

Zestine's eyes narrowed as she scanned the room. "Where's Tris?"

"He's… around. I do suggest you come in, because I plan to close the door in three, two—"

She darted inside and the door banged shut behind her.

"Are you part of a war party?" Mrakzlo asked, resting his chin on clasped, thumbless hands.

"I'm here to see Tris."

"Oh yes. I'm aware."

Zestine huffed. She'd not play games with vermin. "Tris? Tris! He's behind this wall, isn't he?" She walked past the Dark God and slammed her hands against the mirrored back wall. "Tris! I know you're in there. Too much of a coward to face me, huh?" Pissing him off was risky, but she just wanted a reaction, even if it was a bad one. Slinging invectives his way had spurred his anger when he was a good guy, so assuming he still got offended, why wouldn't it work again?

She was about to continue the verbal onslaught when an icy hand covered her mouth and pulled her against a likewise icy body. Not about to balk, she slid a knife from the sheath of her belt and stabbed her assailant, though she wasn't sure where she'd hit him. Zestine tried to grab another knife, but her weapons belt slipped off her waist and sailed through the air, landing several feet away.

"Shh. Don't worry, dear. I assure you, the fun is just beginning," Mrakzlo whispered, his chilly breath slithering over the shell of her ear as he draped something cold around her neck.

Shift! She tried, but it didn't work. She tried again. And again, but nothing happened.

Oh no. Oh no, oh no, oh no.

"Can't turn? How disappointing that must be," he said in mock discontent. He twirled her around and guided her to the front of the room. Seconds later she heard the whir of the rising wall. Her stomach clenched as she tried to turn her head but Mrakzlo clutched her chin in place with his giant hand. "Uh-uh-uh." He used his grip of her chin to shove her into a chair.

Before she could fight or flee, he knocked her upside the head and everything went black.

CHAPTER 39

Tris, who'd been behind the wall as the she-beast thought, walked around to the front of the chair Mrakzlo had tied her to. Silver chains hung from her neck and bound her wrists and ankles. The right side of her chin was swollen, but she was otherwise unharmed. Since the Dark God had inflicted the injury, it'd heal at a human pace. Not that the imperfection interfered with her beauty…

"Fuck," Tris muttered. *Not that it interfered with her beauty?* Where'd that thought come from?

"Interesting," Mrakzlo said, garnering Tris's attention. The Dark God stood by his own chair, inspecting the contents of the woman's weapons belt.

"What?" asked Tris.

"Now we know how she got here without any trouble." He held up a thin gold ring, raised his other hand and slid it on, promptly disappearing.

Invisibility charm. She had to have gotten that from King Lachlan. Tris hadn't remembered until now he'd worn one of those charms the night of the battle. After his transformation, he'd forgotten about it. He had no idea what'd happened to his clothes or weapons. It hadn't mattered, but now his curiosity got the better of him.

"I had one of those too."

The Dark God reappeared and shoved the ring into the pocket of his black robe. "I know."

He crossed his arms. "What'd you do with it?"

"That," he said, situating the belt neatly on the floor, "is none of your concern."

Tris didn't like that answer, but let it go. He'd rather be belittled than permanently maimed.

"You'd better leave before she wakes," said the Dark God.

That'd been the plan, but now that she was here, he couldn't recall why he shouldn't stay. He looked at the female, who moaned the instant his gaze landed on her.

Tris clicked his tongue against the roof of his mouth. "Actually, I think I want to stay." He hadn't informed Mrakzlo about her weakening his Darkness because he hadn't wanted to give the Dark God justification to see him as more inferior to him than he already did. But Tris no longer knew if that was a legitimate reason or a mere excuse. "I'll watch."

Mrakzlo wouldn't simply behead her. Too easy. He'd torture her before killing her. Inflict pain and suffering until she begged him to end her misery, then he'd convince her mercy was coming only to continue the torment.

Don't let her see you! Mrakzlo's voice thundered in Tris's mind as the Dark God used telekinesis to pick him up and move him behind the chair.

From his new position, Tris wouldn't be able to watch, at least not from the front.

"Welcome back," Mrakzlo said to the woman, his mouth parting in a malicious smile.

She released another moan, the sound of which triggered a warm, tingly sensation in Tris's chest.

"Fuck you," she said.

The Dark God's stygian eyes flared before he chuckled. "Is that an offer?" He parted his robe, revealing a grisly sight of near translucent skin housing several pairs of ribs. Sixteen, to be exact, they started below massive, jutting collarbones and ended at his hips, the intercostal spaces concave. It was a wonder he could stand upright. He didn't really have a pelvis, just legs and in between them a long, skinny red-skinned penis pulsing with black veins. It appeared hard, but pointed down instead of up.

In the back of Tris's mind, vicious anger mixed with overwhelming jealousy. The two vitriolic emotions fed each other, threatening to break the surface of his consciousness and erupt into a gory manifestation of sadistic insanity. Uncomfortable heat flooded his face and neck.

"I'm here to see Tris," the woman said.

The Dark God closed his robe and nodded, then to Tris's surprise said, "You're in luck. He's right here."

Tris furrowed his brows and stopped breathing, unsure of his master's motives.

"Where?" she asked.

Mrakzlo held his arm out to Tris and used all eight fingers to wave him forward. Not knowing what else to do, he obliged and stood before the redhead. Upon meeting his gaze, her indigo eyes brightened, as if his presence awoke her soul.

The Darkness within him abated, only to surge back in abrupt force, launching him into action.

He bared his teeth with a rough snarl and thrust his finger in her face. "You should've left me alone. Now, bitch, you're going to pay." He bolted forth, stabbed his claws in her neck and raked them down to her collarbone. Bright-red blood spurted and poured from the deep slices. Her hands jerked within her bonds as if by instinct to cover her wounds. She choked, then coughed as she searched for a breath, but kept her eyes on him through the pain and struggle.

You won't be able to kill me, she told him via telepathy.

The cuts he'd delivered were already closing, so he reopened them. His Darkness was fighting—and winning. Tris felt like he'd burst if he didn't inflict misery unto the beast.

"You're wrong," he said. *Get out of my head!*

No, she countered, and he didn't know if she meant she wasn't wrong or that she wouldn't get out of his head.

"It doesn't matter. I don't have to kill you. That's why Mrakzlo's here." He grabbed her ponytail and pulled, cocking her head at an odd angle. He heard a crack, then a puff of air he thought came from between her lips. "Now shut. *Up!*" He yanked her skull forward, then smashed it against the back of the chair again and again. Yank, smash. Yank, smash. Yank, smash.

Triiissss! Her shrill voice rang between his ears.

With a growl, he paused his assault and spoke through clenched teeth. "Tris. Is. *Dead.*"

"Not *my* Tris." She shrieked when he continued to pound her head against the wood.

After he'd done it so many times he'd lost count and the smacking sounds turned wet and crunchy, she screamed louder and once she fell silent, he let go. Her head rolled and hung forward as blood leaked down the front of her neck, adding a third coat to the first two.

A maelstrom of emotions, some of which Tris believed had been obliterated with his former self, wrenched his stomach and crushed his chest. He sank into a crouch and pressed his fingers into his temples, trying to center himself. Then a warm and soothing energy emerged inside him, morphed into a sharp weapon, and chopped at his Darkness.

The female was unconscious, but soon her wounds closed and she lifted her head. "Is that all you got?" she asked with a daring grin. A glint of tenacious intent shimmered in her eyes, as if she knew something he didn't.

"You have to die," Mrakzlo said calmly, but she acted as if he wasn't there. Her gaze never left Tris.

"Fuck your disgusting Darkness! I love *you*, Tris. Fight it. It's not *you* hurting me! It's the shadows. *It* is pulling your strings, feasting on your mind and leaving you without a choice. Doesn't that piss you off, *Tris?* You conquered it and now it's conquering you. Fight it!"

Tris froze as her words played over and over inside his head. *I love you Tris. It is pulling your strings. I love you, Tris. Fight it! I love you, Tris. It's taking over your mind and leaving you without a choice. I love you, Tris. It's not you hurting me. I love you, Tris...*

"Enough!" roared the Dark God, who stomped forward and got right into the beast's face, forcing her to look at him.

Zestine blared a jarring shriek. Fury shook her bound limbs from the Dark God blocking Tris from view and hindering the progress she'd made.

Mrakzlo's eyes blazed a murderous gleam, his proximity flooding her nostrils with a noxious odor. Her stomach rolled, its contents threatening to rise, though she welcomed the possibility; surely vomiting all over the Dark God's face would be satisfying.

"Tell me what the First Tribe have planned for me," he demanded.

She tossed her head back and laughed. "I'm surprised a creature as vile as you has a sense of humor."

He smiled, the corners of his lips almost touching the corners of his eyes. "Not going to tell me? Oh, but I think you will."

He moved away and Zestine instantly sought Tris, whose expression was no longer vacant, but tense, his shiny black gaze flicking from her to the floor and back again. She couldn't discern how he felt, but she knew her presence—or their love's presence—affected him. She needed to keep talking to him, but her mind was blanking out.

Think, think, think, think!

Mrakzlo returned carrying two of Zestine's swords, one katana and one saber. He touched the end of the katana to her sternum and slowly slid in along her skin, producing a sting, followed by the warm flow of blood. Gliding the blade lower, he cut through the black cloth of her top and stopped between her breasts. She stiffened, her lungs frozen in expectation that he'd spear her straight through.

The Dark God hummed an eerie tune as he severed the front of her bra and moved the cups aside with the tip of the blade, exposing her bosom. "I think this is sufficient."

What does that mean?

The hideous behemoth cocked his head, pressed the sharpened steel to the inner curve of her right breast, and carved a path around the entire swell. Zestine couldn't contain a yelp.

Though she fought to keep her focus on cajoling Tris, anger surged, tinting her vision scarlet. Why did such evil have to exist? "I fucking can't wait to kill you," she told him.

The Dark God laughed and behind him, Tris took a step forward.

Zestine didn't have much time before something horrific happened to her.

No more fucking around. She must get through to Tris, or prepare to die.

CHAPTER 40

Tris, I love you, and I know you love me. Remember, you confessed your love in the shower, then pushed me against the wall and made love to me? Remember how good and right it felt? You can have that again with me. Forever.

The female's voice swirled though Tris's mind. As she spoke, he relived the memory she'd described in explicit detail, making him near delirious. Sweat streamed from his pores. A horrendous ripping sensation sliced him from shoulder to hip, passing through his heart, jerking his hips one way and his shoulders the other. The black shadow that had lined his vision since his awakening faded the slightest bit. He shook his head hard.

What's happening to me?

"Tell me what I want to know or I'll hack off your tits and fuck you with every one of your blades, starting with this." He pointed the sabre at her core. "I'll raze your insides. Can you imagine how much blood there'd be?" He chuckled, lifting the sabre and marveling at the blade as if it were already dowsed in crimson.

She was resolute, even in the face of heinous threats she knew Mrakzlo could deliver on. "I'll never tell you *anything.*"

Tris's eyes popped wide. Why was she acting so senseless? "Are you crazy?" he yelled. "You won't heal!"

The Dark God whipped around. "Shut your mouth, scoundrel. Why do you care if she heals?"

Tris stepped back and dropped his head.

"It doesn't matter, Tris. He'll kill me anyway. I won't give them up. Besides," she said, appearing almost bored, "I don't know their plans. Even if I wanted to tell, I couldn't."

Zestine continued the mind assault. *Help me, Tris. This isn't you. Remember us. Remember how we make each other feel. Remember! What it's like being inside me, how it drove you wild when I rubbed myself against you in the pool by the waterfall. I want to fly through the clouds with you and revel in that magic again. I can't do that without you.*

A flash of a scene from a different existence besieged him. Words jolted through his mind: beauty, love, safety, forever…

She persisted, *You told me you'd never get enough. I feel the same way. I'll never get enough of you, either. I need you by my side. You're my everything. What can the Darkness give you that I can't? I can give you life. The Darkness can only give you death. We're in each other's minds and hearts, right? That's what you said the last time you held me. Remember?*

"What is this?" said Mrakzlo, approaching Tris with his nostrils flared and pointy teeth bared.

"Something more powerful than *you,*" Zestine said.

"Silence, harridan!" Mrakzlo boomed.

Tris looked down to see a gooey black substance leaking… from him? He stood in a small pool of it and its stench was an overwhelming mix of soot, gasoline, and body odor. Was that what he smelled like?

He turned from the female and scrubbed his forehead. Feverish waves coursed through him as two vastly different forces warred within him—one a malicious presence and the other bursting with benevolent vivacity. Both were equally powerful and ravenous for dominion. Part of Tris was flummoxed as to why he was overseeing a grotesque creature torture and revile the woman he loved. The other part didn't understand why he hadn't killed her already.

You have the power to end this! she screamed in his mind.

Then a different, magnanimous entity, carrying an aura of undeniable nostalgia, rushed into form and joined the other. The two noble forces melded and, shining as bright as a billion suns, towered over Tris's Darkness. The entwined energies ascended while morphing into a giant sword, then dropped like a guillotine blade and sliced the black mass in half before tearing into and gutting the halves, reducing the Darkness to scraps.

Tris sucked in a breath as warmth expanded from his chest to the top of his head and tips of his toes. Searing heat hit the surface of his body at the same time he convulsed with a violent lurch.

"Enough!" Mrakzlo said with a snarl before turning to the female. He lifted the katana, grasped her right breast in his revolting hand and brought the blade down.

"Tris! No!"

The hot sensation faded as fast as it'd come. Spectacular white light exploded from his flesh and struck the Dark God with a thunderous sizzle.

Mrakzlo turned from Zestine with a roar, the sound mixing with the sizzle to near-deafening proportions. Dark-red smoke poured from the monstrous deity Tris had helped create.

With a mad bellow, Tris tackled him to the ground. The Dark God landed on his front.

"You ruined me! *Ruined me!*" Insane rage consumed Tris as he straddled the imp and punched the back of his head repeatedly, smashing his face into the rocky floor again and again until an unseen force launched Tris through the air. His backside hit the stone wall with a smack. But he was crazed. It would take *a lot* more to stun him or hurt him. With a savage growl, he sped for Mrakzlo.

A knife pierced his shoulder and next thing he knew, the Dark God, who still poured rank crimson smoke and emanated that angry sizzle, advanced with the katana. He swung and swiped at a blurring speed, slashing Tris on the hip, then on the side. The pain didn't even register.

Focus, Tris, the woman said in his mind. *He hurt your female, your mate. He planned on raping the woman you love with knives!*

Untamable wrath bubbled to the surface of his awareness. Tris batted away the dagger stuck in his shoulder and clenched his hands so hard he thought his bones might break. His heart pounded in his ears, where the humming swish of rushing blood sang. The glorious flavor of vengeance danced on his tongue.

Zestine continued, *Remember, you made him with your Light blood. Find your Light and expose his imperfection.*

Her voice and reasoning centered him. A strident clap rattled the room as shards of brilliant violet materialized and danced within the glow seeping from his body.

The Darkness was gone, *really* gone. Evanesced to perfect nothingness as all Darkness should be.

Then… clarity struck him. Pure, blessed clarity.

The sword Mrakzlo held hit the ground with a clang before he cowered, hands rising to shield his face. He emitted a scream that raked the air with hysterical wrath and crude promises.

The violet fragments shot toward the Dark God, penetrating the red fog with wet clonks and throwing him into the wall. Inside Mrakzlo's body, the fragments scraped together. With shrill peals and scratching moans, the shards chorused a ballad of vengeance.

"Yah! Hahama mm-mahuk-k-k," uttered the Dark God, his face twisted with agony while his body went eerily still. Tris couldn't enjoy the sicko's pain, too sick himself.

With his mind, Tris lifted the katana the Dark God had dropped, turned it around and launched it forward. It pierced the fiend's torso, skewering him to the wall.

He walked over to Mrakzlo, careful not to slip in blood and the puddle of black goo, which had grown exponentially since he'd first noticed it, and used telekinesis to retrieve Zestine's weapons belt. He dropped it at his feet and withdrew a second katana. Pointing the blade up, he thrust it into the bottom of the Dark God's chin and pushed up and back, up and back, up and back, his rage adding undue strength to his effort, until the tip breached the top rear of his head.

Mrakzlo's black eyes bulged to more than twice their size, his nose collapsed in on itself, and his ever-present smile shriveled into a wrinkled gray pile. A resonant whine droned through his buried mouth.

Using the bottom half of the impaled sword, Tris glided his now luminous forearm width-wise over the blade, cutting deep to yield an adequate amount of blood. He ripped open the Dark God's robe, reached through the gushing smoke, and smeared the blood over his disintegrating torso.

Mrakzlo let out muffled howls and pitiful whines as his remaining intact flesh melted. Tris cut and smeared, cut and smeared until the entire front upper half of the monster he'd helped create eroded underneath Light's essence.

The dark-red vapor thinned. Tris's Light beams illuminated the Dark God's insides. Comprising bones, clusters of intertwining black muscle—shredded, thanks to the violet fragments—and tissue that vibrated and *chittered*, it all inflated and deflated in unison, as if breathing. Mrakzlo sparsely bled a sticky black substance and lacked even a single vital organ.

All at once, the shards slingshotted back into Tris's aura with metallic pings.

"This isn't the end of me," declared the Dark God, his voice reverberating around the room. "I was born from blood. Death is not part of my makeup. I do not live according to any rules. Can't snuff me out! I'm eternal, *undead*. I'll be back! You'll never get rid of me." He let out a haunting chuckle. "You'll spend your entire neverending lives looking behind you!" More grave laughter.

Tris had had enough. He grabbed the Dark God's skull and snapped it off, but the laugh continued, so he threw the corpse to the floor and withdrew a dagger from Zestine's belt to cut the Dark God's wings from his body. The instant both wings separated, his laughter ceased and his remains vanished in a puff of smoke.

~

Tris knelt on the black stone floor, half shocked and wondering how his life had become such a mess.

"Tris? Um, will you please unchain me?"

Unchain her... He turned to peer at the speaker. The moment he saw her, it was like a vacuum opened and sucked the muddle from his head.

"Zest-eee." He couldn't even get her name out before emotion robbed him of speech. He rushed over and undid her restraints. The second she was free, she ripped the silver chain from around her neck and jumped into his arms. She kissed his lips and cheeks, nose and chin, forehead and eyelids. Unshed tears glistened in her gorgeous eyes.

"It's you. It's really you." She cupped his cheeks. "I thought you were gone."

Tris still couldn't speak, so he busied his mouth in a different way, slanting it over hers for a deep kiss while caressing her waist and holding her tightly against him. He never wanted to be without her again.

I hurt her. Badly. Intentionally.

Though ecstatic to have Zestine back, he drowned in guilt for what he'd done to her under the influence of Darkness. How could she even look at him after he'd manhandled her, harmed her, and almost killed her *because he'd wanted to?*

He broke away. Swallowed. "I'm so sorry. So, so sorry." It didn't feel like enough. Wasn't close to enough.

"No," she whispered, shaking her head. "You don't have to be sorry. It wasn't you. And I'm the one who should apologize." She averted her gaze.

Tris cupped her chin. "Look at me."

Zestine obliged, her eyes still ashine with unspent tears. "I'm sorry I didn't keep my promise. I was going to—I almost did, but you suddenly decided not to kill me and the Darkness… seemed to lose its hold on you. I just… I wasn't strong enough."

Recalling that moment, he wished he could puke. He rubbed her back. "It's okay. If I was in your place…" He shook his head. "I would've been tempted to let you kill me."

She took the hand holding her chin, opened it, and closed her eyes as she pressed her cheek against his palm. "I love you. Even then"—her voice cracked—"I loved you."

Heaven to his ears. "Zestine." Her name came out a sigh, then he slid his hands around her waist, pulled her close, and kissed her like it was their last kiss. This woman owned him. She was as precious as Light. She was forever. She was life itself.

When they finally parted, he nuzzled her nose with his. "I don't think I'll ever get over what I did."

"It wasn't you, Tris. Not even close."

Though he agreed, he knew it didn't matter. The regret wouldn't ebb anytime soon.

"Hey, don't be like that," she scolded.

His expression must have betrayed his thoughts, but her ire was a small price to pay.

"I came here to get you back. I risked my life *knowing* you came to Noctis to kill me. If it bothered me, I would've kept my promise and you—*we* wouldn't be here right now. Tris, look." Zestine pried his hands from her waist and displayed them to him. No claws.

He unfurled his wings and curled them around for a look. They'd returned to blue and white. He ran his tongue over his teeth. *Not sharp.* "My eyes?"

"Blue," she said with a grin. "And how about that Light!" The streams of light that'd shone from his flesh had faded after Mrakzlo vanished, but its warmth and reassurance remained.

"H-how is this possible?" he asked.

She kissed him. "Us. Our love saved you."

Okay. "But… our love killed…" Not wanting to speak his name, Tris pointed to where the Dark God's body had been. "Him?"

"That, I don't know. Is he even dead?"

He worked his jaw. "He better fucking be."

Zestine looked down. "Did… did you…" She met his gaze. "*Decide* to do it?"

"Do what? Turn? Turn into a monster?" *That's what she thinks?* That crushed him, and he couldn't mask his horror.

She frowned and raised her brows. "I thought that's the only way it could happen."

"No. No, no, no, no. I didn't want it. The Dark God did it. Free will can't stop him."

A slight smile curved her lips. "That's… a relief. I was so confused after I first saw you. I didn't know what to think." Then her eyes widened and she stepped back and smacked her forehead with her palm. "Shit. How are we going to get out of here?"

Tris released her, approached the Dark God's robe, and dug inside the pockets until he found the ring. "Here," he said, offering her the invisibility charm.

"Okay. That means one of us will get out alive." She circled the chair she'd been shackled to, folded her hands together and rested her chin atop them. "Fuck. We've gone through all this shit and now… ugh!"

"Here," he repeated, still holding the ring out to her. She took it, then collected her blades and secured them to her belt, donning it when she'd finished. It looked similar to how it'd looked when he'd stocked it prior to the Corrupted offensive. He pointed at the belt. "Did you do that yourself?"

She glanced at the portable arsenal attached to her hips. "Uh-huh."

The corners of his lips lifted, but the smile felt wrong to wear. Undeserved. *The things I've done…*

"We've got to figure out a plan," Zestine said, not about to be distracted.

Tris pushed his self-pity to the back of his brain. "Do you have one of those red-gemmed rings?"

She scowled. "No."

"Okay." He bit his lip and ran his fingers through his hair. "Maybe… we can use your beast?"

"What do you mean?"

"Like when we escaped the first time. I could… I don't know, *wear you* somehow while also wearing the invisibility charm?"

Zestine considered his suggestion with her finger pressed to her lips before nodding. "It should work. Unless the charm can tell I'm a living thing and not a garment." She clapped. "Let's try it." After handing the dainty golden ring back to him, she shifted into a small multicolored domestic feline, white with brown and black spots and a black patch over one eye. She sprang into his arms and he lifted her over his head and was about to drape her around his neck when she stopped him.

Wait. Try facing me backwards over your shoulder. I might have to dig my claws into you, but it'll make it easier for me to hang on.

"Okay." He didn't care if she raked him raw. If this worked, they were home free. Never would they have to return, which was a freedom he could almost taste; a sanctuary he needed to devour.

Tris gently placed her belly against his shoulder and let go. She used her weight and flexibility to cling to him as he donned the charm. Once he disappeared, he turned his head and saw her there, appearing to hang onto nothing. He settled his hand on her back and a split-second later, she vanished.

"Whew."

Are we invisible? she asked.

"Yes." He turned to the door and opened it with his mind. Though he wanted to sprint from there as fast as possible, he needed to ensure Zestine didn't become visible. He traveled at a clipped, but careful pace, out the back tunnels into the commons, past the Pit of Teeth and several Corrupted, into the front tunnels, and finally out of the cave.

Tris flew them near to the cave King Lachlan had pointed out housed a portal.

Zestine jumped off his back and shifted forms. "Where are you?"

Oh. Duh. He removed the ring and offered it to her as she hurried over. She slipped it into a small zippered pouch on her belt.

"What are we doing here?" she whispered, looping her arms around his neck. Like him, she didn't feel safe yet. Like him, she needed to savor the heat and comfort of their touching bodies.

"There's a portal inside one of these caves."

"Okay." She scanned the area. "Should we split up and search, or—"

"No. We stay together." Tris laced his fingers though hers and they walked from cave to cave. Piled high inside each, save the one with the portal, were corpses of slain Corrupted.

"The king and queen refuse to give them a proper burial," Zestine said, which didn't bother Tris. He'd done *a lot* of bad shit, both as an actual Corrupted and to fit in as one. If anyone knew how much evil they harbored, it was him. If anyone didn't deserve honorable burials, it was them.

Darker thoughts threatened to smother his newfound relief. When he killed that first innocent 'tawk, a void had opened within him and functioned as a dumping ground for uncomfortable emotions. During his time Corrupted, the void had grown exponentially, all but eclipsing his very soul as it collected everything that made Tris who he was. The void had made it easy to not care; it'd made it easy to be a merciless, selfish, insufferable, and downright nasty individual. Now the void was gone. It'd left with the termination of his Darkness. And neither Tris nor his Light could suppress the negative feelings ambushing his conscience. He didn't know how to cope or how to forgive himself.

Zestine squeezed his hand. "Hey. It'll be okay. We'll work through this, together."

Pull it together. I have Zestine back. I should be thankful. It's more than I deserve.

For her, he smiled and nodded. "Noctis, I presume," he said as they approached the misty passageway.

"We have to meet with King Lachlan and Queen Dia right away. They were aware of my plan to rescue you."

He looked at her, feeling a pang of disappointment that their reunion would be delayed, but only inclined his head. "Okay."

This time they walked through the portal together, joined hand-in-hand.

CHAPTER 41

The reunited lovers headed straight to the king and queen's throne quarters, informed the guards—this time two male fae—who they were, and waited only a short while before being ushered inside.

"I have to admit, I'm impressed," Lachlan said after they gave salutations.

Dia nodded with wide-eyed enthusiasm. "I'm shocked! I mean, I don't mean to offend you, but damn. That was quick!"

The king held out his hand. "Please, have a seat. I'm sure you're both exhausted."

Keeping her hand tightly wrapped in his, Tris led Zestine to the right side of the couch and they sat.

Lachlan's gaze landed on Tris. "So, you're the same as you were before? Nothing's lurking…"

"Nothing lurking." Tris looked down at himself. "I'm still in shock, I think. I feel like this can't be real… like that wasn't me back there."

"It *wasn't* you," said Zestine.

"I agree," said Dia. "The real you would never hurt her."

Zestine crossed her legs and leaned into him. "Show them your Light."

Tris hesitated. Then with his cheeks burning, he directed his will toward his heart and blood. *Shine,* he commanded. Gleaming white brilliance erupted from his skin, stretching a good three feet from his body on all sides. Slowly, violet shards materialized within the beams.

"Oh." Dia covered her mouth. "My."

The king bobbed his head slightly as he examined Tris's radiance, his lips twitching in an almost-smile. "I truly don't know what to say. Now, I'm only a little over a hundred years old, but I've studied Pirmas history extensively. And this…"

"Is unprecedented," said Zestine.

Tris pushed his lips together with his teeth and dimmed the shine. Though thankful for his new gift, to be graced with such a blessing after everything he'd done wrung the pit of his stomach.

"The purple fragments," said Lachlan. "Do you know what they are?"

"The Pirmas bond," Tris and Zestine replied in unison.

Dia's mouth parted with a faint smack of her lips. "Wow."

Lachlan nodded. "Thank you for sharing that with us. We'll look into it." He pursed his lips and furrowed his brows. "What of the Dark God?"

"We're not sure," admitted Zestine. "We think he might be dead, but…"

"My aura of Light really fucked him up. Then I put a sword through his skull and coated him in my blood, but even after I beheaded him, he was still talking, without a head, so I cut off his wings and he just…"

"Vanished," said Zestine.

"Vanished." The king looked at Tris, who nodded. "There's nothing left of him?"

"Nothing."

"Did he say anything before he vanished?" asked Queen Dia.

"He said we can't get rid of him; he was born from blood and doesn't exist according to any rules. He called himself eternal and undead," Tris said.

"Hmm. Then why did he disappear?" Dia questioned.

Zestine narrowed her eyes in thought. "Because he was too weak? To escape because he knew he'd lose?"

A moment of silence settled upon the group before Lachlan, who'd been staring off into space and tapping his fingers against his leg, said, "Unfortunately, I doubt he's dead. Weakened? Yes. I don't believe he was trying to fool you when he said you can't get rid of him. From what you've told me of this Dark God, he can exist in spiritual and physical form, which explains how he spoke while lacking a mouth and tongue. It probably takes less energy for him to exist in spirit form."

"So he's in spirit form now, you think?" asked Zestine.

The king's cheeks inflated on a heavy exhale. "Hard to say for sure, but if I had to guess, yes."

"But he said he'd be back, like he was going somewhere," Tris pointed out. "Going somewhere to refuel? Is it possible he's able to die, but can also return when summoned, or through another blood ritual?"

Blood ritual...

Zestine gasped, garnering everyone's attention. "The blood ritual!"

"What about it?" asked Tris.

She uncrossed her legs and straightened. "Don't you see? You helped make him with Light blood. Maybe this is his weakness."

Tris gave her a quizzical look. "What's his weakness?"

"He cannot fully exist all the time. Maybe he needs to go into hibernation, or whenever he's severely incapacitated in the physical world, he can't regenerate right away." She looked at the king. "Does this make sense?"

Lachlan's narrowed, light-teal eyes, which were on Zestine, flicked away and widened. He leaned forward. "I'm intrigued. You could be onto something. I also think Tris's blood impacted his own transformation." He moved his gaze to Tris. "Your blood made the Dark God imperfect, making his Corruption of you imperfect."

At hearing that theory, Zestine felt like the air had been knocked out of her. She closed her eyes and rubbed her temple.

"What is it?" Tris asked.

She shook her head. "I just can't believe it. If he's right, the only thing that saved you was… you. If you didn't spill your blood for that ritual…"

He palmed her cheek and turned her head to face him. "It was supposed to be Konrad, but you killed him, so if you hadn't done that…"

"Crazy." Zestine gave a bemused chuckle.

"It's just a theory. Besides, I'm here now, aren't I?"

"That you are," said Lachlan, making them start and redirect their attention to the king. "We could speculate all day, but we know he's idle, at least for now. He doesn't know where to find you, or us, right?" he asked Tris.

"He may figure out how to get to Noctis, but he's unprepared for confrontation."

Lachlan nodded. "Anything else you'd like to talk about?"

After a few quiet seconds, Tris cleared his throat. "Fuck. Uh, yes. There's something I need to tell you."

~

As everyone focused on him, Tris forced saliva past the lump in his throat. "Um… so, I just realized something. It seems I can divulge information I couldn't before."

"What are you talking about? You've been withholding intel?" Zestine's wide, shiny eyes were rapt on him.

"I had no choice! I was under coercion and I couldn't even tell you I was keeping something from you, but now obviously I can. I don't know what lifted it…"

"What is it?" asked King Lachlan.

Tris bit his bottom lip and closed his eyes. "When I first met the Ravager, he got into my head and facilitated a… meeting, I guess, with six demons."

"Can you name these demons?" inquired the king.

"The Keeper of Secrets, Shredder of Sins, Forger of Fear, Inflicter, Wrecker of Truth, and Snatcher of Souls." As he named them, each of their disgusting faces assaulted his mind's eye.

"What'd they tell you?" Queen Dia asked.

"They're all responsible for creating Corrupted. But King Soren was too, more so than anyone. In fact, Dia wasn't the only reason he launched an extermination mission on Earth. She was the initial reason, but along the way, demons influenced him to do their bidding. According to them, Soren was preparing for an all-out war against the High Lord, which he started by turning His sons against Him.

"I also learned about Light to Dark transformation. Corruption is essentially an infection, only once you're infected, nothing—not even time—can cure you. Soren used Dark magic to make a supernatural agent and convinced some poor raptatawk to drink it. After that, Corruption spread through bites from 'tawk to 'tawk. The Ravager was the only other who ingested the toxin, and it allowed him to turn 'tawks." The fleeting glimpse he'd gotten of the Ravager's long, bloodied teeth flickered in his head. Tris sighed. "Now he's dead, and the first infected 'tawk died a while ago."

"But the Dark God can make his own Corrupted," said Zestine.

"Right, but when the meeting took place, that wasn't discussed."

"The Dark God hadn't existed yet," said Lachlan.

"Right."

Silence fell, and Tris looked at his lap, jiggling his leg as he waited for someone to ask the inevitable question.

"Tris." Zestine stroked his bicep. "How did the Dark God turn you?"

He sniffed. "Stabbed his claws through my ribs, below my heart." He pulled in a deep breath. "Something, o-or m-many *tiny somethings*, scattered from the tips of his claws throughout my body. I became numb and paralyzed… and eventually passed out. When

I came to, I was Dark." Before anyone could ask it, he added, "I bit raptatawks to turn them." Nausea gripped his belly and throat. His muscles were so tense he thought they'd snap. At that moment, Tris wished he had an invisibility charm. Even if they weren't judging him, their gazes were like knives to his flesh, leaving him desperate to escape them.

"And how did the Ravager do it?" Zestine said.

Tris swallowed. "Bite."

"Thank you, Tris, for sharing that. Did the demons reveal anything else?" asked Dia.

Looking back up, he nodded and gave a brief smile. "They're searching for fire fae—or *hunting* them is a better way of putting it."

"The demons, or the Corrupted?" Lachlan asked.

"Both. The demons scry and the Corrupted physically search for them, but so far every fae they've intercepted has gotten away."

"Shit," said Zestine. "To have *fire* fae on their side." She whistled. "Not good."

"Wait. The Dark God can turn only raptatawks, right?" Dia asked.

"Light creatures, so yes."

All other Light Pirmas had gone extinct in wars of millennia past, which had been the driving reason for the High Lord to start His own race by creating spiritually related, thus Light-born, sons who'd yield only Light-born sons, and so on.

"They need people on their side and the only way is to turn Pirmas Dark or otherwise Corrupt them," said Lachlan, who nodded, then gave a slight head shake. "I don't know how they'll manage Corrupting fire fae. This is good information, and I don't fault you for not bringing your rendezvous with the demons to our attention earlier." At Tris's nod, the king asked, "Anything else we should know? Do you have questions before we part ways?"

CHAPTER 42

Zestine and Tris exchanged a look, and she sensed his carnal desire all the way to her aching core. If acceptable, she'd have tackled him to the floor and fucked him right there.

But there was a question she needed to ask before leaving. "Should we remain in Noctis, or can we leave whenever we'd like?"

"We said once you helped us battle the Corrupted you were free to do as you wish, and we're keeping that promise," said Dia.

"Before you leave," said Lachlan, "stop by for a couple of hyx compacts. I think it's wise to stay in touch, but please know this doesn't mean you're obligated to do anything for us."

In reality, they'd *always* be obligated. As First Tribal rulers they could keep her and Tris on as tight of a leash as they saw fit, but Zestine appreciated the sentiment. She trusted Lachlan and Dia to respect their desires as dutifully as possible.

After kneeling and saying good-bye, the lovers walked into the Noctis night, the world and its endless possibilities theirs for the taking.

~

Once outside, Tris snatched Zestine around the waist and picked her up. He cradled her shoulders with one arm and slipped the other beneath her knees.

"What are you doing?" Hit with a potent wave of happiness, she giggled before inhaling his heady scent and sinking against his steely muscles.

"I'm carrying you."

"Uh, yeah. But why? You've never carried me."

He met her gaze as he walked toward the Noctis sea, and she nearly melted. How'd she last a second away from this man?

"Maybe I should have," he said, raising his eyebrows.

She laughed. "Why?" Not that she was against him carrying her.

The corner of his mouth quirked up. "It's romantic, isn't it?"

"Um…" Zestine was not someone to ask about romance. "I wouldn't know, I guess. You're the first man to give me a taste of *romance*," she said with dramatic articulation.

"The first and the last." He winked.

Unable to stop smiling, Zestine rested her head on his shoulder. Her body hummed with buoyancy, flames of both love and lust licking her skin. "Where're you taking me?"

"Where do you want to go?"

A shower sounded fantastic. A shower with Tris sounded downright sublime. Followed by some lovemaking… no, *lots* of lovemaking. In bed. In the kitchen. In the shower. On the beach…

"Let's go to my place."

"Mmm." He touched his lips to her ear and whispered, "You're already drenched for me, aren't you?"

"Yes." Her voice was a husky whisper. All of a sudden she was breathless with anticipation. Without thinking, Zestine lifted her head from his shoulder, stuck out her tongue, and laved a hot trail from his collarbone to his ear, making him moan. She took his earlobe in her mouth and suckled. Adding a naughty edge to her tone, she said, "I'm aching for you sooooo badly. I want you to touch and kiss every inch of my body."

Tris gave a fervent growl. "I'll do whatever you want me to."

Her pussy tingled and wept, the need for him near intolerable. To her relief, he took off at a run, the landscape blurring by. She didn't realize until then how fast he traveled on land. Faster than she would have thought, or maybe his desire for her gave him extra oomph.

Inside the cabin, Tris set her down and she took his hand and led him to the shower. She needed to wash the blood and Dark Dimension ick off her body.

He joined her under the spray and they lathered each other up between desperate kisses and teasing touches. Tris soaped up her tits, paying special attention to her nipples by circling his calloused thumbs over them until they became firm and pointy. Once the water rinsed away the suds, he fastened his lips around a nipple and strummed it with the tip of his tongue until, pulling his hair, she mewled and forced their contiguous pelvises into a rock. Then he switched to the other nipple. It felt so phenomenal, she barely noticed the sting from the cut Mrakzlo had made around her breast.

Zestine cleansed his loins, sliding her hand up and down the rigid length and petting the head with her thumb while caressing his heavy scrotum. He shuddered under her touch, whispering his love for her, his total abandon heightening her already-profound desire.

After rinsing away the suds, they clung to each other skin-to-skin and exchanged sultry kisses for a time before Tris went for more. With one hand spanning the small of her back, he sneaked the other between her thighs to stroke her slippery folds. When he pushed between her lips and skimmed her clit, she gasped, then sighed.

"Oh… yes." Eyelids descending, Zestine hummed in pleasure, imagining she could see his fingers rubbing and kneading her most sensitive flesh.

The lukewarm water cascaded over their bodies, leaving unique and titillating sensations in its wake. She broke into a pant, then Tris lifted and flipped her upside down, making her yelp.

"Hang onto me," he told her.

The next thing she knew, she faced his lower abdomen while he secured the tops of her thighs against his shoulders. She threw her arms around his waist. He tightened his arms around her torso and emitted a wanton, purr-like sound, skimming his parted mouth over her sex right before latching on and devouring.

"Ah!" she exclaimed, the sensations majorly potent. He alternated between slow, savory licks and lapping at her clit. The stirrings of an orgasm arrived without delay.

"Triiiis," she moaned, digging her nails into him amid a lazy slide of his tongue. "Don't ah, ah. Drop, mmm, mmm, me."

Only upon completing his lick did he respond. "Never," he rasped, then returned to taste her cleft in a most erotic manner. Before long she climaxed hard on his tongue in a burst of wet heat, his arms crushing her to him as she trembled and cried out in ecstasy.

"Oh, fuck," she said afterward, cherishing the post-orgasm haze while raring for what was still to come.

With care, Tris flipped her right-side up, his mischievous face coming into view as he placed her on her feet.

~

Zestine gave him a saucy smile before falling to her knees and taking his cock into her mouth, deep-throating him right off the bat.

He groaned, mesmerized by the beauty at his feet delivering such incredible pleasure. Closing her plump red lips around the base, she added vibration by humming, then cupped his sac and grasped the area below her mouth. First, she twirled, flicked, and curled her tongue as she slid her lips up and down. Then she sealed her sliding lips ultra tightly and applied suction while using her grip around his girth to squeeze and stroke.

After a few minutes, she took him out and lovingly kissed and licked every inch of his shaft and balls only to swallow him whole and speed up her stroking and sucking.

"Oh… ah, feels so good," said Tris.

She cleaned the pre-cum from the tip and circled the head with her tongue, peeking up at him as she did. "So big… and hard…" She took him deep and moaned around his hardness, released him, and said, "and *mine*."

"Mine," Tris echoed, his eyes going wide. "Come here." She stood and he picked her up, left the shower, and walked dripping wet to the massive bed.

He placed Zestine on her back, rested her ankles on his shoulders and kissed them while gazing at the swollen pink pussy waiting for his cock, *made for* his cock. Fisting his erection, he teased her by sliding the head up and down her slit, making her buck.

"Tris," she moaned, and when he noticed himself shaking with need, he pushed past her folds and sunk balls-deep.

"Mmm, yes." He rocked back and plunged to the hilt, and again, quickly finding a rhythm as his thumb found her clit and rubbed. Maybe a dozen thrusts later, she exploded, crying out in wild abandon, but he didn't relent. Instead he sped up, fucked harder, hit deeper, her perfect, silken cunt taking, tightening, and giving again and again.

After Zestine's third orgasm, he withdrew and flipped her onto her stomach, gently scooted her toward the headboard, then got on the bed and entered her from behind.

Draping his body over her, he kissed her back and shoulders as he moved, slowly at first. He swept her hair to the side and nibbled her earlobe. "My Zestine. Sheyn. Forgive me for hurting you."

She whimpered and craned her neck, bringing her mouth closer to his. "Oh Tris. I forgive you. I was never mad in the first place."

He captured her lips for a deep kiss. "I want this to be forever, you and me." He slipped his hand down and caressed her ass cheek, while the other slid underneath and cupped one breast, then reached farther and squeezed the other. Her pussy clenched around him, and he released a low moan into her ear as he slid all in, filling her completely. He'd really never get enough of this woman, this treasure of a being who'd found him.

"I do too." Another lazy slide out, and in. "Oh! Gods, it feels sooooo good."

He dragged his lips and tongue over her shoulders, pausing once to close his eyes and breathe her in. "Never letting you go."

"I couldn't bear it if you did. I love you."

Spoken by her, those words released a wave of happiness through his chest. He slammed into her hard, touched his mouth to her ear and said, "I love you too, so much. Now hold on."

Tris lifted himself upright and put a hand under her belly to help her to her hands and knees, then pummeled his cock into her tight sheath at a fierce pace. Soon she screamed uncontrollably, enjoying one orgasm after another.

"Tris!" She fisted the blankets and undulated her hips, her perfect ass swaying with every thrust. Her muscles closed around him for the umpteenth time.

Looking down, the sight of him ramming into her sinful body yanked him from the cusp and he came, throwing back his head. "Zestine!"

Never get enough.

CHAPTER 43

"Which looks exciting to you?" Zestine asked Tris as they studied a comprehensive list of Otherworld realms.

Noctis was nice, and she'd found a friend in Queen Dia, but she and Tris wanted to avoid royal life, as well as reminders of the Corrupted, Dark God, and Underworld.

Not that they could evade the Dark Dimension completely, as they'd gone there to get the realm directory pamphlet. King Lachlan had glamoured them prior to the excursion and sent two glamoured guards with them as escorts.

For each realm, the pamphlet listed info such as usual weather, time from sundown to sunset and vice versa—Zestine rejected every dimension listing weeks or months—types of Pirmas inhabitants, life satisfaction rates, entertainment options, and population density.

They stood outside a portal booth on the Noctis shoreline, ready to go as soon as they figured out where.

Tris had suggested they travel from place to place before settling down. Although she was more than ready to find a home and start a family with the man of her dreams, she agreed to explore a handful of realms and see which fit best. After all, they had their whole immortal lives ahead of them. As far as they knew, their time was unlimited, so Zestine decided living in the moment a bit longer wouldn't hurt anyone and may prove positive for their still-budding relationship.

"Shtot looks interesting." He stopped on a page with pictures of a bustling metropolis with flying vehicles, tall towers, and from the looks of things, lots to do. "It says it's like a futuristic Earth."

"Hmm." It *did* look fascinating. She wanted somewhere to laze around enjoying nature and breathtaking landscapes, like Noctis with less variance between sun and moon rise and set. But after checking how long the days and nights lasted, she nodded. "Okay."

Tris dog-eared the page. "Your turn." He absently combed her hair with his fingers as she flipped through the pages for the perfect spot. She stopped on an image of a waterfall that looked similar to the one they'd found by chance in Noctis. Gistyll's sea-green sky spread above a land comprising rocks and fresh water with sporadic vegetation. The realm was home to three different suns—a gold one, a white one surrounded by a hot pink atmosphere, and a small light-purple one with silvery rays, making for three consecutive days lasting six hours each. At night, an electric-blue moon rose, plummeting the land to frosty temperatures for seven hours before the golden sun ascended and thawed everything for eighteen hours. The population was dense enough to not get lonely, which suited her perfectly.

"I like this one." Zestine folded the page's corner and passed the directory to Tris, whose second choice was Awan, which, like his home realm of Sohvic, existed in the sky.

Zestine's next selection was Ejavii, a dimension comprising a gigantic sea and millions of islands, where if one traveled far enough, they experienced every climatic extreme, from volcano-dominated terrain to frozen tundras.

"So, where to first?" Tris asked after Zestine had closed the pamphlet and they'd joined hands in front of the portal.

"You picked Shtot first, so we'll go there. Then Gistyll, Awan, and last, Ejavii."

He squeezed her hand. "All right. Shtot." They stepped into the swirling white mist to officially begin their lives together.

~

Six months later they arrived in Ejavii. Zestine tilted her face to the warm, golden sun and smiled. "Which realm is your favorite so far?"

"Hmm." Tris stood behind her and massaged her shoulders. They'd landed on a beach of sparkling peach sand greeted by foamy turquoise waves. "Honestly, I've liked them all."

"Me too." Every place they'd visited had been special in its own way. The fast, never-boring life in Shtot, the gorgeous days and phenomenal sights and smells of Gistyll, and the thrill of living among the clouds in Awan. Maybe Ejavii would be their last destination and maybe it wouldn't be. Zestine had never considered how difficult it'd be deciding where to make a home when there were millions of places to choose from.

The beast and raptatawk had gotten to know one another on entirely new levels since departing Noctis. Zestine had told him about the crazy things she'd done throughout the centuries, the important lessons she'd learned from different creatures, the times she'd almost died and how immortality had, on numerous occasions, brought her close to madness.

She'd confessed how, if it weren't for him, she'd be a lost, incomplete soul endlessly wandering through time. Being with him taught her that loneliness linked to a consistent search for purpose didn't qualify as living.

Though not all had been blissful, as the shame eating at Tris ever since overcoming the Darkness grew with every setting of the sun. Guilt chiseled at his conscience, accumulating into a mass of abrasive sorrow until he couldn't take it anymore and purged his emotional anguish through copious tears.

One night in Awan, after heading to sky and making love suspended by only Tris's wings, they'd settled for a relaxing interlude on a grassy knoll edging a deserted rock island. That's when Tris had broken down, torturing himself over the atrocities he'd committed during the mission, both to Zestine and others. The amount of brothers he'd slain was so great, he'd lost count.

It was then she'd admitted feeling guilty as well.

"If it wasn't for me, you'd have never killed them," she'd insisted. But he'd shushed her and they'd agreed dwelling on the past would only hurt them and their relationship.

"I don't blame you, but I forgive you if it makes you feel better," Tris had replied. They'd lain side-by-side, tangled arms and legs keeping their bodies flush.

"And I forgive you! Ask your Father for forgiveness. Perhaps He can relieve this burden."

So that's what he'd done, and one Awan day later the High Lord let Tris know He'd received his plea by speaking into his mind, something He did under only special circumstances. The majesty and relief of it had brought Tris to his knees.

"Be at ease, My son. Your pain is My pain. You have done nothing beyond living the life fate dealt you. You tasted the Darkness and returned to the Light. Focus on that, for it's a major achievement. Look forward. Do not look back."

And then, "One day new life will grow inside your mate. I augur your first child will become a mighty warrior, champion of raptatawks, and his existence will be vital to the balance between Light and Dark. Cleanse yourself of shame or risk tarnishing those you love with it.

"Though I do not and cannot always answer, speak unto Me whenever you wish. The time has come for you to move forth and prosper with your beloved. And do not forget, I am always with you."

Hearing from his Father had helped soothe his despair. There was no changing the past, so the next-best thing was to accept it. As difficult as that was, he was on his way. It helped to have Zestine's positivity to guide him. He surmised nothing was unconquerable with a faithful and doting mate by his side.

Now, Tris sighed in content as he rested his hand on his beloved's belly. She wasn't pregnant yet, she'd assured him, and he didn't complain. He was happy just knowing someday their life essence would combine and produce an incomparable gift. Who would their boy resemble? What colors would his wings be? Would he be brave and selfless like his mother, careful and loyal like his father, or all of the above? Tris delighted in entertaining the possibilities.

"Actually," said Zestine, "you're going to think I'm crazy, but… maybe Shtot would be a good place to make a life."

"Shtot, really?"

"Yeah." She giggled. "But who knows?" She turned to him and slung her arms around his neck, spreading her luscious lips into a smile that still had the power to hypnotize him. "The possibilities are practically endless."

They kissed, moaning and melting into each other, then lay on the sand and he made slow, passionate love to her, the woman who'd saved him from death and Darkness, stealing his heart along the way.

After he'd given her multiple orgasms while swallowing her cries with tender, tongue-sliding kisses, she met his gaze with those beguiling indigo eyes and whispered, "Never get enough."

The end…

…for now

Made in the USA
Las Vegas, NV
25 November 2021

35261347R00208